Best wishes
from Peter Abbasova
30/12/2014

SILENT SINNERS

GW00542014

Peter Abbasova

Grosvenor House
Publishing Limited

This book is published by
Grosvenor House Publishing Ltd
28-30 High Street, Guildford, Surrey, GU1 3EL.
www.grosvenorhousepublishing.co.uk

A CIP record for this book
is available from the British Library

Front page art work by Veronica Abbasova (original)
Back page by Lauren Abbasova
Marketing Sharon Abbasova

All the characters are fictitious as are the locations apart from the city.
However, some aspects are based on fact.

ISBN 978-1-78148-711-2

Foreword

As with all wars, they have their casualties and destruction. Buildings that once stood proudly were reduced to rubble. The immense scale of this destruction after World War Two was evident wherever you looked. This story is set in the Midlands, where the progress of rebuilding was slow; by 1950, it was well underway.

Five years on, there were swages of houses in ruins. Boarded up and fenced off no longer were the eerie sounds of bombs falling and sirens ringing out. They were replaced with the sound of children playing, soldiers, friend and foe, oblivious to the dangers around them. Unexploded bombs and other ordinance, the most dangerous areas were fenced off. Unfortunately, the lack of materials available and resource's large areas were open, and there were signs everywhere, 'Danger! Keep out', useful if you could read, but many children and adults could not.

Jan Probernoskei, he was a brute of a man in his late twenties, born in Provazka Bystrica, situated within a mountain range that dominates the skyline. His tall, heavy build and muscular frame set him apart. Dark jet black olive oil swept back hair; bronzed body with deep-blue eyes defined his looks, transforming him into a lady killer; a glance in their direction jellified their legs and despite the fact, he couldn't speak a word of English; it did not prevent the ladies from flocking to his feet, their were disappointed when he generally showed little interest in their advances.

His parents and immediate family, as far as he knew, had been killed resisting their aggressors or sent to Nazi's work camps, none to his knowledge had survived. He was a displaced person among many, who was facing an uncertain future, British men, scorned people coming from Europe, the country that was in tatters. They feared what they did not know or understand and felt they were being invaded, so they did not trust anyone that did not look English or could speak it.

Zimmer Swaranowich a polish refugee landed in Britain at the port of Grimsby. He spoke perfect English on top of several other languages. He would fit in quite easily anywhere and be labelled as a country gent, his linguistic talents were in demand, when those abilities weren't needed, Jan and Zimmer worked in a fenced off demolition area, clearing the bombed-out buildings, in the North East side of Leicester, a dangerous occupation as there were many un-exploded devices. While clearing rubble on this site his life would change. There were displaced people from transit camps that were put to work in such environments. No British person would want to deliberately risk their lives. They were cheap, disposable labour and there were thousands of them. Jan and Zimmer both lived with the polish landlord Maciej Berderick, wounded towards the end of the first Great War. His left leg was riddled with bullets by German soldiers shooting people for fun.

Spine Avenue was in the suburbs of Spine Hill, composed of Victorian terraced houses on one side and the Zanzibar hotel opposite, set at the North end of a large park, which was once an affluent area, many of the buildings in need of repair. Previous occupiers having lost their love one's, killed in action or unaccounted for. They were unable to maintain these huge five and six bedroom houses with little in savings or income.

It was while working opposite a hosiery factory on this particular demolition site on a blistering hot June day. Some people's lives were about to be changed. Doris was going to do that, unwittingly at first, this shy and quite naive girl, unworldly in the ways of men, but with the influence of her sister and others, would turn their lives and those they encountered upside down, spinning the web of the silent sinners.

So our story begins, based on some truths and facts, with factious characters and fictitious places, portraying no person living any resemblance are purely coincidental.

"Look at the time; I'm going to be in trouble again." Doris was always late for work and everything else. She was a tall garden rake on legs, a small bump in front for breast's and the backside of about the same proportion. Violet her mother, Vi for short, thought Doris had hollow legs, with a matching head. She was, apart from her dad Frank, the tallest at almost six feet, but at no means elegant. Etiquette for Doris was none, Manners also none, and friends, there were none. With an IQ rating of zero and clothing sense that would make tramps appear to have a good dress code, she lived on a street of houses, that all looked the same, different coloured painted doors were. The only distinguishing features setting them apart, If you had taken one drink too many for the road, as long as you were not colour blind. It's probably the one way you would find your house in the dark. These Victorian habitations were created just before the turn of the century. By a builder confined to this singular one design, they all consisted of four good-sized bedroom's scullery with stoned cobbled floor and a copper, one main entrance hallway, a kitchen, a lounge and a lone outside toilet not forgetting the brick built coal bunker that you couldn't deliver coal to except by bringing it through the house. The occasional bombed homes, charred and boarded stood apart. Children played cowboys and Indians in them, throwing bricks into the garden pretending them to be hand grenades, the occasion child, got indisposed at the local infirmary, with a broken something or other.

When Doris opened her mouth, it was poetry in motion. Where's my toast, can I have my tea, where's my coat, I am going to be in trouble, "Doris; you're always in the wrong at work, one of these days you will get the sack" her dad remarked; you would be late for your own funeral; that's a fact my girl. The meat wagon will be going down the road, with you chasing after it by the time you got there, they would have filled in the hole, and the vicar would be down the flaming, pub everyone will then have to put up with your ghost scaring the life out of them.

Frank was a six-foot six, well rounded man, wide as a door and taller, but a gentle giant, he had hands would put an Irish man's shovel to shame, a deep thinking man; He would always think answers out carefully when questioned. If confronted, He was not a man to get on the wrong side. It took a lot to wind him up, his wife Violet, could do it without effort, jokingly, he would tell his chums, how he'd never clocked the woman in the gob, is a bloody mystery, Vi would put the patience of a saint to the test, and the Saint would lose hands down. He would not dare to say it front of her, despite his size; he'd get a copper stick beating of the first class order.

Vi shouted, the street heard, "I'm not your servant, my girl, neither a skivvy, if you were, to stop day dreaming and get out of bed when the alarm goes off, you wouldn't be late, would you. I can see I'm wasting my bloody breath. God gives me strength Doris, and I could swing for you at times." Vi's morning statement was delivered. It wasn't difficult to understand where Doris got her poetic language skills.

Vi was a fiery red head of Irish blood, which ran in her veins with a mix of ninety eight per cent of tea it was the first thing to come out of her mouth if you had just walked in, 'tea?', and even if you said no, you would still get a cup anyway, wind her up. She would crack you with, her usual tool, the copper stick which rarely left her side. A five-foot nothing, quick-tempered mighty mouse who always spoke her mind, her best friends were her nine moggie's, and whilst partially blind she knew them all by sound. She could knit quicker, crochet faster than a racing driver. Behind that old and delicate frame, she had a caring heart, despite her bark, and would help anyone who really needed help, except for Doris. She deemed her beyond help.

"Yeah, yeah, yeah, mam, love you too," Doris replied, "I'll give 'yeah' across your bloody ear in a minute, my girl."
     Doris should have been in the circus. Grabbing her coat, while juggling and eating her slice of jam and toast in one hand, that stuck out one end of a coat sleeve, at the same time trying to drink her tea, on the other hand, her mother chasing her, to retrieve the cup, while she walked down the path, trying to put the rest of her coat on, the girl was a disaster. The jam would be around her mouth and the tea over her front.

"See yah dad!" Doris shouted there was no reply, there never was, on any day, any opportunity before work, he would be out of the back door to his beloved garden and allotment, anyone looking for him; It would be the first place to look, in the garden or in the allotment. It was a serious hobby that kept him busy and provided much-needed food for the family. It was the peace and quiet he sought from the world and Vi, if he didn't have something to do, she would find him a job in the house. Many hands make light work was a favourite saying of hers, caught sitting on your backside, would earn you a job to do. Frank didn't like indoor jobs. He stayed outside whenever he could; even when the weather was poor, he would stay out or take shelter in the shed, otherwise. He would be in bed or at work as a respected engineer, who spent more time fixing the front door than machines. Doris would slam the door behind her so hard that dust, cement, and bits of brick were ejected from the door frame surround; screws came out of the hinges. Frank used counter sunk bolts instead of screws, within a month she had managed to break them, how, only God knew.

Doris marched along the road to work at a fast pace every working day. Only a circus performer or demolition man would understand how she had managed to get through life without bowling someone over. The sound of, the factory siren belted out, when she was at least five minutes further away than a five-minuet journey. It denoted the start of the days shift and the start and finish of tea as well as lunch breaks, only. Her mother's voice rang out a pitch higher often seen chasing Doris down the road with her lunch box. Her voice put the whistle to shame, "Don't bloody mind me. I'm just the floor rag, come and go as you please! Don't you don't mind me chasing you down the road Doris you lazy cow?"

Doris was fearful of one thing; turning up late and actually getting caught, she was a good worker so Megan, the line supervisor, would clock her in although the pair of them knew it was a sacking offence. She considered her worth the effort, Despite Doris's many other faults. She did not want to lose her best worker, that aside, regardless of who you were, what you did or how important you might be; it would be instant dismissal and no wages. Doris could not afford to lose her job or the money, for the ultimate of all fears having to face her mother, who ruled supreme with the aid of the copper stick. One crack from that was enough put any man or woman onto their knees. She never missed. Vi, for her age, had the reactions of a greyhound out of a dog trap at the local stadium, and would be a bookie's favoured choice to chase the rabbit down.

Doris never looked left, right or up and down when she was in a hurry. It was one gear full speed ahead, for some unexplainable reason, not even understood herself to this day, she caught a fleeting glimpse into the corner of her eye a half-naked man, his torso running with sweat that glistened in the morning sun on his muscle-bound body, rippling with his every move from the neck down to his sweat-soaked khaki shorts. His every move was a fine-tuned rhythm as he worked in the hot sun, she found herself with every step slowing eventually coming to a complete stop. Her head turned more and more to her left. She could not help herself but look and stare; she was frozen in that moment.

There he was this bronze god, tossing bricks two at a time into a dumpster, a good ten yards from where he stood, rarely did his throws miss. Every muscle twitched and tensed, the veins standing proud of the skin as he went about his business behind the wire chain-link fence, his swept back jet-black hair and piercing blue eyes struck her in both eyes, cutting to her very soul. Her feet were bolted to the pavement. Doris felt a sensation in her stomach. She had never felt before, her heart pounded against her chest, there was an aching in her groan another strange sensation intensifying, when he suddenly stopped working, turned and looked straight at her, she could feel her legs buckle as they went to jelly, in desperation she grabbed at the fence, clenching it with both hands, hanging on for dear life.

Jan Probernoskei spoke, "Pozdravljeni, kako ste" "Hello, how are you?" "Err," Doris replied; nothing else would come out of her mouth. Her feet would not move, in slow motion as if bound like an Egyptian mummy trying to escape the constraints of the bandages she could not wriggle free of his magnetic hold on her soul. She tried in vain to move, but could not.

Jan continued to stare at her with those piercing blue eyes, stop. She murmured "please."

"He repeated himself" "Pozdravljeni, kako ste," "Hello. How are you?"

The voice of Megan, shouting Doris several times, from across the road eventually broke the spell; He had over her err, sorry got to go. She bolted across the busy road to the factory gates, not looking, in any direction as she crossed running full pelt into the arms of Megan

Howstha. You'll be the blooming death of me Doris. Apart from causing mayhem crossing the road, do you know what time it is? Come on for god's sake "snap out of the trance, you are in, you bloody idiot. She tried to speak but not a murmur that would make any sense was forth coming. Megan shook her by the shoulders. Are you sick, she shouted? A lightning bolt must have hit you. Let's get you inside and try to make sense of this.

Megan was a very large breasted some said at least a fifty, as broad as a door and barrel shaped, at only five feet. She could pack a punch with her right hand, sugar ray, would have been proud of, even more with her mouth, her mass of red hair, was always in rollers and needed a cargo net to contain it, the shape resembling a laundry bag strapped on her head, ready to go to the launderette. When let down it covered a hump of a backside larger than an elephant's ass and the huge breasted front, wobbled like an over-sized pregnant duck struggling to drag its frame along to the duck pond, despite this, men found her hugely attractive, there was no shortage of admirers. Her soft voice seemed to magnetize them into her presence,

They had not travelled beyond the first set of swing doors, the other side the clocking in machine, when they were confronted by Ben Grubb "he Snarled and growled. His lips curled back revealing a set of gnashers that would match a hunting dog's teeth. He had the tongue to go with it, often hanging to one side. When he set about you, he was like a dog with a bone. He wouldn't let go" do you know what this is, he exclaimed, holding a clocking in card in his left hand, well, yours to be precise, Doris; he yelled "marching towards them. It's bloody yours, explain yourself, speak up. I haven't got all day. Tears started to trickle down her face as Doris muttered under her breath this is it. I'm going to get the sack, sorry she blurted out.

"Doris Buntie "The card says 8.30 am," The time is 8.50 am. That's half way through the day "he snarled, showing a full set of clench teeth, saliva was dripping from them, "who the bloody hell stamped you in."

"Just a minute Mister," Megan bellowed, Stepping forward, using her weight and size placing herself between Ben and Doris, cupping a hand around his neck. She pulled his ear to her mouth. "I clocked her in because I had to take her across the road and get some stuff," "what stuff," Ben enquired, "you know" she pulled his head over again whispering in his ear, "be more bloody sensitive. Ben She has got bad ladies problems."

Ben Grubb "huh he sighed typical," as he moved away quickly putting distance between them both, then went about his business. If there was one topic, he did not want a discussion about, it was lady's problems, if it was up to him, he would have all women's private parts stitched up and their mouths as well plastered over for good measure, "bloody woman's problems," he muttered walking down the corridor.

"That was a close call, good job I can think on my feet," Megan stated, Doris, "what's in your head girl, you could have got us both sacked" "if he was more a deci- sive man, thankfully he's not, which is lucky for us." Ben shied away when the monthlies are mentioned, his sick side kick, however, Van strudlewinkle wouldn't hesitate, catch him in one of his fowl moods, and we would be history, in the blink of an eye.

Van Strudlewinkle his real name was Ulrich van Schiegl, got his English name from being a mad as a hatter. He walked with a funny swagger more female than male, his small privates, exposed when he ignored a warning sign, walking passed them, then falling into an open inspection trench. The belt loop and belt on his trousers got caught on a grate covering hooks.

Which removed both trousers and underwear in a blink of an eye, lucky to escape with his life, apart from some bruising. Embarrassment and a dented pride, he was fine, fortunate not have broken his neck, one of the factories deeper trenches, would have been certain death, a bastard after the incident, from that day forth, because the women laughed, so did the men, but he picked on the female gender, considering them the easier prey, making their working lives a misery.

So Doris, what's the drama, Megan asked? "I saw a naked man, I, couldn't take my eyes off him," across the street, when you, shouted at me, "I couldn't move. It felt like my feet were glued to the pavement." "Is that all the fuss is about Doris." "I have seen bloody loads of men over the years, apart from, the tackle, hairiness or lack of it, fat, thin, or tall, young or old; they're mostly all shits, in public though, bare wearing nothing, now that takes some flaming believing." Doris went to say something, but Meagan placed her right hand over her mouth, "tell me later, there's work to be done, and I do mean now, the lines behind thanks to you. We'll have to go like the blazes if there's to be a tea break or lunch today," there rest of the girls hissed like snakes as she took up her position.

The sun shines out of your arse it surely does, Doris. Matilda said yes it really does. Others agreed with her. Aunt Matilda, whom Doris wished, worked somewhere else, preferably on another planet. They were poles apart, for two people who were so closely related. They didn't think the alike, or even look mildly similar, speak or have the same manner. She wouldn't snitch on Doris to her mam, but didn't care for her either. Matilda was the eldest of the three aunts, who thought she was born to the wrong family, a mistake at the hospital. She swore she was swapped at birth, her aunt thought, little of the rest of her related family. She thought Frank was mad, her mother Violet, certifiable and Christine the youngest of the two girls, the most daring, outgoing, frivolous sex maniac of a girl she had ever known and then, she openly said, if Doris had a brain, and it was made of dynamite, there wouldn't be enough in her head to de-wax her ears.

Matilda would have given anything to be related to another family. She was a dreamer who thought in different dimensions to anyone in the real world, especially if they were well to do, she would constantly dream of a man with money to the extent of pre asking on any promising date the range and extent of their wallets or the extent of their family's wealth and the prospective candidate's ambition.

"No" Aunt Matilda said it was no Surprise. There weren't any takers; she saw both Frank's girls as a shovel short of a full load, when they were dishing out children, they were hospital rejects no doubt, and they had to give to some unsuspecting fool.

"I'm sure Megan is your second adopted mother" Matilda stated with a toss of her head, her jet-black hair streaming away from her like a cast fisherman's net, flowing from behind her, there were times Doris wished it would cast itself into the loom and rip her head off. Such was the love for her aunt.

Alice, Helen, Pamela, Beverley, Shayla and Iris, They made the rest of the line, who mouthed in agreement with Matilda." This was the standard practice for talking over the noise, without sound.

Iris, said, "I'd like to know what you've got on Megan, err yes," Helen said. "It must be something big, perhaps you two are lovers" Beverley mouthed. Doris, her eyes wide and fixed as a hawk, waited, for the right moment to attack. "I've got nothing on her; she snapped, "you conniving cows." Putting a finger up, to each one of them one by one, she got her head swivelling round from one and then to another, mouthing it across the lines, "the girls on the line all knew, when Doris was angry, not to antagonize her further she wouldn't let it rest ,and ,at break time had any of them ,had persisted with the conversation, a smack in the gob's would be a certainty, pushed , Doris had a short fuse, she did not got on with any of them at the best of times and the rest of the girls on all the lines did not get on with her either it was a two way street evident during the tea and lunch breaks,they would all hovel and gather in groups some ten yards away, while Doris would puff on her cigarette alone at the other end of the yard, she always knew they were talking about her, if she took a slight look, cat glance were coming her way, a particular group would all look at the same time snapping away quickly when caught then carry on their chit chat, Doris gave the impression she didn't care, but deep down it hurt, to the soul.

Pamela was the groupies troll. She cowardly slipped from one group and then over to another. she limped because of an iron attachment on her right leg. Polio striking her when she was a child, She was really the groups errand girl, collecting gossip, spicing it up, then reporting back, as to keep favour, hense why she had casually strolled over to Doris, "so, why was you late then," "nothing better than being blatant about asking a question, is there Pam," "I saw a naked man across the road in that compound, behind the chain link fence, he was clearing bricks from the demolition site, alright, now you know," Pamela not sure of her hearing, said, "naked man", aloud," every head within ear shot, suddenly swung in her direction, the yard fell silent, tell more, Pamela enquired, Doris was about to tell, when, "That's enough, Pam, go collect your gossip elsewhere," save it, Megan commanded, "Doris they will only take the piss out of you for the rest of the bloody month," "besides, he wasn't naked he had shorts on" laughter echoed around the yard, then died down to faint size, all groups returning to their chit chat, their opinion of Doris, was very low they considered her of sub normal intelligence, no one actually called her thick, but the bitchy comments may well have spelt it out in neon lights.

That's the end of another day, Doris said aloud clocking out, it had been as any other day, for the Squawking chickens at the end of the yard. Hunting for some fool to ridicule, and that's why she and her park drive fag stayed at the opposite end of the yard. Doris recorded these images playing them back when walking home, she could see Pamela, drifting for one group, then to another group. The stories ended up as legends, a little added to every piece of gossip as it passed from one group to another, it was quite amusing, if you had a scratch on your arm, by the time it got to the last group of gossipers, you were having your arm amputated.

Today had been a little different, the sun was shining, and it was turning towards another hot day. She could see the man in his shorts just, in between the piles of bricks. Doris, she felt, a churning in her stomach she had felt before when she first saw him. The more she gazed across the street to the compound of bricks, the stronger the feelings got. The ruminants of bombed houses were being torn down by a swinging ball at the end of a crane. The man stood there just a few moments ago. The falling masonry, created dust clouds. Obscuring her view, she felt uncomfortable with this experience, dodging around the yard, trying to see him, what I'm I doing. She muttered, finishing the fag, quickly before lighting another from the smouldering butt end, she dragged on the fag with every great inhalation, lighting a third before she realized what she was doing, her lungs were overcome, by the extra intake of smoke. The image of the man was burnt into her mind. A bike horn blasted out as she was about to cross the road, "snap out of it," Doris said aloud, she had been day dreaming.

The next-day Doris felt she needed to talk to someone, to get an understanding of what she was feeling, but who? Doris knew they were all blabber mouths on the line and could not be trusted. A small story in the morning would be a film epic by lunchtime, but whom, but whom? Stamping her feet like a spoilt child, she spotted Shayla, "Hey up" Shayla;" Doris grabbed her by the arm. Leading her to her end of the yard, "I need to talk to you please." Doris had decided to confide in her Shayla because she was a mute, Doris assumed she wouldn't be able to tell anyone, later it would be a lesson to be learnt, the stress, a pair of ears to pound without reply, how good was that.

Shayla lost her tongue, in a freak accident, some years ago. She tripped on a steep curb stone running to the park, ahead of her mother. Shayla hit the pavement chin first, almost severing her tongue, while lying across the pavement with part of her tongue hanging out, a terrier type dog ripped it away from her and ate it, shit Doris thought, talk about bad luck. The image gave her the jitters. She always had to plead, practically on bended knees, for a conversation with her sister Christine, who had no time, to spare for anyone. You had to make an appointment, then if you were lucky, if she turned up at all. One thing always got her attention money that would get you an audience. Doris knew; her sister would never snitch to her mother. Chrisi was no rat, therefore, considered her a good confident, while not telling to her mother or father, if the price was right she would tell the rest of the town. Doris weighed up her options and decided to confide in Shayla, because it was free.

"Please Shayla, just need a mo. It's important, come on!" Doris pleaded, dragging her by her coat sleeve to the furthest end of the yard. Shayla leant against the wall while Doris spilled the beans, the girl always got her tongue twisted when she was nervous and under pressure, but explained in detail to Shayla about the man she had seen working across the road in the compound behind the chain-link fence and how she had felt inside when she looked at him. "Ha ha ha." Shayla could not contain her laughter. The yard went quite except for Shayla's bellowing laughter. An eerie silence fell, and you could hear a pin drop. Once the laughter ceased, everyone wanted to know the story behind it. The jokes were going to come thick and fast, and what Doris was unaware of, Shayla could sign and two of the girls understood sign-language. A chit chat with Shayla, hey presto a legend was born. By break time, the groups had a fresh material to chew over the groupies troll feeding one circle then another, each passing of chatter more was added, coming back full circle.

"There a new virgin friend was born." "Doris she has got the hots for a man she has seen once, over the bloody road there." Shayla pointed at the demolition site. "I'm pissing my pants over it. She has him burnt into her head and her knickers. Perhaps, he might, put a bit of fire in our knickers, hey girls?"

"You are a bastard." "Shayla." "You are a Bastard!" Doris screamed.

The rest of the women in the yard burst into hysterical laughter as Shayla unfolded the story. Doris had confided with her, adding her bits to make it Spicer.

Doris burst into a flood of tears; she felt about less than an inch tall, vowing she would never speak to her again. She ran back into the factory and into the ladies' toilet, almost bowling over Ben Grubb, the factory charge hand. She was like a bull that had just had the red flag waved in its face, "Bloody women's problems, and pain in the backside the lot of you."

Doris almost took the toilet door off its hinges. The door slammed against the wall; the impact rang out echoing across the empty factory floor. "What the bloody hell is going on, Megan?" Ben Grubb asked. "Bugger if I should know; more importantly do I want to know. Ben I bet, though it's something to do with frigging women's problems, wouldn't you think." "It usually always has" Ben pointed towards the women's toilet, "the lot of you should be stitched top and bottom. If it was up to me, you would all be going to the infirmary this afternoon. I'd shut the factory to make the time and surely God would understand, hopefully, that he had made a mistake. He could make an exception and come down here to fix this for me. I've prayed, more than once, it won't be the last time I'll ask God. I would surely think after all the thousands of years, He'd admit he was wrong when he nicked one of our bloody ribs, which may have been the only mistake God made." Ben was giving men two heads to think with, most of the time neither of them useful.

Megan entered the ladies' toilet. Doris sat in a cubicle, sobbing her heart out; She gave an account of what had taken place in the yard with Shayla, Megan, Doris said whimpering, they're all going to take the Mickey out of me? I don't know why I have these feelings or why I'm having them, all I did was look at him. I'm not worldly or smart, what had happened, was nothing, but something, Doris it's called growing it's time you asked you mam about the facts of life, sometimes referred to as the birds and the bees, she listened to Megan attentively, but knew in her heart? She wouldn't dare to ask her mam anything to do with men? She knew her sister Christine knew about men but was discrete about her encounters. She was younger than Doris but appeared to be so much more, womanly in her ways, after the episode with Shayla, well dare I, she thought, should I talk to Christine, at least I know she won't blab, but at what cost.

When they were both at school corridor chatter spoke of Chrisi, taking boys behind the bicycle sheds, often being referred to as the village bicycle. Doris thought she must be teaching them how to ride. Chrisi worked part-time at local chip shop. She told mam that she had another job in town waiting on tables. That would turn out to be a lie as Doris had seen her taking grown men and older men into the back room of the chip shop, often wondering what went on in there. Whatever it was; they seemed to come out pleased with a smile on their faces, often patting Chrisi on her bottom or frequently kissing her on the cheek. She would always be counting up money on her way back to the counter where she'd dish some up to her boss and pocket the rest. Considering she worked only Friday and Saturday night, she took more money in those two days than dad took in a month, seeing she'd meet at least six or eight men every week, some of the new, other's regular visitors. The rest of the week she didn't know where she went, but it wasn't home. Doris never told or passed this on to her parents; Chrisi had sworn she would break her legs if she spilled the beans.

Chrisi told Doris she was giving them private lessons, and her boss had let her hire the back room when they were quiet, which was most of the time, as they were an absolute terrible takeaway. The worst there was in the city actually. Few people went there to buy food, and if they had, they didn't again. Doris thought whatever it was she was teaching them; she must be good at it, because they kept coming back. Chrisi would often treat Doris to some fags, hush money it was called. For sure, it helped, mam taking most of her pathetic wages. She questioned herself 'why can't I get a job like that?' The rest of the day went without further event, and in fact; she had completely dismissed the thought from her mind, going home to relax for a while, then heading to bed to where she slept like a log.

Friday, was pay day, after work and after taking out her keep, buying any essentials, she would go meet Chrisi at the chip shop. This week, Doris thought it might be a good time for a chat. Besides, she was now broke; the hush money was a life line, and right now she needed it. Chrisi would be flush, most weekends they would slip into the local pub for a drink, the sort of place any respecting man wouldn't be seen dead. Looking older than her age would get served without question. Doris, on the other hand, would get refused. She did not drink since alcohol made her giggle, so she always got a lemonade, and when no one was looking, Chrisi often spiked the lemonade. She didn't do it in the past. Doris had seen her on occasions poring something into the lemonade bottle that looked like water, after she drank some from the bottle, "Chrisi, you know that stuff makes my head turn funny?" "The room spins, drink it slowly. I never listen, do I?" Chrisi said giggling. "It's the curse of my life." Doris didn't complain, secretly she enjoyed the feeling.

Doris told Christine about the man and what had happened at work, and to her surprise, she was calm and understanding. "See, if he asks me out, go for it, get shagged." "What's getting shagged, Chrisi?" "You will know soon enough. He sounds like a hunk. One day, you'll have plenty of shags, keep what I tell you to yourself, Doris." She had no idea what Chrisi meant, her head was fizzed out. "Would you teach me, Chrisi, about things? You know everything. I can't pay you; mam takes all my money. Please Chrisi!" She pleaded. "Ok Doris, next weekend. I'm far too busy this week, but it's between me and no bugger else, ok?" "You're the best, thanks Chrisi." "Someone's got to teach; you can't go through life blind." "There's nothing wrong with my eyes." "Doris, you take the biscuit, as idiots go. Now don't cry, please, I was only joking." "No, you were not joking. I'm thicker than half a dozen planks" "no, Doris, a baker's dozen. Kidding."

The weekend gone, it was Monday, and Doris felt sad. When the weather was nice, there was so much to do in the garden or down the allotment. It was hard, but enjoyable work. After roast dinner, she could still smell the chicken, and it always went so quickly.

For a change, she was up and out early, with her thoughts about the man. 'If he speaks again, I'll speak back.' Doris sprang into her normal sprint walking pace eating up the pavement, full of joy in the early-morning sunshine, turning the corner to cross the road to the factory gates on the other side. She had not a care in the world then.

Jan Probernoskei spoke, in a soft gentle voice. "Pozdrav-ljeni, kako ste" "Hello, how are you?" Doris stopped in her tracks and spun around. It was like she had just been struck by lightning for a second time. Her heart was pounding; her stomach had become knotted, her mouth parched and agape. Doris was bolted to the spot where she stood again, unable to speak or do anything, except stare at him, "Err." She murmured.

"Pozdravljeni, kako ste" "Hello how are you" Jan's soft voice spoke again. Sweat was running down his face, chest and the arms. His muscular body flexed; the veins stood up proud on the forearms. He was God's perfection, and he knew it. His hands were covered in lime brick mortar, his olive oil jet-black hair also had a sprinkling of the same that sparkled in the sunlight when his head moved. Doris stood there motionless, like a puppet that had just had its strings cut the fence coming to her rescue; she grasped onto it for dear life, supporting her fragile frame.

Speaking in Slovak, "Please don't go, if only, she could understand, what he was saying, "bugger 'she replied grabbing the side of her dress with her left hand, pulling it up well above the knees, in readiness to bolt across the road. She noticed his eyes fall to the hem of her dress, staring at her bare white legs, "bugger me," If gold medals were being issued for the hundred-yard dash that day Doris would win hands down, from where she was standing, to the clocking in point she would have set a new world record. Slow down, Ben Grub shouted as she slammed into him knocking Ben to the floor. "Have you shit the bed girl" Ben chuckle getting up and regaining his composer, Doris was frantically trying to feed her time card into the clocking in machine.

Ben could see her frustration; Doris was creasing and bending the card,"they'll be nothing left of that, "for heaven's sake. Doris give me the bloody card, there that wasn't so difficult." Was it, snatching it from her hand, clocking it, then putting the card back in the rack "when you women get on heat your pathetic," I thought your backside was on fire, yes that's it, he said, you had a curry, on top of your other woman's problems, must be hell for you, thank the Lord? I'm not a woman, exclaimed Ben, go on get to your dam station pest, "bugger me. Doris carry on at this speed you'll melt the soles of your shoes. Pity you can't work at that speed; She whisked by Alice, who was about to say something, Good morning, piss off Alice; Doris replied, before she could finish, get with the other morons, she what gossip you can cook up today, I'm past caring, "what you arsoles think.

Helen, Pamela, Beverley and Iris, took the advice, making no comments, throughout the day, apart from the odd mouthed wise crack. Doris, demonstrated a composed rigid side, something new, often showing her hand when anyone went to speak, mouthing, talk to the hand, dip shit, each time a fired one-liner came her way, she worked at a relentless pace the whole week, talking to no one and mixing with no one. She was not in the mood. It was not a week to pick a fight with her, unless you wanted a visit to the work's infirmary, the factory siren sounded, sorry can't to stop, Megan, go to go. She bolted to the machine, clocked out, then bolted to the exit, see you Monday Doris "Megan shouted. She stopped, looked at her nodded her head and with saying a word was off running not stopping the whole way home, as she crashed through the front door panting, she was met by her mother clasping the rolling pin.

"Good, your home early," Doris, you can help with the washing. It needs hanging on the line mam, never mind mam, just get on with it, sod it mam. I've finished work; she said it in her mind. She wouldn't have dared to speak it out loud. A bunch of fives or the rolling pin, was the likely reward, if there was one thing, Doris hated more than anything, was hanging the washing. She normally walked home at a snail's pace, which she now wished she had, the choirs they would have already been done. Doris could kick herself for hurrying, but she did not want to face the man, so in some way she was grateful, even if not pleased, at least she was home; it was the weekend.

Friday was also a bath night, a fire up the chimney, tin bath full of hot water and a nice pot of Rosie Lee, sheer bliss. She was second, because Chrisi had to go to work, Doris would get in her water as soon as she got out, a fresh bath was then made for Dad. He would have a bath all to himself, because in his job, he would get filthy, needing a bath every day in the scullery. Mam would shout the same thing every Friday. "I'll come and scrub your bloody necks if you don't wash properly and don't forget to clean behind your ears." "Right mam" There was a wonderful thing about Friday apart from the bath, clean fresh sheets, aired eiderdown, the bed seemed extra comfortable, and it was perfect for dreaming.

Friday evening was the time to meet up with Chrisi at the chip shop. Doris didn't like the winter, especially after her bath, she was reluctant to go out into the cold, having to force herself, although the days were getting lighter, when she went to meet her sister, it was in complete darkness. The odd street light provided some illumination. In the shadows, sown into her head was this fear about someone jumping out and attacking her, the dark unlit alley, was a short cut it wasn't long, but it had two snake bends in it, so you were out of sight at either end for a while, it was these during moments she felt scared. For a short walk, it appeared to take a long time, the alternative was to go around the block; this would take four times longer.

After Chris finished work, they would always go down the pub for a drink, Chrisi bought Doris a stash of fags, she called it her hush money, just as well, without a fag, Doris thought she would die, from the stress and boredom of work. It was the reward. This would take her mind also off the walk; down the alley, it made taking the short cut worthwhile. Free chips were on offer at the chip shop. Chrisi had been warned only to eat them at your own peril, good idea in the week, if you wanted to be laid up with the heaving trotters.

"Hi Chrisi." "Hi me duck." Chrisi replied, "be ready in a mo." Doris; she never stopped admiring how attractive her younger sister was. Even in her white fat stained chip shop coat, she looked elegant. The coat, however, was very short well above the knee, and it exposed her cleavage, with buttons down the front spaced far enough apart, that from any angle, it exposed peeks of more than skin when she moved or bent down. Doris commented how dangerous it was. "A splash of chip fat is going to hurt. I wouldn't worry too much about the chip fat, Doris. We hardly sell any sodding chips. I'd be far more worried if dad saw me, he'd have a fit, if you blabbed your mouth."

"Chrisi, I'd never snitch; I'm no bloody grass." "She replied, no matter what you did, I would not tell," "I'm glad to know it Christine remarked, come into the back room while I get changed." Christine unbuttoned her work coat, revealing no bra and a pair of loose fitting knickers, the skimpiest she had ever seen, "sodding hell Chrisi; Mine are like air field, wind socks." Christine put her top coat on, done it up. "I'll just put the rest of my clothes in this old potato bag, right ready, she remarked." "Good grief Chrisi you couldn't go to the pub like that." "I can, watch and learn Doris. You wanted an education you're going to get one, not a bloody word either, to anyone, ok Doris." She nodded in agreement. "You know I would swear on the Bible if you asked me." Good enough, I'm ready let's go."

The steam tramp public house is just three or four minutes away. "Aren't you cold Chrisi," "bloody freezing, a drink or two will soon fix that, they have a raging fire," "let's hope we get there before you become a lolli-pop." It was a clear sky night sky, frost, sparkled on the cobbled stones, walking a fast pace arm in arm quicker than usual, in an effort to keep warm and escape the cold rapidly.

The log fire greeted them like a sunny day, as they entered the snug. Chrisi pushed her way through the men at the busy bar, dragging Doris with her by the arm. "Brandy straight, single vodka no ice and a lemon-ade Harry, on second thoughts make the brandy a double." "Is she of age," the burly barman asked, "old enough for you to have wet dreams, bloody hell Harry." "She is older than me believe or not; She doesn't drink booze anyway she becomes violent, hence the lemon-ade," make her scarce, up in the corner somewhere, not too far from the back door, got you Harry, come on Doris follow me. The pub was a dark dingy place, the light of the log fire providing most of the light. Hardly, any of the gas lamps worked or had wicks or glass shades, engineered that way, no doubt. Electricity to this neighbourhood was being restored. War time bombing destroyed a lot of the infrastructure. "I've got some business Doris, stay here, drink your lemonade and turn a blind eye." Chrisi beckoned a guy, who was close buy to join her. Doris notice he followed them to the darker side of the room. Where there was an alcove about two yards square an oak wooden bench on one wall with a small iron table at one end and a shelved arm at the other to stand a drink on, Chrisi "shush Doris, remember to keep your gob closed and remember nothing," "ok she muttered softly." The other bar end of the alcove had a floor to ceiling fretted panel, narrowing the entrance to the alcove standing on that side, rendering it private from the rest of the bar. Chrisi pointed to the bench indicating to sit with her fore finger. Doris did as directed.

The guy was directly behind her; he placed his arm around her waist and drew her close to him spinning her around to face him. Doris couldn't make out his face. The flickering light from the fire was behind him. She could she in the shadows Chrisi dress being on buttoned. The guy suddenly lifted her; long legs wrapped around his hips. Her back was to the wall; the light intensified as new logs added to the fire burst into flames, Doris could not see enough having to strain her eyes most of the time, there were lots of movement between Chrisi, a bobbing up and down motion, ceasing as quickly as it had started, she made no sense of what they were doing. Chrisi buttoned her dress and coat the guy took something from his pocket threw it on the table, then walked away. Chrisi sat down on the bench beside Doris. Chrisi picked up the paper from the table taking one sheet, giving it to Doris, "put it in your bag Doris, not a bloody word." Chrisi poured the vodka into the half-empty lemonade bottle. "You've had it before, now drink your drink. I'm just going to the toilet to get dressed, there's a decent café up the road. We can get a bite before we go home, you are you hungry," "a little Chrisi," I'll be five minutes.

When Doris got home, she went straight to her room. The drink had not affected her as much as it did the first time, she sat on the edge of her bed, taking the paper Chrisi had given her, from her handbag. She was dying to know what it was bugger me, ten bob, that's a week's pay. Lots of thoughts with no real answers, went through her mind. What had she done for this kind of money? Her head was in turmoil. She could not get to sleep. The night was passing; various thoughts went through her mind, as she lay staring at the Ceiling, thinking of this and that, about the week gone and the man, she saw in the rubble on the demolition site.

Her stomach began to churn again oh shit she muttered. I'm going to go a different way to work on Monday and every other day as well. It was no use. She tried to think of something else, the more she was drawn to that moment. Dawn was breaking. The sun streamed into her room; She could see and feel his eyes burning into the white flesh of her inner thighs. She remembered him looking there. Doris put her hand down between her thighs, there she could feel the burning sensation; she drew her legs up to and elevate the knotting of her stomach; that's it. I've had enough of this she muttered to herself; she crept out on to the landing, snuck into Christine's room, getting on the bed beside her; she didn't want to think about the man.

The ache wouldn't go away; she whispered in Chrisi ear "I can't sleep." Chrisi pulled her nighty up around her waist and put her right hand between her thighs rubbing herself, "have you hurt yourself Chrisi; Doris enquired," "no shush. She whispered, see the chair in the corner, place the bow of the chair under the handle." She did as instructed, get on the bed and watch, "this is pleasure let me show you how." Chrisi placed a finger over her lips, "shush now Doris, watch" She took her hand put it down between her thigh, guiding her hand, showing her the motion; then put her own hand back between her thighs. Doris went to speak "shush; It's nice the first time, Hey; I love to pleasure myself."

What "Doris whispered" "shush, whisper, you have to whisper and put one hand over your mouth, or you'll wake the whole bloody house up." "I'm not daft enough to do that," "you have to Come." "I haven't been anywhere; I'm still here," "no. That's what you have to do down there, where I put your hand, it's called the sweet spot, come you'll see, you do the same," just watch. Chrisi continued the motion on herself her thighs eventually lifting her legs as her movements accelerated, suddenly her body went rigged, a muffled noise emulated from her mouth suppressed by her left hand.

Christine chuckled, quietly as they lay there together "give me your hand Doris. She whispered, place it down between your thighs. Now feel there, put your fingers there, do the motion I showed you." Doris quickly pulled her hand away, "it's wet; I've pee'd myself," wiping her hand on Chrisi nighty. "I can't believe what I'm doing," "no you haven't pee'd, I do all the time; it's a truly wonderful thing, but you have to put one hand over your mouth, remember that always a must, in this house its important, get caught. We will both have the sticking of our life." "Look outside its doesn't matter and better still, get a bloke to do it for you Doris." "What," "shush, she whispered, remember you have to whisper. Lift your nighty come lay here with me. Chrisi placed her head on her shoulder and proceeded to massage her left breast. Chrisi took her

hand, placing it down between her thighs, see "massage
that place gently with your finger, now you do it, put
the other hand over your mouth, before you reach your
peak you'll know that time," "ok what," "Doris said
again" "Just do it, "they were the last words; she could
remember. The feeling and glow in her body, words she
could not express the sheer pleasure she had experienced. The morning sunshine broke through the gap in
the curtains burning into her eyes, blurring her vision.
Still half naked her nighty around her waist, she quickly
got out of bed, picked up her bloomers, from the floor
and was about to put them on. She noticed the stain
on the bed sheets. shit pity Christine hadn't told that
would happen shit, 'what to do, what to do, panic
stricken" Doris wrenched the sheet from the bed, virtually clearing the stairs in one leap. She hurried into
the kit, going directly to the copper to see if there was
any hot water in it; Hell it's empty, shit I wish I was
a magician, "Doris muttered," "wouldn't we all,
language girl." She did not see her dad at the table in
her panicked rage. "If that's what you've done on the
sheets, I hope it is a girl. He laughed, or I'm going to
wash your mouth out with carbolic soap," "sorry' yes"
dad. She replied sheepishly."

Her face was burning. With embarrassment, "wash it
quickly before your mam comes down." "Thanks dad"
Doris, kissed him on the cheek and went about the choir,
filling the sink and washing the sheet by hand "put the
soap back when you're done," "yes dad," "or the cat will
chew on it, and you know how that makes him sick,
bloody strange moggy, strangest I've known." "Morning,
what was that about the soap Vi enquired?" Who chose

to be deaf when it suited, if she didn't want to listen your tripe, as she would put it, but Vi had radar ears as fine-tuned as any animal alive, when she wanted to hear, that meant you were probably in trouble? "Cat messed her bed sheet. That's why she needed the soap "Frank said," "got a tongue" "yes mam, Doris answered," "how comes she needs you to speak for her."

Vi on that note decided to go into one of her rants. It didn't take much, don't know why I bother. "I've worked my fingers to the bone, am I appreciated, no, you lot come and go as you please, bloody cats, wafer's and strays." "Enough about me, I'm off then, interrupting her." Frank smiled riley. He supped the last dregs of his tea, then headed for the front door. He knew it was better to go and not stand and argue a fight you couldn't win. Although it was too early to leave, once Vi got on her soap box, you could not get her off, she would go on and on and on, "bye love. Frank chuckled." "That's sodding it leave me to it, you just go, I'll deal with it, never you mind me." Frank shut door on the way out, knowing that wouldn't be the end of the conversation. He had given it attention; it deserved, none; he had barely shut the gate at the end of the path, before the front door opened. "Frank, Frank! Come back here, I haven't finished with you. Frank, Frank! Don't you walk away when I'm talking to you? Frank! Do you hear me?" "Hear you the whole bloody street can hear you" muttering under his breath, two streets away I'll still bloody hear you.

Going back, was pointless, a slanging match would just erupt into the street. The neighbours would hang out the windows and doors, to see who was getting the verbal public roast from Vi, as she was un affectionately known. If you got the tongue pie from her, you were on the losing wicket and was just as likely to get a crack from her favourite tool the copper stick which rarely left her side. "Sometimes I think I'm talking to the walls" violet muttered. She looked in the living room, then the kitchen, outside-in garden; the house was empty. The only thing moving was the sheet on the washing line, Vi had that effect; everyone had evacuated the house. German bombs during the second world war would not have been so effective.

Chrisi had got dressed in double quick time, escaping through the back door, then legging it across the garden with Doris climbing over the fence into the gully that ran down between the gardens, backing onto the allotments. During the summer, it was a pleasant walk, but you had to watch out for the stinging nettles and blackberry bushes, if you had bare legs, you were in trouble. Vi stood in the garden for a moment, typical, hasn't even mangled the sheets, bloody half the job as usual. Still mumbling to herself aloud despite her sharp tongue, her heart was in the right place, most of the time, everyone knew her cats were her life, she loved them. They were her children, all six of them, despite her sight poor through diabetes. She knew all their names by sound, frequently having conversations, with them as if they were attentive children.

In the evening, they would curl up around her legs and in front of the fire on the rag rugs she had lovingly made for her moggies as she would refer to them, while she

PETER ABBASOVA

knitted or crochet the fire crackling and the kettle hiss-
ing, on the iron grate, ready for anyone who wanted a
cupper. Vi was a grafter and looked after the house,
with military precision. All the meals were cooked by
her every day from fresh produce. Nothing was ever
wasted, rationing had taught her that, the allotment had
been the life line during the war, still was the case now,
not an inch of garden was wasted either; fruit bushes
and fruit trees were in abundance in the long garden
and was worked by her and Frank everyday as was the
allotment baking onto the garden behind the Anderson
shelter a short walk from the house. Jan was made from
the fruit, pies, dessert, flowers, scent, vegetables, rabbits,
chicken for meat, nuts from the hedges and wine from
the berries. During the summer, it was a harvest to
behold. A feast fit for any family, the result of hard toil,
if you spoke to either of them, they made the work
sound easy; it was clear that they enjoyed the labour for
the rewards they got.

Doris, asked Chrisi as they walk along the back of the
allotments, "You know I had a stain on the sheets. I had
to get them in wash and blame it on the cats," "Shame
on you. Chrisi replied," was that really the first time.
She felt her face flush up, "yes," "what about you and
this naked man. I'm hearing about have you done
anything with him, what an earth was he doing out in
the middle of the day in his birthday suit, birthday
suit." "No he was in shorts," birthday suit everybody
owns one of them, Doris. I don't she replied." "Where
do you buy one of them," "bloody hell Doris? I sometimes wonder if mam had an affair with the milkman,
you being the by-product."

"Wouldn't dad be upset about that, Doris said, if he knew, Chrisi did she have an affair with the milkman." "It's an expression, Doris, there's no doubt. You're as thick as shit, that why I don't tell you jack." Doris began to cry. "Oh for pity sake turn off the waterworks," "but I'm not worldly like you Chrisi. I don't have any friends, not, anyone, none that I can trust, there're you and that's pretty much it, if I didn't have you to talk to I would go mad." "I need you to help me Chrisi." "Look Doris, as she wiped her eyes, with a hanky, your birthday suit is your skin. When your bare, with nothing on at all, everyone has one, now was that man naked or not," "no; Doris muttered; he had a pair of shorts on, like I said and some boots," "so why have you made such a fuss over it," "I haven't Doris remarked sobbing. It's just when I see him, I'm breathless, my stomach churns, my heart pounds. I can't move for a minute or two and there a funny feeling down in my bloomers," "Oh Doris, really you've got the hots, and you don't know it." "Hots Chrisi" "boy have I got to teach you everything. When, you have the hots, it means you have feelings, within, in your case not knowingly, look come to the pictures with me my treat, you're going to have an education, about men and the birds and the bees, she perked up with a half-smile on her face.

They took deep breaths, taking in the scent of the mid-morning sun. Treading with care along the gully laced with the vines of the blackberry bushes and nettles, whilst the road could be clearly seen a short distance away the journey played havoc on their bare legs, not matter how far you could make your ankle socks stretch, the quick escape route and the pain, you had to be sure it was worth it. Just to get out of the house when the need arose, sometimes it was the only route you could take.

"My legs are stung to buggery. What about you? Doris remarked." "Don't worry about it, when the lights go out at the flicks, you could be sitting in just your knickers; no one would give a monkey." "You would be in the shit only if the usher could be bothered, or put the light on you." "They're so bloody lazy, in particular, when the girls are on, which is always in the afternoon session, there'll stay at the back for fear of falling over their own feet." "Doris you know when you felt yourself. Doris chirped in," before Chrisi could elaborate, "remember it all too well, Doris, bleeding shut up and listen, and maybe you just might learn a thing or two." " I'll start again when you pleasured yourself last night, today you're going to do the same but with a man, don't worry I show you the ropes, means how to, Doris, men are different down there." "I'm not that stupid Chrisi. I do know that much, I've heard the girls talk about it at work." "What have they said, exactly Doris," "that men keep their brains in their trousers, some do Chrisi, Doris was quick to remark, and they're all dick heads." "Christi could not console herself with laughter, Doris you're going to make me piss myself, sit down on the wall." "I need a bloody fag, look, Doris. Men have private parts. It's called a penis," "what do you do with it." "Good question, for a better word, think of an ice popsicle, remember how you want to suck all the juice out of it until you only have ice left, think along those lines, mind you sometimes they want to put their popsicle elsewhere, when the time comes you and your man will figure that out." "For God sake what I'm I doing, telling you this" "No don't stop Chrisi. I'll do whatever you say or ask, could you show me, ok?" "Please Chrisi," "let's have that fag, once we get to town. I'll find a man that's as some sugar." Is he going to make the tea Chrisi, Doris you're a national treasure, dimwit it's a man with spare money?" "That's rare, fortunately; I know how to separate the weeds from the crop," Doris, all you've got to do is watch me and learn, ok, just follow my lead.

In no time, they were in town walking past the foot of the castle a short cut alley across the road would lead them into the inner city. Chrisi, did not like this part of town, like most people, She found walking by the bombed out ruins was too eerie to stomach; it would bring back memories of the blitz. Neighbour's friends, children and relatives were killed here. Spending night after night in a cold shelter during the relentless bombing, there were few roads or buildings that were unscathed, the loss of life was terrible, and the worst they had known.

The market was filled with elderly shoppers, looking for bargains spending the little they had. Men were leaning against pub doorways. Throwing up in the drain gullies before drinking more ale. They were eyeing up the women as they passed by, wolf whistling making sexiest comments. Chrisi stopping at one to hitch her dress up so it showed a bit of leg just above the knee, attracting her own brand of Wolfe's whistles and comments. Never mind, the leg, show us the us, the menu darling and your mate to, this was the men's play area in this town, at the weekend they owned, in these two side streets, no respecting man would be seen here; it was hard to believe it was only a street from an area with affluence.

Doris grabbed Chrisi arm tightly, every few yards the occasional man would step into their paths, and pat their backsides. With shouts of how about it then girls, Chrisi would just brush them to one side. "You couldn't afford me," ignore them Doris." "She chirped were not eating dog today, thanks." "We want fine wine." They turned into London road, here there were restaurants of good standing, Doris stopping to browse the odd one. "Sodding hell, Chrisi, have you seen the prices." "I'm not intending to pay, so don't worry about them." Dance halls, picture houses, museums and a theatre, there was also money, two streets separated rags to riches. "This is where life is Doris, time to relax, its ok here, we'll have a ball." "Chrisi chatted to one group of men and then another. Doris felt a prize prune acting as a mute every time a man approached her. They were shunned away focusing their attention on Chrisi. They would put their arm around her drawing her close to them while she put her arms around their necks, then pushed them back when they didn't measure up to the mark of her requirements. She whispered in their ears, whatever words were spoken. They soon let go. When it was not to their liking, lips pouting blowing wind and muttering as they pulled away. Doris felt uncomfortable, but at the same time intrigued, every time a man got close to her. She shuffled along the pavement lengthening the gap quickly between

herself and the men to disassociate herself with Chrisi.
It wasn't long before she triumphed arm in arm with her
catch. "Come on Doris, latch onto the other arm, where
off to the Odeon."

They strolled along the pavement, boldly arm in arm
chatting as they walked like long lost lovers. Doris
felt she was in tow, a sheep, what I'm I doing as she
eyed the man her sister was attached to. "Christi
said his name was Johnny." They're all called that,
you don't want you to know their real name, or that
they are married, the man paid for the tickets, "Chrisi
whispered in her ear, were alright here Doris He'll be
good for a few bob."

They followed him up the stairs to the upper circle. The
usher guided them to their balcony seat, a first class
area; completely private and exclusive, Johnny sat in the
middle seat; he had just sat down when Christi leaned
over his lap. "Doris this is the best seat in the house; she
whispered, remember to do what I ask." Doris nodded
her head, ok Chrisi," as she moved back to her seat
taking Johnny's hand, she placed it on the inside of her
thigh, looked straight at Doris with eye and hand
gesture to do the same. Doris stared at her with a blank
expression. Chrisi leaned over Johnny, taking his other
hand placing it of her knee, "oh; Doris mouthed." The
lights dimmed and the Pathe news light up the screen, as
did the sensation of Johnny his hand rubbing gently on
her inner thigh riding higher up the leg as each few
seconds passed, Doris felt her heart starting to pound.
She looked across at the lap of Chrisi; Johnny's left
hand was already at the top of Chrisi leg. She watched

in the flickering light, but she couldn't make out what Johnny was trying to do, both his hands withdrew the light partially coming back on before the start of the film. Just before the lights had dimmed again.

Chrisi turned sideways placing her left her on Johnny's trouser buttons on doing the first, quickly undid the rest, then lights went off, for a few minutes. Doris couldn't see a thing, when the light from the screen intensified she could make out Chrisi hand inside his trousers. She couldn't help but turn, to get a better view as she did the Johnny hand was back on the inside of her thigh working its way up. Doris just let her legs spread apart her heart once again racing. She looked down at the his trousers, as Chrisi leaned over, "face the screen Doris, she whispered," it distracted her for a minute she had forgotten what Johnny was doing until he touched her sweet spot, she suddenly clamped her thighs shut on his hand and grabbed his arm. Chrisi leaned over took the wrist of her right hand guiding it to Johnny's trousers, manipulating her hand and fingers around something firm but soft, guiding her hand, teaching her what was required. When she stopped Chrisi was quick to restart the process. Keep it going, she mouthed, during the action. She relaxed her grip on his hand, immediately continuing his action of pleasuring her. Chrisi had repositioned herself her head was in his lap; Chrisi cold nose touched the outside of her hand her long hair a masking Johnny's lap from her view of the action, which progressively increased in speed. Doris still had a firm grip on Johnny's right arm; Her heart was pounding it was the same feeling as when she had pleasured herself, only better, Doris buried her mouth onto his shoulder to suppress her squeal, as she reached her peak, expelling a gasp of air, Christi was sitting upright, wiping her mouth with his hanky. Johnny pulled his hand away from Doris adjusting himself buttoning his trousers. She couldn't bring herself to look at him, for a while. However, she did notice his wallet open. Johnny took a few bits of paper out dishing them to Christi. He got up and left. Chrisi moved over to where he had sat, but never said a word, just stared at the screen.

After, as they exited the cinema. "Christi said, well Doris how do you feel," strange. I couldn't see much, there was little, in the way of light." "However, I saw enough and felt him, oh boy when I reach my peak, it was unbelievable." "Doris it was also rewarding," showing her six one- pound notes in her right hand. "Chrisi that's more than I make in wages in two and a half weeks with overtime." "Don't get over exited Doris, after we have been shopping, had a decent nosh, a drink or two most of it will be gone." "Doris you must tell no one, and I mean no one." "We have done our weekly sin, if mam or dad ever knew I be disowned." "Perhaps both of us, thrown out, onto the streets, then we would be well buggered." "Chrisi. I swore to you. I wouldn't tell a soul. I meant, but please you must teach me more." "Ok Doris, it's a deal now let's go eat?

"This Bistro will do, Doris." "I haven't been in a restaurant before, are you sure we should be in here Chrisi." "Been before Doris, I' m careful; I chose places where I know mam, dad and their friends would never come." "They couldn't afford to, not anywhere down this road." "The menu please cameriere," Chris commanded; I'll order." "Chrisi I can't understand a word of this menu, its Italian. What's fagioli soup? It sounds like something you'd smoke." "The menu is in Italian, as is the wine, that's why I'm ordering, enjoy." "Chrisi. How do you know about the place" "Doris, Patrizio the owner's nephew works here? That's why I sit here at the back away from prying eyes, and it's next to the staff room door see? The one marked private. We might get a cut price banquet if he's here; he is Patrizio. Chrisi called him as he came out of the kitchen.

"Hi baby, Che piacere vederti, how nice to see you" Patrizio walked up to Christi, kissed her hand then on each cheek. "Are you ok for a while, staff room, five minutes." He'd forgotten that Doris was even there, "err." She made herself heard. "Oh, so sorry didn't mean to ignore your friend hope you don't mind I have a little business with Julie." Doris was about to say I'm her sister when Chrisi, butted in. "My friend will be fine for five minutes or so, get her a glass of red wine." What's here name, asked Patrizio," again before she could answer, her name is Helen?" "Maybe I can do I little business with you both hey." Christi stood up shaking her head, "not today big guy." "Perhaps another time Helen, Patrizio said." Who knows Doris replied," "A nice glass of red-wine Patrizio, will ease the pain of the wait," "of course he replied, on the house, good boy." "Darling sip, the wine, our business won't to take long." Chrisi went with him into the staff room the door. She heard the door locking behind them. Doris felt so out of place it gave her goose bumps, the wine soon took the edge off adding a warm glow in her belly, wow. I could get use to this, talking out loud.

Five minutes had hardly passed when they exited the staff room first Patrizio to ensure the coast was clear, then he waved Chrisi out, Patrizio, well ladies look at the menu I will be back shortly. Chrisi what sort of business did you do. Don't, ask that question here Doris, I'll explain when we leave, ready to order ladies, I'll have the fettuccine allay romana, and Helen will have ravioli manicotti, with two slices of garlic bread, Patrizio red wine please, of course he replied. Err there will be a discount make sure it's one hundred percent; That's a good boy. Doris whispered, Chrisi why do you keep referring to me as Helen, he thinks your Julie, never tell a trick your real name. Now eat drink and shush, ok. When the bill came the total was a mere nothing, perfect Patrizio, Chrisi left half a crown on the plate, "please ladies come again" "See you patrizio."

"Chrisi that wine has gone to make head." "Don't worry about it Doris, a walk around the shops will soon wear it off." "Chrisi I saw the prices on the menu a glass of water, came to more than what you paid." "Please what did you do for that," "well best you know I let him stick me. I let quite a few selected men to stick me, you will know what I mean one day, that's what I'm good at and the pays not bad either." "I didn't see you complain when you shovelled the food down your neck." "What you do is up to you." "However, all the money and favours mam and dad will latch on at some point. Surely, they're going to wonder where the clothes come from." "Not a chance Doris as long as you keep your gob shut, I don't take it home anyway." "I have a locker that I rent at the station, once I'm twenty one. I'll rent my own place and work the tricks there." "I don't spend it all. I have some savings at the bank. The rest goes for living, my style." "Shit Chrisi, I wish I was as smart," "Doris you're a good kid, don't become me. I take chances, but I'm street wise. You're not." "I love you to bits, but you're not quite the full load, no offence." Doris smiled "I know; I'm stupid, but you're my friend not just my sister; that's important to me." Chrisi put her arm through hers, "come on let's go treat ourselves to some nice stocking, hide them, make sure if you're going to wear, then you stick them in the back off your knickers." "I only have those bloody bloomers." "Well, then it's time to put that right, don't forget to take them off put them in your hand bag, change into them when you're out."

"Before we go home, should forget, Chrisi. I've had a fantastic day." "I've got some lipstick, knickers stocking and some great perfume." "God I can't believe what these cost," "just keep them out of site. "Make sure mam does smell it indoors; She'll have your guts for garters."

The reality of home life was a blow on the nose, the minute they walked through the door, and where have you two be all day, yes you two; that's right just treat it as a hotel, never mind me. I just scrimp scrape and work my fingers to the bone; You enjoy yourselves; I'll be the donkey. Doris tried to block out her mother's voice, for a moment thinking. This is the same-old shit, she looked at her mother putting her head in her hand. Please God, don't let that be me in years to come, as she went on and on, at times, stopping occasionally for a new tank of air, Doris blurted out without thinking, for God sake mam, shut up "it's enough to give you a bloody headache."

She barely finished the sentence when a crack from the copper stick connected with the funny bone of her left elbow. The pain filled her eyes immediately with tears; she saw Chrisi out the corner of her eye vacating the room smartly, "sodding hell mam that hurt," her mother about to crack another blow stopping midway. "Hurt; it was meant to bloody hurt, and you don't lip me and expect to get away with it." She clasped her left elbow with her right hand rubbing it to try to soothe the infliction. Doris might as well not have bothered, as a second shot, came when she was least expecting it catching the other elbow, sending her into a hopping dancing jig, she leapt from one spot then to another, tears bellowing from her eyes; she squealed, gritting her teeth, spitting bubbles, feeling the pain. She gave her mother the devils look, grimaced again, as she crept towards her mother, if her looks could kill, her stare would have buried an axe in her mother's head. "Have you got anything else to say, my girl," Doris had slumped into the rocking chair, rocking back and forth her knees drawn up to her chest? She shook her head, whispering a quiet no. "Good, didn't think so" you probably hate me right now, don't worry it will pass. You'll thank me one day, when you have children of your own, you just wait and see," I won't treat them like you, cow bag. She thought in her mind, bugger off mam, leave me alone, you evil witch, still wincing from the pain, which slowly subsided, her mother s went off to the kitchen, muttering. God knows what.

What a lovely day it's been, until now, then that cow spoilt it for what, she thought one day. I will pay her back, wait and see if I don't; I'll be like Chrisi get out of this house sooner rather than later wait and see she kept telling herself.

Dinner was eaten in complete silence; she had to force herself. The meal she had in the city with Chrisi still weighed heavy on her stomach. There was only her and her mother at home. Doris dare not say I'm not hungry and have another copper stick session. Chrisi went off to do her stint at the chip shop lucky sod. She thought her dad was out at work. His dinner plated up, ready to put on the stove to warm it through, shit this is boring sorry. What did you say Doris, nothing mam?

She cleared the dinner plates away, washed up, then went to her room, sitting for a while, looking out of the window, at murky sky. Doris curled up on the bed; she couldn't remember falling asleep, when she awoke, it was pitch black; the house was silent. However, someone covered her up. She jumped out of skin. The grandfather clock struck out, one, two, three gongs normally it would not bother her. Its three bloody hell she thought; I need a pee, bugger she thought again, why can't we have a lock on the damn doors, creeping along the boards on the landing, without making a sound? Would be like try to walk through a minefield blind folded. Typically, every board groaned and creaked not matter how careful she was. Standing on the cats' tail at the bottom of the stairs didn't help either, meowed leaping out of its skin its faint shadow disappearing into a dark corner, surprisingly no one was aroused. God she thought I could be a burglar, who the hell would care. Someone could come in and murder us all. Having had her toilet, getting back to her bed, was a miracle considering the noise she had made going down. Thank god she thought, getting back into bed a hand came out of the dark clamping her face, over her mouth. "It's me Doris a voice whispered," "Chrisi, I've had enough punishment and scares for one day." "I know Chrisi replied I felt bad about hop scotching it upstairs thought I would cuddle you for a while." "I couldn't sleep me neither Doris said." "I'm still thinking about yesterday. It was great wasn't it, until we got home. the cow bag." "Doris, you are a little bugger," "come on turn round put your back to me and cuddle up." Chrisi put her hand up her nighty and between her legs, "that's perfect," putting her hand on top of hers, closing her eyes.

Chrisi took Doris with her each weekend for the company. They didn't always go man hunting; going out with Chrisi, was now the highlight of her life. She was teaching Doris how to live. They went to museums, art galleries, on the train to the next city, restaurants and window shopping, in a short time they had become very close. She was ready to take on the world it was late September, harvest festival, church time, thanks Doris thought it was bad enough to have to go there without the extra hype.

"Come on lazy bones, get up, we've got to go to church remember, come on." Christi was "shaking her by the shoulders like a rag Doris." I don't want to get up Chrisi," don't give mam another excuse to stick you, shit your right." The thought of it would be enough to spring a corpse from a coffin." Come on Doris; shake a leg" "ok, what the rush" "It's nearly nine, that's the rush." The familiar Sunday morning calls from their

mother echoed around the stair well, are we in need
of the copper stick this morning "no mam came the
universal reply. I'd like to put that stick where the sun
doesn't shine and her in Billy when its full of boiling
water, oil would be better still, old Billy, was the name
of the copper, but nobody knew why, apart from Vi and
she wasn't telling.

"Don't know why we both have to go to church. You
could go." "Chrisi, ask God for a double forgiveness, see
whether he will do a special." "Doris I won't go to
heaven will you." "Chrisi, I don't think there is one."Doris
as for hell living in this bloody house is at times hell,"
let's hurry." The church will still be there in a hundred
years, so slow down Crisis, so that I can catch my
breath." They descended the stairs together; you look
great girls, thanks dad; they replied. Vi, on the other
hand, had different thoughts. "Hair looks like she been
dragged through an edge backwards; it's in needs a cut;
clothes look like you've both slept in them." "The pair
need cracking into shape; a good hiding now and again
don't hurt anyone, let me crack your bloody elbows and
knees with the stick see if that hurts or not." Doris
thought; mam give us peace just one day of the week.

"A goody two shoes there pair of them, but there are
evil thoughts in both their heads Frank." As they made
their way to church Chrisi, looked at Doris smiling
half breaking into a giggle, she knew exactly what was
in her head, "It's no laughing matter, Church you know,
you two, do you want to get struck down by a lightning
bolt." "I'm your dad; I know about the fear of your
mother" she is a puppy compared to God."

The Vicar spoke from the pulpit "There are today, among us sinners." Great. Doris looking around the congregation, while the vicar threw down the fear of god from his box. If only he knew, how many hypocrites where in today, which he probably did. There wouldn't be anyone attending church today, he'd be out of a job. I suppose most of them thought; if they came to church once a week, the slate would be wiped clean. Then out of here and down to the pub, the vicar would be leading the sprint to the white horse for the first drink. If God was cleaning their slates, who was doing his, she chuckled, exiting out into the grave yard.

Doris liked to walk among the grave stones, reading one every now and then. As she walked she saw Johnny, the man from the cinema, she turned taking look around, the cores of the congregation were chatting outside with one another, the vicar was mingling in among them, some were leaving by the south gate. Her mam, dad and Christi had already left, which was not unusual. She would often go for a walk after service for an hour or so, Doris turned and looked again for Johnny, catching a glimpse. He had been walking around to the north side, to the wooded area by the old Iron Gate; leading to the public foot path across the fields. She followed seeing him pass through the gate and out of sight. She looked around again, making her way through the same gate onto the foot path, which led to spinney in one direction and Houghton to the left, the path to spinney turned about a quarter of a mile exiting the woods onto open farm land. It was a wandering path that went in a half circle eventually leading to burnt house lane about a quarter of a mile from home.

At this time of the year, it was a pleasant walk as there were few obstacles. She looked for Johnny. He was gone; she took a slow walk to the end of the woods and was about to turn back, when Johnny appeared from behind an oak tree. Doris leapt about two yards to the rite falling on a grass mound showing off her skimpy knickers. She could see he was looking, but made no effort to conceal herself. "Johnny you scared the bloody daylights out of me," "sorry Julie; I didn't mean to frighten I wanted to make sure we were alone." I wasn't sure you would follow me down here. "Few if, any people come this way, except the odd occasional dog walker, you were nice to us when we last met." "I was curious, about you, your friend. She appeared to be very professional, what about you."

Oh, I'm just getting started." How much will it cost me Johnny inquired," "will you become a regular? She asked." I don't think so." I'm, not sure even if it's what I want, but for now perhaps you'll show me what you want, your friend Mary. I saw her at church, didn't think professional girls sort forgiveness." "She was with her grandparents, Johnny. They are church people, are you a regular here" "no I was putting some flowers my mother's grave. It was coincidental. I saw Mary first and then you, had I left a minute earlier I would have missed you both." "That's fate sometimes Johnny, is it." "I don't live here; I live and work in London. I was bored too I went for a walk around town. That's how I met you both, when do you go back Johnny, tomorrow, my names not really Johnny?" "Oh? That's all I need for now, mines not Julie either, It's better that way?

They walked briskly only stopping occasionally to take in the view, making small talk along the way about this and that, nothing specific, there it was, the pillar box, grey concrete covered partially by moss and lichen, bramble and thorn bushes where on two sides, all the slit holes were visible. Johnny went inside emerging a few seconds later it's quite light inside with a good view in every direction, perfect; he drew her to him planting a firm kiss on her lips, "wow you're a fast worker," "why not he replied I know what I want?" "Do you now," Johnny had a look around, then went back inside the box? "Come on Julie," there was a raised platform in the Centre. It looked as though it had been designed for a mounted gun emplacement. Between the three iron fixing plates, there was enough room to lay Johnny's spread the coat he had been carrying over his left arm.

"It's nice and dry in here; it's not too uncomfortable." "You see all the way down the path, what shall we do first he said." "I'll sit on your coat, do what you did with my friend, she nearly blurted out sister." He interjected, "Mary," "yes my friend Mary." Johnny sat beside her, leaned slightly undoing his trousers buttons."let's explore and kiss for a moment," "ok Johnny," they both leaned toward each other and started to pet. His hand went straight to the top of her knickers. "Why don't you take then off, he said softly?" Doris arched her back, drew her legs up, slipping them over her ankles. His finger went straight to the sweet spot and inside of her. She gasped, "oh Johnny, don't stop," he kissed her gently on the lips, pulling his hand away when she had been pleasured, he rolled from right to left taking a look through the slits, "just making sure he said." He pushed his trousers and pants down stopping at his knees, "wow" "glad you approve." He took hold of it with his right hand, with his left brought her head to him, she opened her mouth to speak. However, she remembered what her sister had said to suck it like a Lolly, until the juice has been taken and only the ice is left.

In the cinema, she remembered Chrisi actions; she thought I would do the same. Johnny sighed; This is not too bad. She thought, not quite like the taste of a Lolly. After what seemed like an eternity, he pulled her head way; she was glad her jaw was starting to ache. Johnny pushed her down onto the slab pulling her legs apart and cantering himself between them. He pulled her by her hips more to the edge lifting her legs her feet were now planted on the concrete wall behind him. He reached then pushed against her. She gasped feeling him inside; he drew back and pushed again." Err she muttered," as he drew back and forth repeating the process at first it hurt a little, but became pleasurable, her feet lifted from the wall and back to the wall with every stroke; without thinking, she pushed her pelvises to meet each incoming thrust, "oh god she sighed," reaching her peak again and again there was one final thrust; Johnny let out a roar. She could feel Johnny pulsing; a gush of warm liquid entered her. His body went limp, laying his full body weight on her. Johnny; I can't breathe; he lifted himself up on his hands; sweat was on his brow, are you ok she said, fine, absolutely fine. He got off, took out a handkerchief then tossed it with her knickers onto her stomach; she took them and put the back on; Johnny threw the used hanky into the corner. "Don't you want that, no? I don't think so." Johnny pulled up his trousers, redressing himself, "that was truly wonderful." "It's a pity you don't live closer Doris, replied." "I don't think my wife would approve, do you Julie," "no I suppose not." As they emerged out of the box; Johnny took out his wallet, placing two five-pound notes in her hand and walked off trust that's enough. She was in shock, staring for a moment at the cash in her hand, how cold she thought, walking back home to the church, how bloody cold, now she understood, what Chris meant, by getting sticked, not quite the same as mam's copper stick.

Sunday typical bloody Sunday mam asleep in one chair feet up the chimney, moggies curled around her feet. Chrisi looking at her, what's up Doris you've got a smile on you like a Cheshire cat, nothing she replied, just enjoying the day? She had made her mind up, not to tell, either about the money or Johnny, if they knew what had taken place, she would have ripped my head off? Sunday dinner was always the same, roast whatever, with roast everything and gravy and let's not forget the toping Yorkshire pudding. Chrisi would wake mam ten minutes before serving time, out came the same-old thing, wash your hands properly and table now.

No conversation was allowed, unless mam had something to say, or dad, with her consent, then wash up listen to the radio, bed, sleep work the next day. This was the boring part; every weekend was the same, you could write about every weekend as it happened, compare notes over a whole year, they would be identical. The only difference was Christmas presents or when anything important said. Doris helped as she always did washing up or drying. Afterward, to her room, an escape zone from everything, bloody hell, she thought laying there, the man. That's not so bad; I'll leave early. The man behind the fence, no worries she made her mind, bah, the bloke behind the fence, bah. She thought who cares. Doris felt full of confidence, what could be worse than what I've done, bloody nothing? She thought, bugger it.

"Bye mam, see you," with a new-found bounce in her step, as she bounded along the pavement at her usual but with much great vigour. She marched straight up to the fence, "please come out, wherever you are." Jan appeared from behind a half fallen building, "hello. I'm Doris. She shouted," Jan Probernoskei dumbfounded, there she was speaking to him, instead of running away, "English please, then I could understand you." I want to understand you. Jan hand signalled her in a manner beckoning her to stay; He turned his head and bellowed out through cupped hands across the compound."Zimmer, Zimmer," "Zimmer, Zimmer.". "I'm Prichard, pockajte I'm coming, wait."

The noise of someone walking towards them over the loose bricks; echoed among the buildings. In the midst of partly standing bombed-out buildings. They both looked among the ruins, the scruffiest man you could ever imagine emerged on top of a pile of brick's about thirty feet away, his hair looked like he had been electrocuted, a goatee beard protruded from his unshaven and wrinkled face; his shirt was in tatter's one sleeve missing; the trousers were no better, patches covered patches; he looked like some mad professor assembled from various discarded rag dolls. I'm Zimmer Swaranowich and your Doris; she stood back a pace from the fence; you speak English, and nine other's...

"Good morning," I'm Zimmer and this is my friend Jan; he likes you very much." "I believe he has spoken to you before, be it in Slovakian." He speaks no English, my friend; we would, be happy that is Jan if you came and had a drink with us. So he can know you better. "Why not, when, Doris replied," he was about to have a discussion, about the where and time. When the factory whistle sounded, "bloody hell she said, I'll see you both at lunchtime, sorry got to go." "Later hey here twelve thirty, ok," "not the quiet shy timid girl you described Jan, hey, Zimmer said, see you later."

On entering the factory at a brisk stride not the old Doris but a new decisive and purposeful Doris. Ben Grub, was standing in his usual place by the clocking machine as she strode into the factory with grace, and her head held up high. "You look full of bean's Doris." "Yes, Ben I'm on a new diet, "is it any good he enquired," "yes brilliant and simple, kill men and eat them. I Wouldn't turn your back if I was you, especially if it was that time of the month. Hey Ben," bloody hell, it's just one thing after another with you women." "Anyway about the diet, had a plateful for breakfast, tasty sausage, exquisite meat balls, with bread sauce and some onions cooked slowly with a little liver, makes it more interesting when you add flavour, hey Ben," as she turned, Ben was legging it down the corridor.

"What's gotten into you Doris, that no way to talk to Ben or your work mates," "work mates, Megan you Bastards, you who speak to me when it suits you." "They stand at the other end of the yard at break time taking the piss, treating me like a leper, you sorry looking shits, hey, tell me If I'm wrong," well, language Doris." "Megan they make me sick, go on you lot; piss off and go about your business you shit heads." Megan smiled at Doris, "you've started something now, about time you stood up for yourself girl, go about your tasks. During the morning, we'll have a chat, just one to one you and me" "a little bloodletting never hurt too much Doris."

Break time was as any other day, Doris, alone in her spot, she could sense that she was the topic of the day. During the cosy little group chats, multiple glances, every other, half minutes were in her direction. Shayla would break from one chat group then go to another. The gossip by the end of a break was well circulated, if it was you, they were discussing; everyone in the factory would know your business or thought they knew. The elastic would be totally stretched in imagination and creativity. A new legend was born every day. "Hi, Megan," "Doris what an earth has made you change like this and so suddenly," "life; I haven't lived it. Everyone's been living it for me, Doris, do this, do that, go here, go there, fetch me that get me this, get up, go to bed; it's enough to make a mad person insane." "That's life for most people Megan replied," "well not for me, not from today; it isn't that's all I have to say for now, sorry Megan." "I'll come and do my work. That's, that. Doris walked back into the factory," before the break had finished. There wasn't the usual mouthing after the morning, break the air was normally full of mouthed chatter, maybe they're waiting for another outburst from me; she thought, there were stares in her direction, but that was all.

Looking at the clock on the gantry at the end of forward loom, did nothing to stop that feeling in her stomach was churning. The same one she experienced the first stay. She had laid eyes on him, that feeling when Johnny when took her, the feeling was nice, but was blurring her concentration at times. She had to get a grip on herself; time was slowing down the clock seemed to be stuck. She was thinking of calling the line charge hand over, to see if it had stopped, each minute that passed was an eternity, the last five the worst, the siren blurted out its eerie sound. She was at the exit door faster than a greyhound, road sense, any sense, there was none. Her heart pounded more and more with every step; Doris felt her heart beating in her head, every breath of had exhausted her lung; she hits chain-link fence and hung to it like a bat to a cave.

Jan, Jan, Zimmer, trying to regain her composer, while puffing and panting was almost hopeless. Zimmer she belted out her lungs with a fresh gasp of air, abruptly, turning, focusing his eyes firmly on her right side. She could feel those stunning blue eyes burn into her soul, her legs jelly, her mouth open, her bosom pounded. Zimmer's voice bellowing from within the compound, "a moment please, one moment; I'll be there." The sound of his voice, was the distraction that snapped her out of the trance. God, she thought did he go to bed and get up in the same outfit. He looks exactly as the first time she cast eyes on him a bloody tramp. "Sorry, so sorry, I'm not very good on the feet on the rubble." "Never mind, no matter, I'm here, let's talk brass tacks," "let's not Doris said, let's talk me, him and your wallets, seven thirty this evening, by the clock tower, in the city, town Centre, is that yes in town and yes by the clock tower." "Yes, my English is not perfect. Zimmer stated," "your English was not good, or you didn't like the answer, not everything in the world is bang on is it, there lots of things not perfect about you mate."

"Where should we start, your attire perhaps?" "Oh. I don't always look like this; he laughed." "Really, seen you twice; you've looked the sodding same both times?" During their conversation, Jan had been prodding Zimmer, asking what going on; his muscles flexed the sweat reflecting the sun like a worn mirror. He turned to Jan and spoke in Slovak. The smile on his face needed no translation. It's; ok Doris asked yes its fine. Bang on time the factory siren sounded, "until tonight then boys." She ran across the road into the factory out of there sight. "She is a fiery woman Jan, good luck, see you later."

Doris conjured up her plan during that afternoon, dads out, first of the month, union meeting. Great mam will be asleep by the if fire she wakes up, she'll think I've gone to bed. Doris pondered all the possibilities and scenarios, never before had she concocted such a sneaky thing, once side of her condemned what she was doing as stupid, the other new-found devil side was going, go for it sod the consequence. During the rest of the day working like a trogon keeping her mind focused. However, from time, she couldn't help herself. Her mind for a few seconds wandered back to Jan's body, sending shivers down her spine, knotting her stomach, like a wet towel being wrung out on wash day, the feeling in her knickers, squeezing her thighs together. The feeling passed, but really she didn't want to let the feeling go.

When the siren sounded marking the end of the day. Doris was in a trance, in and out of her own special dream world, stepping out into the sunshine, she stood for a while, other factory workers hustled by every one of them invisible, a tune sprung onto her lips, Doris had heard it on the radio. She couldn't remember all the words, no hurry to go, humming in between words filling the gaps for those she couldn't remember home to my sweet heart. The air was full of summer fragrances along the path leading to the pillar box; where Johnny had taken her. She buried herself into the crop of ripening wheat, making a bed, laying on her back; she made out pictures from cotton the clouds in the pastel blue sky. Her mind wandered back to Jan's rippling muscles; she pressed her hands onto her stomach to suppress the ache within, down between her thighs tugging at the cloth a handful at a time to pleasure herself; her mind flashed back and forth, Jan, then Johnny, images of muscle and thrusting hips. Her voice rang out as she peaked, birds in the hedge rows took to flight, breaking her thoughts, wow, oh, wow. She took a deep breath of air, and played for a while longer, she was a peace with herself. She listened to the orchestra of nature bursting into song from the hedges and trees. Bee's and butterflies danced to the tunes of nature; her eyes dance with them from one and to another, there just like working folks going here and there, she stood, looked around at the view, so beautiful, she said out aloud, there was no rush to go home ambling her way along the winding foot paths.

Her mother's voice greeted her when she opened the door. "Where the hell have you been; still think it's a bloody hotel, don't you" she bellowed. "there the day was perfect now its buggered she muttered softly," "what that my girl, what did you say, she bellowed," "can I have some bread and butter," "get to the table," "yes mam" she smiled" and take that smirk of your face, bloody bread and butter, to many fancy work-mates, bloody bread and butter, your dad's money, doesn't stretch to bread and butter?" Doris tucked into her dinner, when she'd finished, her mam was still prat-tling on about bread and sodding butter, mam she thought if you were a cow, which you are, your mouth would sour the milk; that's it, why we have no sodding bread and butter.

Dinner served, her father, quick to exit the table. "See you later Doris, union meeting" "I know dad" she replied, "you said a hundred times, see yah." "Help me clear the table and wash up Doris," "yes mam," "may be your dad, can bring it up at his union meeting, Bread and bloody butter, see what they make of it." She took a knife from one of the plates, following her mother into the kitchen, gesturing a stabbing motion into her back; it would be the sodding right thing to do she thought, for the sake of humanity.

The excitement of her pending adventure was all she could think of, every time her mother spoke it was a pure wasted effort. As soon as the dishes, were put away and table cleaned; she knew; the next event would be, let's put the kettle on, then radio, stoke the fire, peck on the cheek and see yah later love, hello moggies and settle by the fire, within few minutes snoring would fill the air. The radio would do nothing to dampen the sound or wake her no matter how loud the volume would be. Her stomach churned; she sat on the couch watching her mother sip her tea by the fire side, then, a few rows of knitting, her head bobbing up and down as her eyes closed, bang the lights were out.

Doris wasted not a moment; she sprang into action. It was the only time of the day her mother was out for the count. Falling bombs wouldn't wake her mam when she was asleep it was equal to death itself. She dressed herself up, slipped the perfume Chrisi had bought her into a handbag she borrowed from her room; I'll put that on later, thank God. She not here; Doris knew getting out wouldn't be a problem. She crept around quietly just in case, getting back in would be a different matter, if she did wake up. She would just assume Doris had gone to bed. Doris closed the door behind her. It's sods law whenever you tried to sneak, out everything you did either creaked or made a noise of some sort, it's a good job. Mams dead to the world; Doris chuckled under her breath got away with it; legging it down the pavement. The concern was catching the tram to town and not be seen by anyone that would know her, if that happens, I'll cross that bridge when we come to it. Town Centre Miss; the conductor asked, yes please she replied, err the return time, last tram ten thirty me duck, four pence please, missy. This is the most bloody uncomfortable ride for cost she thought, but better than walking on broken glass, but not by much. The seats were wood, the tracks buckle and the road uneven, at this time of the day it wasn't very clean either. Other travellers had left their rubbish when they had disembarked, she would normally avoid them for that reason, alone, the turnpike by the three bells hotel, was just short of the city Centre, the clock tower about a six or seven-minute walk. She would have liked to window shop if there had been time, the building occupied were brand new. With the latest fashions, many others were under construction. The new installed electric light made it glitzy. She loved it, apart from prices, which were out of her league.

There they are, twiddle Dee and his side kick Hercules. The white shirt he was wearing, seemed to look to be a size small, she giggled; she thought, if he flexed now, it would rip open everything up to the top he would be exposed, that would get him arrested, Zimmer, wow that was a real shock. He looked a city gent with style a banker maybe or professor, some sort of professional, what shock, not looking a guy who worked on a rubble site, what a shock, she kept repeating to herself.

"Been waiting long," "yes, it's him, Jan. He's so on the edge, wanting you, so we've been standing a long time. An hour or more," "patience Jan," tell him Zimmer, Jan didn't need Zimmer to tell him anything. He knew what he wanted, taking her hand, he then put it under and around his huge biceps. "God Jan it's like putting my arm around my sister's waist, what an earth does he feed them." Good food and exercise, press ups, Zimmer chirped," perhaps he could show me some of those later." "no Zimmer said he'll ruin his clothes," "oh. He can take them off first. I wouldn't mind a peak" she said. I reckon, that hours going to cost him, about thirty bob." "What they charge you for waiting here." "No, that's to entertain me Zimmer," patting his face with palm of her right hand, "that seem fair, he said ha, English humour," she thought someone's dafter than me, where we off to Jan will lead, it's a bit of a walk, but it's worth it. Lead on then muscles, she said "let's go be sinners, It's Zimmer." "I said a sinner, it sounds similar, if you're not one, you, soon will be, let me introduce you to hell."

Zimmer looked at Doris bemused, scratching his head, "don't worry your head about it. God doesn't understand me either," "you English women; you are all mad," "do you know plenty of them Zimmer" she enquired, "no. I try to live healthy; I've found women will harm your health" "I'm interested. How did you work that out," "they befriend you, take over your life and everything you have and leave? You're a broken man." "You are a sad bastard Zimmer?" He translated as they walked their conversation to Jan as they made their way through the narrow back street and passages, it was the first-time Doris heard him laugh. "He has a sense of humour," "yes he has" Zimmer replied.

The area was not known to her, around every corner. There was a new smell of a different food being cooked on the street. It was a bustling area, jewellery, silks,

spice, in small stalls set up on the curb side of pave-
ments and doorways. The variety of colours was stunning. Jan stopped now and again to look at the wares.
Jan guided them through the people mingling around
stores to the Zanzibar hotel. "It's has a club Zimmer
said I know the doormen, its private, but they will let
us in," Zimmer leads the way, palming money at the
door, to gain entry, Doris and Jan followed behind,
the bar to a dimly lit, there was a long bar to the left.
Waiters were serving drinks from there to the tables
and booths, another palming of money. "Yes Sir this
way, this is your booth," a table waiter said. Doris
seated herself opposite Jan next to a window, Zimmer
sitting next to Jan, ordering from the waiter, "two
whiskey's with soda and two large glasses of medium
sweet wine," Zimmer leaned across the table. Doris
make sure you drink your first drink the second one
for ladies is free, are you hungry," "a little" she replied,
"they only serve food to the booth's," "it looks expen-
sive Zimmer," "it is, but don't worry about that, the
food they serve is basic, how do you say, simple but well
cooked?" He beckoned a waiter, "I'll order you a snack.
The food is polish hope you will like it."

"Four gulasz, please" "its stew of meat, noodles and
vegetables, potato, seasoned with paprika and other
spices, usually eaten with buck wheat kasza,if they
have it, cooked seasoned wheat, it's a side dish." "Doris
said, sounds interesting." I'm going to speak to Jan for
a minute,"Doris notice he hadn't taken his eyes off her
since they sat down. Zimmer paused, for a moment,
leaned over and whispered to Doris, "if anyone should
ask your twenty two," it's important you understand

Zimmer; "I'm not stupid" I've been in bars before, I've drunk vodka," "very good Doris; I'm impressed." He resumed his conversation with Jan.

Looking out the window, she could see the Victorian terrace house across the road. A lamp lighter was firing up the street lights. A few people gathered around an organ grinder; she couldn't see if he had a monkey, like the one down at the market, there were too many background noises in the bar to be able to hear any tune. As, she strained her ears against the window, a piano behind her further down the bar room burst into life, she leaned across the booth pocking her head into the Isle to get a glimpse, a burly old gentleman of African origin was playing a tune she heard before, but could not recollect the name. Zimmer tapped her on the back. "Sit up Doris" she snapped at him."I was only taking a peek," he went to say more but Jan interjected, spoke to Zimmer and smiled "Doris, look if you want when food arrives; I want to talk to you; Jan has some questions I will translate, a go-between for you and him."

Ah, wine and whiskey, wine for you dear, bottoms up, as you say or is it cheers and here comes the food Doris had never had wine before, she took a large gulp from the first glass. She felt her the cheeks of her face instantly glow to the touch and the warmth in her stomach, nice stuff Zimmer, yeah bottoms up, chinking her glass with them, taking another gulp, Wow this is good shit Zimmer.

It's polite to watch ones p and q's; you sound like my mother. If so, he replied, then she had the sense to teach you good manners. Jan wants to know do you have a boyfriend. No Doris replied he put his hand up to signal a pause then, translated to Jan. He would like to be your boyfriend; bugger, can he afford me. With all respect and honour, you may have a chaperone if you wish on times. When he takes you out, are you shitting me Zimmer, no. I will accompany you while he learns English, what do you say, ok Zimmer, is that a yes, yes?

Doris would have agreed to anything. The wine took hold of her senses. She was enjoying that and the food. Zimmer was passing the comments on, of mostly small talk, to Jan. The time passed rapidly, last orders, please, were called from the bar then a bell rang shortly after. Doris had consumed, the first two glasses of wine as if it was water, the third glass was becoming a challenge, "drink up Doris" we need to get out of here before the bobbies do their rounds, she swallowed the remaining wine and tried to get up from the booth. With a slur, "bloody hell, my legs won't work bugger they have turned to jelly and impossible to stand on." The situation didn't improve as she tried to walk, only Jan's quick reactions saved her from becoming pals with the floor, "my hero." She flung his arm around her waist, supporting her weight; she quickly hitched her right arm on to his neck; they made a swift exit.

Zimmer cleared the way to the outside. The cool night air hit her skin; she started to reach as if to be sick "I'll be fine." Doris giggled. Jan spoke to Zimmer, who swiftly turned, a bobby pushing his bike along the pavement was coming in their direction, other people exiting the bar were taking notice of her drunken state.

Jan had already taken the initiative, "down the alley" he said to Zimmer, he lifted Doris by the waste from the floor, pick up her shoes. Doris tried to speak to him, but even her mouth wouldn't work, suddenly she reached, this time vomiting over Jan's back, "never again,"slurring her words, "for God's sake shut up Doris," the alley, they had gone down an alley that came to a dead end. The east gate of the park confronted them. Zimmer said, "if we're caught here, we will be in a lot of trouble." "I know he" replied in Slovak "come,'" he slung her over his shoulder like a sack of potatoes, vaulting the gate in just three moves again she spewed over him, on his way down the other side of the gate. Now you, Zimmer, "you know I can't Jan" he laid Doris on the damp grass. "I'm in no fit state for any hanky-panky" she muttered. Jan ignored her. He would have understood her; he climbed back to the top of the gate and yanked Zimmer by his trouser belt to the top, swung him over and carried him down the other side by the back of his of his trousers.

"Tell her Zimmer, to keep quiet," she giggled every time Jan spoke. "You're so funny," laying there she tried to engage her brain to make her mouth work. She wiped the residue of the sick with Zimmer's handkerchief. She looked at Zimmer smiled, being sick had improved her the situation slightly, words were still slurred but a little more coherent. Jan helped her up from the grass to her feet. She is a little wet Zimmer, but ok; the back of your dress is in a bit of a state, covered in mud, "let's not worry about that, now. let's just get out of here," "what did he say Zimmer," "we'll take a cut across the park to Irvington," she asked, "he said you're a little wet," she giggled, "you have now idea," Jan. She took his arm around her waist, "there that's better," they made their way through the park along paths to the west gate, "my feet are cold Zimmer and wet," "we will look at them in a minuet," on the other side of that gate, can you put my shoes on.

At the west gate, the procedure was the same as the first gate. Jan took the shoes. Zimmer put her shoes, on; "I'll do it; she is still unsteady." Jan supported her, as made their way back to town. Clear of the park they laughed together about the ordeal, all three seeing, the funny side, "what if that Bobby had come down that alley," Zimmer said. "I would like to see how he was going to get that bloody bike over the gate," there were more flurries of laughter, as Zimmer explained it to Jan, they had just turned the corner towards the coach and horses, pub.

"Oh bugger, oh shit" Doris bleated, pointing at the pub door, there was her Dad. His eyes clasped straight onto her. She knew he was going to blow, like factory steam whistle. He's supposed to be at the union meeting, what's he doing in the coach and horses? He marched straight at her. "You're supposed to be at home, in bloody in bed, my girl and who are these two clowns," and "you're supposed to be at the union meeting Dad." "Don't you sodding back mouth me Doris; I'll knock your block off." Frank raised his hand as if to back hand her; his forearm was taken out of the air by Jan; a vice like grip clamping onto it?

Frank was a big man. However, no match for the muscle power of Jan. Stop, Stop; Zimmer stepped between the pair, the two of them. You had to admire his bravery for his size; they could have crushed him like a fly, "don't fight, there no point; you will be hurting your son, pointing to Doris is going to have his babies," "what, he bellowed," looking down at Zimmer, babies, Jan muttered. He knew enough English for that word, repeating it again, "yes babies" he turned to Frank. About three inches separated their heads. Frank grimaced up his face in shock "you're in the Club, girl," "err, you must know I'm in the club, didn't mam tell you." Doris had reattached herself to Jan's arm, as Frank relaxed his stance, "Jan let go."

"Bugger me Doris, your mam; she knew, you told her a month ago," a feather would have knocked Frank over. He slumped his back against the pub door, looked at Zimmer. "He's the feller then" "yes" Zimmer replied. "He's her boyfriend. I'm the translator, his best friend." "Jan doesn't speak any English a couple of words best, how did the you manage it, oh. I guided them," "don't even want to ask about that?" Frank stated shaking his head in disbelief? "God Doris" Thoughts about her being in the pudding club, raced through his mind, in her present state, he assumed, maybe they forced her. Did they make you? "No Doris replied; I knew what I was doing." She thought her dad was talking about the Christmas club at work, where she put money in each week, for a hamper. Not being the brightest spark she thought again, oh God he thinks. I'm pregnant, what the hell do I do now?

"What did you say your name was again," looking at Zimmer? "Zimmer Swaranowich and this is my friend "Jan Probernoskei." "I'm going to call you Zim, because it rimes with Jim, and Jan you said." "Well, Jan, my son looks like we have lots to talk about Sunday, our house, dinner, one o'clock don't be late." Doris tell Zim how to get there, it's easy to find, a tram ride from there, Doris explained the route, ok Zim, what's going on Jan enquired, were having dinner on Sunday, their house? I'll tell you latter "Jan smiled at Frank nodding his head; in acknowledgement, I'd take a bloody bat to that head, if it wasn't for the situation, he thought, how I'm going to explain this to your mother do not know. He bid Jan and Zimmer good night, Sunday then, Sunday Zimmer acknowledged, I'll tell you how to get there. Doris chirped, again tomorrow, to be sure; they waved good-bye. They went their separate ways?

As they waited at the number two town stop, for the last tram home to arrive. "You do know I'm going to have to persuade him to marry you, don't you," His false teeth were chattering, while drawing back on his fag and trying to speak at the same time. Could bloody throttle you, Doris? She dare not back track now for fear of a good beating, instead looked to the pavement as if shame on me. The union meeting excuse, Doris it's the only time I get to go out with my workmates. You know how she'll nag if she knew, spoil everything, please not a word; dad she replied, I won't say anything. Departing the tram, they walked arm in arm all the way home. Doris was puzzled. She couldn't understand it; he had a smile on like a Cheshire cat as they walked home, I have a plan he whispered in her ear, Vi she wouldn't go to bed on meeting nights until Frank arrived home safely, Doris bolted the door went upstairs and straight to bed; her head barely touched the pillow; she was out like a light.

The next thing it was morning, she flew down stairs, quickly washed her clothes out put them in a bag. I'll get one of the maintenance guys to dry them in the boiler room. Doris as usual was in her ever desperate hurry to get to work, grabbing a piece of toast and a gulp of tea. She heard her mother at the top of the stairs, "don't know what was on your; Dads mind last night, bloody union meeting." "He smelt like he drank a brewery more than beer or two would I would say." "All that talking and muttering in his meeting" God if she only knew, before shutting the door, shouted "see yah mam," she was down the path and gone like a flash. I couldn't understand a word of it, every time, bloody union meetings, Vi was still puttering.

She put on her usual brisk pace as she turned the corner to cross the road to the factory gates. She was joined by Pamela, "saw you in town last night, Doris, with my guy. What were you up to, staggering around? Half cut saw you, with that giant and the skinny little rake," "oh. I was getting myself in the mood with a glass of wine or two, then had the pair of them? I find ones not enough, what about you, makes life interesting, Pamela, don't you think."

Doris knew, as she clocked in. She would be the talk of the line, the air today will be burning "hi Ben; How's it hanging," patting his crouch has she passed by, for once he was without words? "Close your mouth, dear, or you'll catch a wasp with it open that far Pamela." She was dumb founded, wait until I tell the rest, she thought.

Doris matched off to her line position, knowing now, that the upper hand worked best. She was the new moll in town, and they were surely going to know it very soon. She hammered her away through the morning sensing what was going on around her, come the tea break suddenly everyone wanted her to be part of their little chin wagging group. She decided there and then to make an announcement bellowing down the yard. "When I was plain old thick, Doris, you didn't want to know me, now that I've wised up. I'm everybody's flavour, well sod! off you lot, are not even on the same level." "Your shit, do you think it smells better than anyone who appears to be beneath you." "Well, you are sick jumped-up fantasizer's, you can kiss my arse, with your little gossip groups." "For your info, your shit ends up the same place as mine, live, you don't know how to live, and you certainly don't know me." Megan smiled a stuck her thumb up in a good for you. She mouthed as the yard fell silent for the rest of the break.

A girl called Alice. Doris did not really know had been designated to make the peace. "Hey, look Doris, we don't want it to be, you and us with bad feeling." "Doris you have to understand, there's a period of growing up and it's clear, all of a sudden chuck, well like you're there; whatever has happened you've changed a different Doris." She couldn't argue with that, in weeks past. She would have given anything to be friends with anyone, now; she thought I don't know. Alice spoke in her broad liverpoolian accent. Doris listens attentively in order to understand her; "I can imagine, what it's like to feel like a black sheep well, I can, oh. I can chuck; they treated me the same way when I got here, down from Liverpool like, they did, see I was foreign to them, talking about which, how are you getting on like, with, you know, then over the road?" Good Doris replied, just eying them up; I will probably use them for sex and fun. Doris giggled out, mostly the fun." She said, thinking to herself about the previous night antics. "What you doing both, even the little tramp," "oh yes I believe in variety, Hercules's well he's main course the other one desert and then there the Johnny from London. I have on the weekend." "Bloody hell Doris, you just haven't come out of your shell, you've been sodding exploded out of it, if you have got any others you're not using pass them my way Doris." "Alice there'll be no fear of that, I can't get enough now; I'll see what I get bored with first and let you know." "You're shitting me Doris, hey," "yes that's what I'm doing Alice."I must get back to the grind-stone," that will give them plenty to mutter on she thought, if I'm going to be part of a gossip group might as well be a legend.

"Hi Christi, haven't bumped into you lately, what you have been doing" hugging her. "Come up stairs I'll tell you," Vi, emerged out of the scullery, "what you two chatting about,"I was telling Doris about the overtime I was doing at the chip shop." Doris burst out laughing, "wasn't that funny girl," "where was the joke," oh it was nothing mam, work, just to get my head around it." Yeah, her mother laughed, "suppose her, working extra, see the joke now." They went to the bedroom, "go on Chrisi tell?" "Well, we met this rich guy, really wealthy, owns a manor out a church Marriott, other sides of thirstone. He has a Bentley, squire of the manor.

Christi went into full detail, only one problem Doris. He's married, two kids." "So what you're going to do?" "What I always do, take the money and run." "What about you," Doris told her about the previous night; Chrisi laughed her head off. It was a jaw-dropping day, a new Doris, Chrisi remarked if that made faces blush, then it is your new-found friend, "good for you Doris" "thanks Chrisi. I'm getting noticed now, not probably for the right reasons, but noticed nevertheless." "I've got a bridge with which to cross the water." "I can build on that," "good enough." "So when am I going to meet this millionaire," "soon Doris."

At work in the afternoon break, against her better judgment Doris became a full member of the gossip circle. The start of the self-generated destruction of others, in the weeks to come, learned in specific detail gained from first-hand experience how to needle the vulnerable and as her gained confidence with a little improvisation from Chrisi, she would become the gossip machine, that would brand her king slut and make her the talk of the factory.

The week passed quickly. She did not see much of her dad; he had been working overtime. By the time he got in she had gone to bed, Doris kept out of her mother's way, spending most of her time in her bedroom, reading a book. She didn't want either her dad or mam finding it, an old book where it had originated, even Molly, who lent it to her had no idea; it was an instruction on sex. The title was part worn off the cover, something asultra. Her mother would have had a fit; dad would have swallowed his teeth, Molly, worked on another line in the packing plant, she told Doris the book was on the banded list or was illegal. However, it was a bloody good manual if you wanted to know about sex. Molly said, make sure no one else gets their hands on it, read it at your own peril and keep it out of sight. I want it back quickly I have to return it, to the person I borrowed it from.

Doris read the book cover to cover. It was a very explicit manual. It had words that she had heard some men speaking them in the pub; she thought their use was taboo if spoken in public, if caught, she would be in the shit big time. Doris decided to hand the book back, giving it to Molly during the break times really do people do this stuff, she said. What people do behind locked doors, god only knew, at night she tried to imagine, did Mam and Dad do some of this stuff, coming up with a big no. It seemed beyond belief, in her mind. She got the notion to want to try some and wished there was a handyman around, so she could.

On Saturday morning as she crept out of room in her bare feet, onto the landing. She was half in mind to go down stairs or stay in bed a bit longer. She could hear her dad asking mam, about Doris being in the club. "Doris oh yes, she has been in the club for a while, Frank," "well she isn't showing much. I thought she would have more of a show by now," "it's only been in a couple of months." "She is not going to have much to show for that time." "When would you notice he enquired, after about five month's she probably has a quid or maybe a little more," "what the sodding hell are you talking about woman?" "I'm talking about Christmas club. What are you sodding talking about," "the family way club, not some bloody Christmas club you biscuit?"

Vi almost chocked herself speechless on the tea, it had now back fired from her mouth, having partly been going down the wrong way, once she and stopped chocking and staggered to a kitchen chair, collapsing into it, like a sack of potatoes, she regained her composer and quietly and calmly said. "If you don't mind, run that by me again Frank, please.

"There are two chaps who are coming here on Sunday. For dinner, one of them the small chap he speaks English." "He is going to translate for the big chap." "He doesn't speak English." "The little chap instructed the big fellow on what to do." "Now she is going to have the big chaps baby." "What's the little fellow done?" "He showed him how to do it; what," "I can't get my head around this, how did you come to meet these chaps in the first place." "Err, well, they were walking through town I caught sight of them with Doris, as I came out the coach and horses." "I had a drink with the lads because the meeting finished early." Frank realizing, what he had just said, knew it was too late to back track. He knew he was in the preverbal shit pot. Oh shit, he thought how do I get myself off this hook, bugger me. "Indeed. Frank Buntie, with hell and damnation, tell me if I'm not wrong you were supposed to be at a union meeting; she was supposed to be in bed and now Doris is pregnant expecting some man's baby." I've never had the pleasure of meeting; bugger you indeed."

"Well, you know what needs to be done, on the quiet. Frank and she had better kept her mouth shut about it," "what would the folks we know think of us? Our names would be shit, we wouldn't be able to show ourselves, best rope these chaps in Frank?" "You deal with that; I'll deal with the arrangement, once they understand the drill, even if you have to put a gun to their heads in the literal sense, then if that's what it takes uncle Kens got a twelve bore, borrow it Frank?"

Oh shit Doris thought, oh shit, what to do, God, please help me. She sat with her legs folded, rocking on the end of her bed. The tension was too much to bear. She crept back onto the landing with her hands over her ears, to block out the inevitable row that was surely going to come. Doris thought what should I say I haven't read anything about babies. I don't even know how you get a baby, well apart from the story of the stork delivering them to the gooseberry bush at the bottom of the garden. That's, what I've always understood happened, my aunty told me, mam told me, heard dad say it, then it must be true, but why are they even talking about me getting a baby, surely they can get their own, so I wonder when are they going to get it. I won't deny it and I won't confirm it, that way I won't look more of a stupid idiot, than they already take me for and see what happens. What else should I do, she told herself, that it was the best plan, it's the only plan, just be my stupid self.

Doris took her hands down covering her ears to listen in, "thankfully. Frank, Doris is not as showing yet." Showing what Doris thought, "it has to be a quickie, Frank and I mean quick, no messing about and no excuses, when these two chaps call, Frank make it clear were not having any bastards in this family." "Have you got your head around that, Frank," "yes dear."

Frank knew who was boss at home. It was a safe plan not to argue with Vi, when she was in this frame of mind, Doris thought, take whatever's coming on the chin; she made her mind up deciding to go down and face the music. It would be better to face the music now and get my thrashing, rather than mam build up steam, the consequences would be far worse later.

Mam, dad, "Doris, how are you, feeling, queasy," "no mam, I'm really fine,"however, now that you mention it, first thing in the morning? I feel a little sick, not much of anything? It only sort of came on yesterday and today, a cup of tea and I'll be fine," "breakfast, a fry up, toast, some jam," "no mam. I'm right off that, just tea thanks," "are you sure Doris, sit down girl and take the weight of your feet." "You should rest," "Dad'" "There's nothing to worry about?"

Doris, couldn't believe how civil and calm her mother was. Breakfast, toast, jam, whatever next; this is not like her, at this time of the day Doris. "I've got the instant cure for that morning sick feeling." Without the second blink of an eyelid; she smacked Doris on the elbow, with the copper stick, not hard but enough to make her jump up, "flaming hell mam," "no one, in this family is going to skip important meal times, you'll bloody eat and like what you're served, it does not matter a shit to me if you spew it all up the toilet wall. However, you will eat when I say, you will take care of yourself how I say, understand," Doris just nodded in approval, while the tears flowed.

This was more what I expected. However, I have yet to work it out, as to the why. To be nice on one hand then, on the other hand, punishment. The being amiable again, just don't get it. Then were back, to can I do this for you and that for you. "I'm going to look after you, now that you're in this condition, you have to take things easy, or you could lose it, then we'll have a lovely chat once you've rested, by the fire in my chair, with a cupper, because you're in the club." Good God, Doris thought. Maybe I ought to get caught with a couple of chaps on a more regular basis. Why no row, and about being in the club, nearly everyone at work is in it. Maybe the money's not safe; I've on got a couple of quids in it. Sod this I'm going to bloody bed.

What a wonderful sunny morning. The sun was lighting the room through the gap in the curtains. The erotic smells of flowers and fruit bushes, that filled the garden burst through the open window. Doris was woken by the smell of baking bread. The aroma drove her mad she was in need a cup of Rosie Lee My aunt had told me it was cockney slang. I had no idea how we came to use the saying in this house, the only way she was going to get a cup was if she got up.

Doris had forgotten that Jan and Zimmer were coming to dinner. She thought it would be a good idea to get out of her mother's way. Her moods had a habit of changing like the weather. She wondered out in her dressing gown to the bottom of the garden. Doris sat on a bench, built by her great grandfather. He told stories here; to her dad when he was a boy; sitting in this very place on the bench by the Anderson shelter. Frank came down and sat beside her. "Doris I love to bits. However, there is something. You must promise me today. You've got to ask for God's forgiveness at church today and his bless-ing, now that you're in the club, there's nothing else for it, you must not tell the vicar you're in the club either, we might get cast out and thrown into eternal hell and damnation, shush not a word." As Doris went to speak he put his finger to her mouth "shush girl, not a word," he got up and walked back to the house.

This is doing my head in, has money suddenly become a sin to own. God, she thought nearly everyone at work will be going to hell. Did the government have something to do with this or the church? She walked back to the house, straight to Chrisi door. Doris didn't bother to knock and if her sister, wasn't still dead to the world, she would have woken her. Chrisi only half awake. She would have torn her head off. God, what was I even thinking. On a Sunday, she would be hell for the rest of the day. Doris contented herself with getting dressed and ready for church. As much as she tried. She couldn't help, but reflect back on her father's words. Why all the worry about being in a Christmas club, if I was going to hell for that, might as well join Christine be as naughty as I can, got to church on Sunday get forgiven and start again on Monday, if I'm going to get blasted for a couple of quids, that's it. That's why the vicar hasn't been struck down, now I know how god and the church works?

"Where's mam, oh she is not coming today, busy with dinner; it's because a couple of chaps coming to dinner remember, in fact, It's more than a couple of chaps coming to dinner it's your future." "Chrisi, stop drag-ging your feet and walk properly" Frank snapped, as they walked along, Doris fell gradually behind deliberately to talk Chrisi, she grabbed her by the arm; her dad looked back, "get her to get a move on."

"Chrisi, Mam and Dad are furious with me, because I'm in the club, It's doing my head in, they said I'm in trouble, even at church." I could be damned, if the vicar gets to know, shit Chrisi help." She had to put her hand over her mouth and stamp on her own foot to stop herself bursting into laughter, but couldn't hold it in, "shit, Doris," the sound having carried "That's enough," "I won't have you blaspheme on church days" "now catch up before I crack the pair of you," Frank replied.

It was not a good idea to challenge their dad. They promptly did as he commanded. Both apologizing for the outbreak with a sorry dad. Throughout the service, Doris was like a cat on a hot tin roof, fidgeting one way and another. She had fear of spitting out loud I'm a sinner, having then to explain, the sin she committed in front of the congregation. She once saw someone else do that, get torn verbally to pieces in front of everyone by the vicar and the senior church members. She said thought sod that, they all vacated the church, for the usual congregational chat, Frank said, "I'm just going to have a chat with the vicar. I might be a while," go home with your sister, hell he's going to tell the vicar, "tell your mam. I will be there as soon as I can."

Doris, quickly made herself scarce in the graveyard, hoping to steer Chrisi to the spot, behind one of the tall grave stones, Christine was with one of the girls and her parents. They had just moved in four doors up from us, new a church. Doris waved frantically; she knew her sister had seen her, but chose to leave with them, for a while she stayed behind, Doris couldn't be bothered and sat down on a bench, she was feeling a little sick, but this passed after ten minutes or so, resuming her walk home.

Doris turned into the Avenue, when her Chrisi jumped out from behind a privet bush, "shit Chrisi you scared me out of my wits. It will teach you, not to day dream" she replied. "Anyway. What's the problem why the urgency, for my affections," "oh shut up you tart," "less of the tart if you don't mind even if I am one?" "Chrisi, mam and dad are worried about me being in the Christmas club." "They even said I was to ask for forgiveness at, church, has money suddenly become outlawed." "No you are bloody plum Doris. They think that you're in the family way, the pudding club, you're not are you." "No Doris said," "even if I was. How would I know?" "Have you been with anyone and had sex," "intercourse no? I haven't been on any courses," "God Doris sometimes you are as thick as shit," "has a man put his thing in you." Doris at first, didn't want to answer, thinking, what will her sister think of her? I might as well spit it out?

"You remember that guy Johnny." We met him at the flicks." " I bumped into him, as I came out of church one Sunday, he, was visiting the grave of a relative." Christine stopped her. "Doris, just get to the action did he or didn't he." "Yes, she replied in sheepish voice, in the old pillar box." "Did you wear protection, in what way, a rubber?" "rubber?" "Bloody hell Doris, did he come inside you, liquid, oh yes, twice or was it three times," "bugger me Doris." "Another question, why do mam and dad think you're pregnant." "Because dad caught me in town, with two men, Jan and Zimmer, outside the pub, they're coming to dinner today?" "You haven't answered the question Doris." "Zimmer told Dad, That I was going to have Jan's babies at first he was quite livid. However, when Zimmer told him Jan was going to marry me; dad invited then both to dinner."

"Oh Lord almighty Doris." They think you've had sex with Jan." "Have you Doris" "no; we've only had a drink or two." "Do mam and dad know about Johnny," "oh no Doris said?" "And do Jan and Zimmer know, of Johnny," "of course not Chrisi. I'm not stupid." "Doris, sorry but I beg to differ, whatever you do don't tell mam or dad or Jan and Zimmer, about Johnny ever, just trust me on this, Doris, swear it" "I swear it Chrisi; ok," "let's see how the dinner goes Doris; dad is either going to love them both or kill them."

"Your chaps will be here for dinner soon." I can't wait to meet him, Just can't wait." I suppose neither one, nor both of you think it might be good manners to go and meet them off the tram, "yes mam" Doris replied, "coming with me Chrisi, why not; this will be interesting, wouldn't miss it for the world let's go."

They had barely got down the Avenue as Jan and Zimmer, came around the corner, "Doris, now I do like Jan's minder." "I suspect the little scruffy looking chap probably needs all the protection he can get," "no, Chrisi, that's Zimmer. The minder has you put it, is my boyfriend." Doris wrapped her arm around his huge biceps and leaned her head on his shoulder, as they walked along the pavement. "If the other thing is a big as his arms, wow Doris, with a bunch of flowers for you as well." "No Zimmer butted in the flowers are for her mother and the beers I have for her father." "I was going to ask you to join with me and make four of us, but I can see already, what kind of girl you are." Don't kid yourself zummer? You couldn't afford me." "That I could believe, and the name is Zimmer" Doris interrupted Chris don't spoil it, please."

They had barely passed through the front door, "Doris go see your dad. Chrisi went with her; he is in the garden." "Good, in the kitchen, Zimmer I assume got that right," "yes" " he replied. I want a bloody word or two with you; your mate may not understand English, but he knows what he has done, and now he's going to do the decent thing and marry Doris. That's ok Violet," he replied."The flowers are for you." Jan shoved his arm out, any further he would have taken her head off. "Beers for us boys, I'd hardly call Frank a boy, Its Vi if you please. Go on out into the garden, Vi she followed them through. "Doris, Chrisi give me a hand in the kitchen," "let the men get to know one another, err Frank get Jan and Zimmer one of the beers."

"Well, Zimmer you've met the wife, yes she's kosher fine with everything." Are you sure about that, does he know?" "He is going to marry her, no, not yet, to answer your question." "However, he is smitten with her," Zimmer said. "So it does not matter what he wants, British citizenship I suppose, and she needs a husband, so let's all be British, so this is a good thing, yes, Frank" was speechless suppose "that's that then, we'll have this, and I've got something stronger in the cupboard. It's called whisky." "I think this is a day I might need it," Vi joined them in the garden, Frank, she said, "the chaps are ok, Zimmer said Jan will marry Doris." "Yes. I know love, but he doesn't know, pointing to Jan," "who gives a shit Frank," "apparently no one he replied."

"You have strange customs in this country." Zimmer wasn't sure how to explain himself. "Jan wants to marry Doris; he is a love-struck child despite his appearance." "He not worldly and neither is Doris, but why must he marry her. That's what I don't understand." "Because she is under twenty-one years of age, at only nineteen, you have taken advantage of her. In the eyes of the law, well at least he has, according to this country." Here you need your parents' permission. It's not a bloody free for all, get it, or do I need to get the twelve bore to spell it out," "show him Bessie," Frank, Vi said." He drew the unloaded short barrel shot gun from the shed, "beauty don't you think," Vi didn't give Zimmer a chance to speak. He had no choice; he agreed with a lump in his throat, "put it away Frank. We won't be needing that hey Zimmer." He stared at the shot gun, "no."

Jan, had gone to the bottom of the garden with Doris, sitting beside her on the wooden bench, he had learnt a few words of English, cheers he understood, touching his glass with hers. "I love you," he told Doris Frank having joined them, nodded, "that's a start chap. The rest will come in time." Zimmer also joined them. "I'm going in to help mam Doris." They spoke for a while, Zimmer translating, before they were called to the table, Frank was clearly pleased with the outcome, showing the relaxed feelings he had for Jan and Zimmer, the broad smile on his face said it all.

"Vi said lets us pray." I assume you understand Zimmer Godly worship," "oh yes Jan had God-fearing parents." Jan's father's name was Joseph and his mother Mary." "They would always give thanks before eating." "In this case," Why don't you say prayers as our guest, no I can't do that Zimmer stated? I'm an atheist." I haven't heard of that religion," Vi stated, at the other end of the table Chrisi had to put her hand over her mouth to stop herself spraying everyone with water, choking to boot, "Jan will say the prayer in Slovak, I will translate."

Jan, please begin. "Náš Otče v nebesiach, posväť sa name. Your Príď kráľovstvo, tvoja vôľa na zemi, ako je tomu v"

"Ourather in heaven, hallowed be your name. Your kingdom come, your will be done, on earth, as it is In the heaven." eaven. Give nám tento deň náš denný chlieb, a odpusť nám naše viny, ako i my odpúšťame svojim debtors.

"Give us this day our daily bread, and forgive us our debts, as we also have forgiven our debtors."

"nám tento deň náš denný chlieb, a odpusť nám naše viny, ako i my odpúšťame svojim debtors."

"And lead us not into temptation, but deliver us from evil."

"A neuveď nás do pokušenia, ale zbav nás zlého."

When Jan had read the whole prayer, it finished with customary amen.

"That was beautiful Jan; you are getting married to Doris," Zimmer said. "She will give you good babies from some special club she is in, let's be thankful for that." This is not our home land things are different here, but I say amen, to that." Chrisi couldn't contain herself, bolting from the table, to the garden, laughing her head off as she went. "Never mind her Vi said, let's eat."

"When is this wedding going to take place, Chrisi asked," taking her place at the table once again? Oh not for ages, Doris, was quick to say, "these things have to be planned. We need to think about where we will live, when we're married. Jan and I have to be engaged first," looking at her mother. "Yes, your right. This is your engagement and celebration rolled into one. Next Sunday Frank, did you fix it up with the vicar," "oh yes" he replied. "I had to tip him five quids though, told him, on account of her being in the club." "He had slotted us in between a wedding and a funeral, said he needs the business." Chrisi almost choked on her dinner bolting out to the garden once again. "You're not in the club, are you, Vi shouted, To Chrisi."

"Doris stood up; I'm not in the," however, before she could finish. Her mother jumped up, "sit my girl and shut up, if you know what's good for you," reaching for the copper stick, "just shut up," she repeated again, "we will decide what's best." "So Zimmer, where are they going to live, got a place have you?" "Yes, Vi?" Doris sat down being somewhat shocked, "a friend, Maceij Birderick, has a house in Spinehill Avenue next to the park." "We have been there once," "hey up to Doris; that's a very to do area," Chrisi stated. "Yes, it is, nice place" "well Zimmer, hats off to you two have been busy." Everyone at the table had a smile on their faces. Except Doris, she was in a state of bewilderment; Chrisi's face displayed, more of an it's unbelievable, smirk?

Jan tapped Zimmer on the shoulder. Jan has asked me to translate for him, "I committed a crime; we took her for a drink." Pointing at Doris, "got her drunk on the wine, then got her dirty in the park, really messy in the mud" "Then we found Frank; her saviour if it may make things, better; Jan will take her for a wife. I will take care of her." Tell them Zimmer. That hadn't come out quite as expected, but his words, Zimmer said. Frank said after that I don't know what to say, "except welcome to the family son."

Zimmer kissed Doris on the cheek, "congratulations." "Up your's she replied, leaning her mouth to his ear you are a bastard. I'll fix you wait and see." "Did that drink you had, get forced on you and did that not cause; the situation; Did you not evade the truth when you set off without their permission." you're supposed to have been in bed," he stated. "Look it's not so, bad, for and Jan." "What you two doing whispering in each other's ear, "it's mam, just talking about the wedding, "hey Zimmer," "yes the wedding. Congratulations again to you both," Zimmer said out loud, making sure that everyone heard.

Jan drifted into the garden with Chrisi hanging on his arm, much to the annoyance of Doris. "You should learn to leave what's not yours alone Chrisi," joining them. "I was teaching him about the birds."

"He mimics the words, look pointing at a Blackbird." Chrisi repeated "blackbird," blackbird he replied, well done you, "money," Chrisi repeated again, once again he replied, "money," "really Chrisi, are you sure that's all your trying to teach him; next word will probably be how much, let's find a quiet spot." "Now, now, Doris, fair is fair we have shared before, Johnny, remember," Johnny" Jan, said waving his hand and finger in the air, looking franticly for the object. Chrisi took his hand, pointing to the toilet, "toilet. "the or John" Jan smiled, "if we're going to have a conversation Doris, do it quietly, not within earshot," "He's learning fast," sorry Chrisi. "these is all my fault and Zimmer hasn't helped much "I could cut his throat at the moment, the slimy bastard, he right up mam's backside; Oh I put that fire out leave it to me Doris."

Frank set an oak table up in the garden placing sliced beef and homemade horse radish, left over's from dinner. With three glass tumblers each containing a three finger measure of old whisky, "boys get that down your necks." Jan took a bottle of Polish brandy out of a bag. High proof "try this, better," 'great there all going to get bloody legless now," "Doris's look on the bright side. You get to get out of here, a place, just you and him." "He'll know what to do when the time comes, left to your own devices." "Chrisi, I'm sure you'd show him some instructions given the chance," "no. He's your

chap. I won't do that, but I promised." "I'll sort Zimmer
out" "you're not going to hurt him are you Chrisi,"
"no. I'm going to give him something though, I'll tell
you later," "Zimmer how about a walk, in the evening
sunshine, you and me." "I thought you didn't like me?"
"I don't," "but that can change, yes or no, make your
mind up. Jan looks like he's managing, give them two
some space, Doris can help him with the words. That's
her job now."

Chrisi took his hand, leading him down the garden path
to the allotments. "Come on Zimmer don't be shy, oh.
I'm not, "where are we going, to a little concrete hut,
I need my oats." Oh yes I can see from the fields you
grow a lot of them." "err, not those oats, my kind of
oats Zimmer You'll see." "ok I'm for something new,"
"oh this is not it's Zimmer its thousands of years old."
After a short walk, they were at the pillar box where
Doris had taken Johnny. "Come on Zimmer, just behind
here there's some meadow grass it is out of sight to
anyone, and it's a nice warm day, go on lay down on
your coat, put your hands behind your head and rest."
He obliged without asking why. She immediately
straddles herself across his upper legs, undid his
trousers'. Zimmer didn't move a muscle, more from
shock than anything, "Zimmer now that's what I call
a nice leg, what a leg should look like, wow." He was
just as he was about to speak, when a sudden harsh
downward thrust, drew the wind out of him as she sat
upon him. She reached over with her hands pinning his
to the ground. She took him like a jockey in the last
furlong, going for the winning post, only the whip
was missing. It wasn't long before he let out a cry that

carried for a hundred yards. "God Zimmer; you're the best I've ever had, and I've had plenty" she said. The look on Zimmer's face was unreal; all he could manage was to pant, to think, she thought I was going to tell my dad, he raped me, good Zimmer. "I want to do it again, can you." "I'm not sure wait until I've gotten air back in my lungs but at a slower pace please." She learned to his lips and kissed him passionately. She was love struck, a man I can feel at last, she thought. They spent the next hour, laying in the evening sun, making small talk.

They walked back the same way they had come; the difference was that her arm was around his shoulder and his around her waist, Chrisi "yes Doris" what the. She interrupted; "love and passion Doris, my new soul mate Zimmer." "Friend, Jan said, pointing at Zimmer; good English, the way to go Jan." "Doris, don't ask, I've found my man, just like that. I know; I didn't expect it, wasn't looking for it either, sure as hell Zimmer didn't expect what happen out there in the field," she was in shock, "shit Chrisi" I know." "I'm taking him to my bedroom," "what for seconds. She laughed joking, "no Doris thirds and perhaps pudding."

Vi and Frank were busy in the kitchen as, they tip toed up to her bedroom. She quietly shut the door, placed a chair under the knob and striped off, again, yeah again, he obliged striping, "stand there a mo. I want to take a good look, wow, that doesn't require much persuasion, wow and wow." They emerged two hours later, didn't see you two come in, "what have you been doing up stairs Chrisi?" "showing Zimmer some pictures, that all, yes mam" "that's all," she sighed, "he's a dish mam, isn't he," "err, about time you visited the optician Chrisi. Don't you think? He would make a good father; we all see different things? When you see something different, well let me know what that is. He is going to make a fine father don't you think mam" "you're taking the pee, right." "You aren't a young man, give it a chance though who knows hey." "I think its copper stick time, no offence Zimmer." "I need to give my daughter a crack on the knee, see Zimmer told you she would be please." They ran out into the garden, laughing Vi in pursuit, "I'll give you laugh; you pair of buggers you."

Doris and Jan were still doing English lessons in the fading light. "What have you two been up to for the last couple of hours" Doris enquired, "oh not much Chrisi said, just testing his pogo stick." "You are a dirty little devil, shall I draw a picture in case you don't know how to find one?" "No I don't need picture's thanks Chrisi." "It's getting late girls" "you'd better walk the chaps back to the tram," "yes mam."

Zimmer and Jan said, their fair wells, "remember boys, suit, shirt tie, next Sunday, you know where to meet me," "no problem," Zimmer replied, "have a good one Frank."

Jan and Zimmer walked along the pavement together. Doris and Christine about ten yards behind,"Doris a feather would have bowled me over, my sister, in the club, whatever next flying pigs." "Chrisi looked to the sky just in case, "stop taking the pee. It's bloody getting serious. I'm marrying this man under a lie,"" well do you like him," "yes I do, but I don't know about love him." "He makes me feel funny inside, but Chrisi. I don't know about the rest." "Doris, that's all in the mind these things strike you, that funny feeling you have been inside, well that's special. I've been with loads of men, you know I have, but, well today." "When I took Zimmer down the garden path didn't expect to come back in love Doris." "Really, I didn't, didn't. He's nothing, but a rag muffin, but when he kissed me, Oh boy just can't explain it and the rest you don't want to know, but it is, the best I've had." "I would never have thought it was possible." "I was becoming a robot for money, that all I ever thought about, was, being rich."

"Chrisi, I was enjoying Jan's company today. Even though there were few words of meaning between us." "It felt like one of those old married couples that you pass every now and again, along the streets. They just seem to get eaten up into the crowds, as no one is looking, until you take the time to really look. Hand in hand, they come to the end of one of a row of shops, stop and talk for a while. They're not young, but notice each other as if time did not matter, not to them and time around them wasn't moving. They weren't looking at anyone else, only at each at each other. Then walked on swinging the hands again, as if they were joined at the hip. That's what I want, it's real, it's love." "Doris I don't know what is and what's not, I get what you're saying, it is magic, but is it just a fairy tale, as they came to a giant oak, pausing for a moment, magic hey, who knows, Chrisi, let's not write the years off just now, hey.

The boys have stopped Doris, think they care, look at him hey, Zimmer. He turned and kissed her on the forehead before moving off onto the tram stop a few yards away. Doris kiss Jan on the lips, see you hunk.

They waved them good-bye they both shouted as the tram departed, Doris, back to reality, let's go home, bloody work tomorrow, what a day, perfect. It was bloody perfect Chrisi as the strode along the pavement down the Avenue, arm in arm in the tranquillity of the still warm evening air of perfect summer sky, suddenly they both stopped, looked up, without words walked on again.

It only felt like it was minuets ago when she went to bed,"Shit; I'm bloody late again." Doris flew down the stairs, her usual routine, "mam, where is my toast, where is my tea, where is my coat, see you?" Wait a minute, why is the road so quiet, she looked at her mother? The clock went forward one-hour Doris, "what the clocks have changed already she exclaimed," "no. I put them on one-hour yesterday Zimmer had the idea." "I told him you were always late, so he said to put the clock back or forward or it will confuse her. It's to get her life on track, clever little bugger, worked hasn't it." "No just means I'm early, see you mam."

Head down full speed ahead, then she slowed, why I'm I rushing. I have loads of time. She looked around in the warm early-morning sunshine. She had never taken the time out before to look, around this was a part of her journey done with blinkers on, the smell of flowers and Colour in the garden. People going about their early-morning business in a casual manner, not like her at race pace. I like this, taking time to say good morning to people she didn't know. It seemed like no time had passed when she reached the chain-link fence. I've got here faster than if I had rushed. She thought well at least it seemed that way. The compound looked like a prison camp. No machinery was going, no dust in the air. It looked a menacing place, eerie, a place where you would probably come to forget, whatever it was you wanted to forget; how does he work here, how can anyone enjoy this? People have died buried in this rubble somewhere in this awful a place? Tears fell freely down her face, a moment ago she was joyful and now sad, that was soon interrupted. She wiped her eyes; Zimmer shouted. She could hear bricks moving. "I'm coming I'm coming, the rag bags reply, what does my sister see in him. "Where's Jan," "he's coming five minutes may be less," "do you live out here Zimmer." "No, we have a place, only feels like it. Doris laughed out aloud I know that feeling anyone who works, knows that feeling. She looked around Jan, there he was same-old shorts, for a moment she had visions; of no shorts, her heart pounded as it had before, must be love she thought. He looked like something out of one of those comic books her uncle once, left on the dinner table, she had picked up, not read but flicked the pages. They had a muscle-bound hero fighting the villains. Doris pictured him with this giant sword swaying over his head as he trod over the rubble laying before him.

"Good morning," that's broken the spell, near enough, the words, he looked at perplexed. Doris went to kiss him, forgetting the chain-link fence was in the way. He pointed to his lips, then laughed he took hold of the fence with both hands tearing a hole big enough for the purpose, just like one of those comic heroes as their lips met she almost fainted. Latching to the fence for support, her heart was pounding out of her chest, at least it felt that way, "do it again she commanded." She wanted to pull him through the fence, "tear a bigger hole,"Doris said, "no, we will get fired, no job, no Doris. This hole is bad enough. "I will fix it. This is horrible Zimmer," break time. I'll make sure he's your side" A tear rolled down her face. She knew he was right, that last thing she wanted was for him to lose his job. How I would feel about that, if I lost mine, she contented herself to watch for a while before walking across the road.

She stood there in front of the gates; that's a first. She thought, before the whistle has sounded. Ben Grub, came across the road, noticed Doris and almost got himself ran over by the coal lorry, silly old fart. The driver shouted from the open cab. She laughed so much she pee'd herself, shit I think I need to lay down, Doris you're doing this on purpose to give me a bloody heart attack, have you got one Ben; she remarked, callous cow you are, your becoming worse than them, you never use to be like that Doris. No you're right Ben. I did not but then you and everyone else use to walk over me, now I don't give shit.

She waved to Jan, then turned with Ben, towards the factory entrance. See what a wonderful day it almost was Ben, you nearly got killed, it was a fringing shocked Doris. Bet that's the first time you have punched your own card this year, isn't it, go on and admit it, Ben, she shouted. If I did that, then I'd have to kill you, now you wouldn't like that. I'd wait as well, you know, until that time of the month, when us women are a little crazy, you know, what I mean, Ben, bloody Nora, he replied, roll on retirement, your all mad.

"Morning Megan, good golly Doris, are you ill," "no, just in love," "are you now, don't worry that will pass, hang onto it while you can." No Megan your absolutely wrong I'm going to one of the old couples you see still holding hands." Doris, trust me, when you get older, you will be lucky to hold your breath; as for your man," "you'll need to hang on to him to stay upright and what you did in a minute will take all bloody day, for goodness sake don't let me not get on my soap box."

Each day during that week, she met Jan outside of the chain-link fence by the bus stop. It was the only place they could find to sit. The wall had been taken down to a sitting level, part of a gate to a factory that had once stood obliterated during one night during the blitz. It was as though someone had intended to rebuild it, but had never quite got around to it. They were both glad they hadn't; It was big enough to sit on and to share lunch placed between them made up of what Jan brought and what Doris brought. They mixed and shared. She liked his, better than her lunch. It was spicy and interesting for a taste's she had not experienced. She craved for some unknown reason for more of the same each day. He didn't care, that she was tucking into his share as well. It took away the sickness that was getting stronger each day. She wanted more at breakfast, but wanted to deliver it back up an hour later. Whatever it was, something that's going around she thought, it would pass as did the week.

"Right young lady, big day tomorrow, come on, no Saturday lay in today." "Mam, what big day," "you know, you and Jan," "what's he coming to lunch again." I'm seeing him later does he know," "of cause. He knows Zimmer knows." "Christi is meeting him here today. Jan will be with him." "Your dad wants to make sure their suits are up to scratch for church tomorrow." I didn't know," unless your dads said anything, how would you, now I've' got this dress?" It is old it was your aunt Sadie's." "It's Victorian, but very pretty, now go try it on." "I'll pin it? I've got a lady coming here later to help alter it." So don't go anywhere, because I want this done and dusted today." "What's the rush. Never mind, your lip, let just get it done." Why, oh, why, is it always bust your lip, break your sodding knee or elbow with you mam, thoughts best kept in her head, biting her tongue. "ok mam whatever you say" "and don't be condescending, if I want your opinion, I'll give it to you?"

"Wow, mam the dress is beautiful. It could be a ball gown or a wedding dress." That Jan, no Doris, he must not see the dress, unlucky if he does. How's that going to be bad luck, mam, copper stick awful luck, shit here we go again? This time she didn't contain it to her thoughts crack went the elbow, bloody told you so, Doris stood up clenching her fist? The pain was excruciating, try it once me girl, hit me, be the last thing you'll do, stop dribbling I don't want water marks on the dress, can't I at least see him, later. He's busy, him and Zimmer with your dad, now shut your row.

The pulling and pushing, on with dress, off with the dress, on and on it went. Four hours later it fitted like a glove, her dad popping now and again. Her question always the same one, "can I see Jan," "not yet, later," "you said that last time dad." "Well, it's, still later," eventually Zimmer walked in. "What have you two been doing all day, Zimmer?" "I thought you were with Chrisi," "she's up stairs trying a dress on." "She should be at the chip shop," "no, not today. We've been to town to get some things a dress." "Bet she's only gone and got one because I have a special dress." "Why it everybody buying things and trying this and that on and done in such a hurry?" "It must something special going on this Sunday, at church." "It must because Jan is going for the first time and dad wanted to make a good impression." Zimmer and Christine were sworn to secrecy, tell her anything but what really up to. "Where is Jan, he's up stairs with your dad, showing him the Slovakian way to do a neck tie.? " I'll go upstairs to see him," "no you can't." "Your dads not decently attired," "I'm sure dad will let me in," no Jan's not properly attired either." "He's trying a pair of your dad's trousers on it wouldn't it appropriate." "Zimmer, my dad's trousers won't fit him." They're too long, that aside my dad's too fat," "well it doesn't matter. You go in" "There'll be down in a minute." "The lady doing the alterations can sort out the trousers" "don't think so Zimmer. She left half an hour ago," bloody hell I would like to know, has everyone in the house gone mad."

"Hi Doris, Jan spoke through the crack of the door, go for a walk yes." Walk please and some explanations please."Do not worry, nice out, yes," this is going to be a barrel of laughs. She thought as they walked it was hopeless. His English was getting better, but not enough to form a conversation. When he didn't know the how to reply, he just shrugged his shoulders upwards, an expression she had come to understand as I don't understand. They found themselves in the midst of a park, neither had taken any notice as where they were going. It did matter not. They walked a little, then stopped again looked into each other eyes. He lifted her up onto her toes and gently kissed him on the lips, placed her arm around his waist. They walked on through the park. Pub he said, pointing across the road. He dragged to a beer garden at the rear. She needed the rest. I'm knackered. Some two hours later when they got back to the house, Doris exhausted. It was as if they had never left. Frank and Zimmer were still locked in political conversation, the government this, the government that and her mother had just woken from her nap. Chrisi was playing patience, sitting halfway down the garden seat by the apple tree, reading a comic book. The wireless could be faintly heard from the next door's garden.

"Tea you two, yes mam, that would be perfect" "Come here," thinking she was going to kiss her instead. She gave Jan a smacker on the lips. The place is as mad, since I left it a couple of hours ago, bloody hell she thought, hope it's not the tea, or maybe they've put something in the water. Doris watching her mother waggling towards the kettle like a duck, singing some tune or other, was the last straw. "Mam what's going on, going on," being happy is going on, try it some-time," "right mam plonking herself in her mother's chair, here comes some more happiness, get out of my chair. "Jan why don't you clear the cats off the chair, then releasing, it's no good telling you, that, is there." "No problem, he picked up two of her moggies sat down and placed them on his lap. She stood there with her jaw open, "mam you'll catch flies if you stay like, "right Doris, tea. Doris, thought for a while, Jan knows more English that he's letting on, or did he just read her mind, that will be a first." Doris said if they don't get a hurry on, they're going to miss the last tram." No they won't, don't worry your pretty little head about that they're staying here tonight," Zimmer, he's brought a blanket or two. It's a fine evening. He's sleeping outside." "Jan's sleeping on the couch, the chamber pot, has been brought in from the shed, it's under your bed Doris" "so don't get any ideas about coming down here. Christi, she'll have to come down if needed and use the toilet, but she's been told not to flush it don't want Jan or the rest of the house woken." "That clear," "yes mam," Doris and Chrisi replied. "Your dads going to set the alarm, the boys, will be dressed and ready for church before you get up, dressed and gone." "They'll meet us there, at the church," "they're going to hours early." "Don't, you worry about that, they have one or two things to do, now bedtime." "After we have some tea yeah, once Churchill and bloody Montgomery have put the worlds to right." "Keep going like that you two and God won't need a job, come judgment day. He'll need them two, just about everyone would be put to the sword, there'd be no need for spaces in heaven, except for the very fortunate, like me, Chrisi your full of it, what charm Doris, no, I wouldn't call it that.

The sun was barely on the horizon, as Zimmer and Jan made their way to the front door. Frank was on his way down to wake them." You boys are on the ball, Jan's

army training," " right boys. Harry's Café is just across
the road from the Victoria paper shop, do you remember
how to find it. "Yes" Zimmer said. "Get yourselves a
breakfast take your time." "There's a toilet in the yard
at the back, see you at that church." "Big day, ok" Vi
hearing the door close, called downstairs, "boys gone,
suited and booted. They've gone to Harry's dinner."
"You make the fire up" "I'll brew up as soon as the
kettles boiled," "the coppers still in, it will need stoking,
you get on with that." "I'll sort some breakfast out and
get the girls up, big, day Frank," "big day Vi."

Cleaning out the fire was one choir Frank loathed.
It had to be done every day from scratch. The copper
wasn't any better, that would just about stay lit, it
didn't have a good draw, but once it was going, it was
fine, without either there was no tea or cooked food,
fortunately they would burn anything, to save the coal.
Frank had several places he got wood from, work. The
saw mill on uncle Kens farm at church Linton, in the
summer the covered wood piles were plenty, stacked at
the front of the allotment, but in the winter if it was
harsh. Frank had to look out for the foragers, that
would steal he kept a catapult and some marbles, if
one-hit anyone, they were going to know about it, if
they did get up, at all, Frank would fire it into the
bushes to scare them. It usually did the trick.

The fires going and breakfast is on the go. Vi woke the
girls, right you two the coppers on, they'll be a bath full
of water soon, you first Doris. "Mam, it's Sunday."
"when I need you to tell me, what day of the week, it is,
it be time to take me down the luneybin." "For now

move it Doris, bath on a Sunday mam I only had one on Friday." "Well you're getting another today, ok, after come through and have breakfast, put the dress on. We altered." "While Christi has a bath, then she'll get your hair done and your face made up." "Mam don't you think the dress a bit much for church." "A touch overdressed, don't you think." "Doris that's far too dangerous; I'll do the thinking for you today, ok, put the bloody dress on when I tell you to, go to it, yes mam."

"Come on Chrisi whatever you haven't done; it's too late to do it now." "Is Doris ready done, yes mam she is waiting upstairs." Don't bloody move from that spot until your dad tells you?" She kissed Frank on the cheek "it only ten minutes to the church, in fifteen the transport will be here." See there my Love." It was the longest fifteen minutes of Frank's life, every other minute he looked out the front door. "Can I come down dad," "no Doris. I'm not decent,"what you are doing down there, having a wash." "If you're having a wash. Why do you keep opening and shutting the front door then?" "Are you flashing dad, I'll bloody come up there and flash your lips in a minute, my girl," "Now shut up and stay put." Finally, he could hear the hooves' of horses and wheels of the coach clatter along the cobble stones. "Right Doris. You can come down, now lass." "My oh my are you a sight for sore eyes," a tear ran down his cheek. He wiped it to one side with the knuckle of his hand."Let's go." He took her hand and led through the door, down the path to the waiting coach pulled by four dray horse from the brewery. A favour he called in from times past. "Dad, is someone getting married." "Yeah you Doris, today you look like a bride, "what, dad," shush, in you get, she didn't know where to put her face, as neighbours and on lookers on their way to where ever, stopped to look. "Dad, this is mad," "shush I said," enjoy the day. The coach made its way slowly down the Avenue, again she tried to talk. Frank butted in "if I have to gag you I will, you will say I do." Before you get any other notions, "but" "no buts, I mean it. I'll gag you, take kicking and screaming if I have to." "You can go willingly or be man handled, but you're going to get married today, "fine dad."

Doris looked towards the church entrance, spotting Uncle Denise with his brownie camera. The flash startling her, as she dismounted the coach. "God Denise you almost bloody blinded me," "language Doris," remember where you are, put your arm through mine and walk at the same pace as me" The organ burst into life, with here comes the bride as they passed through the lobby into the aisle. The church was full. She thought to herself. It's because there were two weddings and a funeral, the vicar had packed them all in together. Doris was oblivious of what was going on around her. There's never this many people her on any Sunday. Where the hell have all these people come from, sorry God? She muttered. She looked out of the corner of her eyes, as she walked with Frank, she couldn't make out anyone she could recognize.

Her eyes watered up. Everything was a blur I'm going to faint, went through her mind. Snapping out when Jan took her hand and let go of it, as the vicar spoke. "Dearly beloved," she couldn't breathe I'm going deaf, all the sounds around are muffled, did Chris take the cotton buds out of her ears. She couldn't remember. Doris, the vicar shouted, Doris, "yes" she replied, for the second time of asking, "do you take this man to be your lawful wedded husband," "I suppose so." He moved towards her and whispered the words are. I do. Then I do, just. I do but louder so the congregation can hear I do. She shouted at the top of her voice. The vicar almost lost his balance standing on the back of his gown, as he jumped back, a choir boy halting his fall to the ground. "splendid," regaining his balance "I think everyone heard that." She returned to her trance, until the vicar prodded her with his finger. "both of you repeat after me," Zimmer may answer for Jan." "Zimmer may answer for Jan,"Doris bellowed out," "no Doris only repeat what I say," she glanced down to her hand as the ring was placed upon it, "I now pronounce you man and wife," Jan caught by the waist, stopping Doris from toppling back, pulled her upright and planted a kiss on her lips, to which she replied "are we done, can I get out of here please I need air." "Are you ok Zimmer asked," "no this dress is strangling me? I can't breathe," Zimmer spoke to Jan in Slovakian, pointing to the exit to the grave yard? He swept her from the ground and carried her to the bench by one of the yew trees, laying her down that's better. "I just need a minute; I'll be fine," Doris swung her feet around to the ground, turned to her left and heaved up, spewing over the bench. Zimmer handed her his handkerchief, held on to the side of the yew tree, doing the same in sympathy. When they look a good few people looking at the flowers next to the hole, which was waiting for a coffin, were doing the it into the hole, it was infectious, as one started so did another, although dead, she couldn't help feeling sorry for whoever was getting buried.

Frank, walked around the outside of the church to look for them, they are waiting. For you the front. Of the church, you'll have to go back in and come out before the bells stop ringing, quickly now, she's sick, Zimmer said wiping his mouth, never mind that, get a move on, everyone has a good heart today, don't they Frank. Zimmer took one arm and spoke to Jan to take the other, come Doris; your audience awaits.

Doris had a look around the empty church, wishing she had been watching from one of the pulpits. I bet it was grand she thought as she walked to the front exit, flashing camera's greeted here and the bright sun light was right in her eyes. She felt something falling from the air looking to the ground to see what it was, she blinked a dozen times to try to regain focus. "Oh shit confetti" she screamed out, "no its first class, top grade confetti. I'll have you know," someone said, the bellowing laughs that came back, made her realized there were lots of people. Jan took her arm leading her into the shade, "now I see you, she blurted," as the camera snapped away, a group photograph. All relatives together please, someone shouted, "dad, where and how did you find time to sort all this, and where have all these people come from." "Some are from Jan's work, friends of mine, aunts and uncles. They all came to help. I'm pleased they did, so is the vicar." "The coach will be here in a while." "It's only going to the swan house." "They have a function room. It's going not going to be much of a reception, but it's the best we could afford." "Dad your amazing," "save some of that praise for your mam." "She sorted the food and drink and just about everything else.

"My husband, that sounds strange," "wife yes," Jan clasped his hand in hers. "I feel like the queen in this coach and the horses. They've been dressed to the nines." "Have place, for us, Jan said, Zimmer, where he." Jan tried to explain, limited by his grasp of the language, room in house, night time, "you have a house for us," "yes" he replied, "room, yes." He nodded with pride, indicating with his finger it was for them both the journey to the swan house public bar was a short brief ride. Zimmer was waiting for them, Zimmer. She shouted from the coach; "Jan's got a house," "yes a room, your new home" "can't wait " she was so excited. Doris leapt from the coach, to run and tell her dad. He already knew, Doris, "Zimmer has already told me you're a lucky girl, that Jan's alright in my book." "He's my hero dad," "look after him, he'll look after you."

"Mam you've out, done yourself, my favourites; beef dripping sarnies on door stop bread cuts and rabbit stew." "I think that's two of the moggies in their Doris, joking just joking." "The cake, look at the cake, jelly, scones, mam," Vi was in tears, unable, to speak, every time she tried, the flood gates opened, that started Doris off, "you two bloody blootherer's, bad as one another, good job a brought a pocketful of hankies," "thanks' dad, look the boy's band from the steel mill are about to do a turn, a bit of Glen Miller, with a bit of luck, better grab your husband, get him on the dance floor, before the old gin totting swing dancers grab him, or Chrisi."

105

"Give this until nine, we'll wrap it up." "You three need to get the tram into town and the bus from Saint Mathews to your new home." "Me and your mam had to share a single bed with my parents. Vi parents didn't think much of me, said I would never amount to anything." "They probably weren't wrong about that I'm still scratching for a living," "Dad, how did to manage in a single bed?" "With bloody great difficulty." "We had a year and some of that, sleeping toe to head, in the summer I slept on the floor." "In the winter well that was worst of all; my feet use to freeze." "Your mam nicked all the covers, so count your blessings." "It looks like Zimmer is ready to leave." "What about all the clearing up, don't worry about it, there's plenty here to see to that." "Love you Dad," kissing him on the cheek. Jan shook his hand, "bloody hell boy Frank yelped, save some bone," "take care of my girl ok?"

They were just leaving, the swan. When Chrisi shouted, "wait for me, Doris" "where are you going," "with lover boy of course," taking Zimmer by the hand. "What would dad say," "oh nothing, he doesn't know?" "He thinks I'm staying around a friend's house, Jean; for the night," Doris turned around, "Jean, you don't know a Jean, do you Chrisi." "She just a few yards behind us, that's who I pointed to, so dad knew who it was," "so that's Jean, bugger if I know Doris," "she's not coming as well Doris uttered," "no she is getting on the tram and getting off at the next stop." "She often gets on this team." "I don't know who she is," noticing her dad at the front of the swan puffing on a cigar. She quickly back tracked latching on to Jean's arm, waving frantically and dragged her onto the tram her dad, who wasn't as it happened taking a blind bit of notice, "what's your game" the girl asked, "thought you were my friend Jean."

Doris couldn't contain herself such was her excitement, every two minutes she would ask are we nearly there Zimmer. Soon would be his reply, soon, as she looked out the window, the bus pulled up outside the Zanzibar hotel, illuminated by the gas lamps outside and in. It was the brightest lit building in the street and the nosiest, piano and song filling the air and the organ grinder, clashed with those sounds in the Avenue as they dismounted the bus "are we having a drink here first." Chrisi enquired, "We can if you like" Zimmer said, it will give the newlyweds a chance to see their new home. "What Doris asked; are we going to live in the hotel?" "No," Zimmer pointing to a house partly in darkness on the other side of the road, the gas lights in the street providing the only light. It was eerie. It looked as if it would be more at home in a horror movie, "see you later Doris," "I think Dracula might live there Chrisi."

"See you later you two," we won't be too late, we have some loving to do," Chrisi blurted out across the road."Have some respect," she just laughed and giggled, dragging Zimmer, by his coat into the Zanzibar hotel.

Jan knocked on the door. "We have no key" he knocked again harder than the firsts time. "Someone's coming Doris "she could see a flicker of light through the glass in the door accompanied by a thud. The light got more intense as the thud got closer to the door, which creaked has it opened. Doris saw before this tall Errol Flynn looking man with a walking stick and a candle, who spoke Jan first in Slovakian and to her in English. Despite the appearance of the house, there was something soothing about his voice. "My name is Maciej, please follow me," he gave Jan a pair of keys, leading the down the hall, stopping at a door half-way down. "Zimmer's room," he continued turning to the right, next floor, is your room. They followed him up the creaking stairs to the landing. The lock is broken, but it will be fixed soon. This is the room; the bathroom is down the hall opposite at the very end. It is shared; Maciej pushed open the door, that also had its own eerie sound. "There he said, nice, biggest room in the house," "is there no light" Doris asked, "yes, but it's broken I'll fix it." "There's no furniture," Doris said, "I know you'll no fix it," "no; you're looking at the furniture, there is a bed. The mattress is leaning against the piano, there" pointing to the wall, behind the door. "No wardrobe" she asked, dressing table, instead of answering Doris, he spoke to Jan, who squeezed by Maciej, picked the mattress up, threw it on to the bed, spoke to Maceij again, who then left the room.

"What's going on Jan, wait, a moment." Maceij returned, a couple of minutes later with bed linen, then left, closing the door behind him. Jan pulled a blanket from the linen pile throwing the rest onto the floor beside the bed. He spread the blanket out onto the mattress. "Come here he Doris," "wow. Jan your English is getting better by the day," as she lifted her arms and hands to place them around his neck, he swept her from the floor throwing her into the centre of the bed, Jan, steady, she turned to look at him in the flickering light she could she he was removing his trousers and the his underwear, he climbed on to the bed pushing back to the mattress, about time she said, he hitched up her dress, ripped her bloomers off with his bare hands, had you asked I would have taken them off, lay be quite, Jan I'm not a dog, he grasped both her knees, lifting them and forcing her thighs apart, that hurts, stop, please she screamed, he ignored her thrusting himself against her, Jan set about her, like a ferocious animal, he full wait upon her, she was unable to move, as quickly has it had started, it ended, grunting like a pig, rolling off her, he turned on his side, asleep a moment later, she lay there crying, the experience had been awful.

It seemed as she had only just gone to bed, when she was woken by a continuing knocking on the bedroom door. Just a minute, rubbing her eyes, she looked around she was alone, the door opened it was Zimmer, "sorry to wake, you. I have your clothes." "Chrisi brought them here yesterday, to my room." Jan he's down stairs having breakfast with Maciej." "Bastard is an animal Zimmer" Doris sat on the bed, looking at the bruises, lifting her dress. She forgot that her under wear was missing. Zimmer the gentleman, he was turned away "your underwear, is err missing," "oh shit, sorry Zimmer, its ok, you have nothing I haven't seen before" not that I want to see it again that is. "Zimmer, Chrisi here, where is she, by the way, asleep in my bed?"

"I never thought you two would end up being a couple." "Doris, please don't read too much into it, she is a great girl, that only lives for the moment." "When it has passed, she will move on to another thrill. That's just the way she is." "Because, she will want more than

I will can give and get hurt in the process." "Come on Zimmer, just look at you two, Doris enough, hey." "You lady must get ready for work remember you have to catch a bus to town and the tram to your work," "Jan you know he's not such brute as you might think" "He doesn't know what he should do, he had little or no knowledge, except what he has seen, you have to teach him, all that you can," "shit Zimmer that won't amount to much, what do I know?" "Married life is a difficult path Doris, quickly, now. You must eat, eat. Breakfast the most important part of the day, see you downstairs, completely dressed," "yes, of course. I don't make a habit of flashing my privates," "see you at the breakfast table."

Doris walked to the end of the hall across the landing, hope this is the bathroom. Slowly opening the door, "what a state, bloody hell this as had a lot of use," she said aloud. Most of the enamel was pitted and discoloured. It looked as it needed a clean, but it wasn't dirty just worn, still it will beat a tin bath, its three the size, if it works, I'll try that tonight. She thought. Maciej was coming out of the kitchen, as Doris entered the breakfast room with a frying pan of sizzling of Sausages. "They smell nice" she remarked. "parówki, sausages, some potatoes and scrambled eggs, there black tea in the pot, on the table." "Maceij I only have toast and jam in the morning." "I can fix that," "no. The eggs and sausage will be fine, today." She looked across the table. Jan had his head bowed. She walked around, sitting down next to him taking his hand in hers. "I'm sorry he muttered. It'll get better. She replied, don't worry." I'll show you. He turned and smiles at her;

he was about to speak. She put her finger to his lips, "shush now. The sausages look good and the eggs; I'll take some tea, please, where's the sugar and milk Maciej?" "We only have black tea, its traditional; it's what we have at breakfast, never mind I will get some milk and sugar to day" "very well." "Jan, I'll teach you some more tonight, English and perhaps other things."

Having arrived for work. Doris crossed the road in her usual daydream manner, "one of these days Doris you're going to get killed crossing this road." Megan took her arm, noticing the ring on her finger, "what's that all, about" she enquired." "I'm married," "bloody Nora Doris, how the devil the devil did you manage that." "I took a knife this, chap's throat, had my way with him, told my dad what he had done." "My dad took a twelve bore shot gun, placed it to the back of his head, said, marry her or else." "Then forced him to the church, "seriously'" "that's what happened, pretty much." Doris said, "good grief," "Doris burst out laughing. Some of it is true, but it wasn't quite like that." "Shame on you Doris," what's up though, I feel sick every morning, I love breakfast Megan, but lately it doesn't love me, "I hope it's just some bug girl, "that, or your pregnant?"

Doris clocked in then ran to the toilet. Megan followed on behind, "breakfast down, breakfast up, I'll just clean that up in a minute Megan." "I didn't make," "don't worry about that" she replied. "Are you alright," "yes it takes my breath away for a moment, then I fine for the rest of the day, I felt like that at the wedding, the dress I was wearing, started to feel too tight I was sick then, I was ok, I don't get it," "you need to have a test Doris, with the nurse at the clinic, if you turn out to be pregnant, then that will explain why you're sick in the mornings," "if that's the case Megan, when does the stork come," "about nine months form the time you conceived," "how did that happen," "Doris you really are naive, have you had intercourse with a man?" "No, someone else asked me that" "I haven't been on any courses," "you twit, have you had sex with a man," "Oh yes," "Doris talk to your doctor soon as you can, get him to tell you about the birds and the bee's, someone's has got to, I'm not the person for that, your doctor Doris soon as you can, in fact go to the surgery now and get an appointment, tell them ,it's urgent and he or she may see you straight away, I'll clock you out, I'll tell Ben you're sick, go on now ,away with you", "thanks Megan."

I wonder what the birds and bees to do with anything. She thought, as she left the factory. Doctor Patel, not her regular doctor had just come in from his rounds. He was new to the surgery. He was available more of than not, on account he was from India; lots of people had their doubts about his qualifications, on the account; he was foreign. "You can go in now, Doris," "sorry. I can't pronounce your name," nurse crackup said. She had got the nickname, because her face was badly damaged from an accident, it resembled a broken plate; nobody called her by her real name; it appeared. She didn't mind one bit. It was the only name she responded to, if you called her Heather, she would ignore you, "thanks."

"Sit on the chair please," now. What's the problem? Doris told the doctor and about what Megan said at work. "I was to ask about the birds and the bee's doc," doctor, not doc. How you people ever managed to reproduce, let alone start an industrial revolution is beyond my comprehension." "Go to the toilet in the lobby, pass water in this, tell the nurse when you're done, give her the container." "What Doctor, this bottle," she did as directed, went to the toilet. "He said I was to pass water, well I suppose walking by the sink would count. She went to the reception desk." The Doctor said. I was to give you this when I have passed water." "there's nothing in it" nurse crackup said, "you're supposed to urinate into the bottle, put it into the bag and then bring it to me." "How do I do that," pee in the bottle please?" "Good grief, but I'll get it all over my hands? "That's why we have gloves and a sink, so you can wash them," "oh."

Fifteen minutes later the Doctor called her back, "after I've finished. See the nurse," "Doctor, so what's wrong with me," "lay on the examination table. I want to take a look at your tummy." "Yes as I thought, you need to see me in another two months, unless you start bleeding." Come straight away if that should happen, your monthly cycle has stopped." "Yes Doctor, missed the last two months I didn't think much about, it, was glad." "It's such a messy time, for your underwear." "Yes I can imagine, that confirms what I suspected, see the nurse, she'll give you the required to explanation, about the birds and the bees."

Doris was anxious, "when the urine is tested and the swab " nurse crackup said. We will hopefully have a more precise diagnosis." "I would say your about two to three gone," "nurse I'm here, I haven't gone anywhere," "no Doris gone in time, your pregnancy; you're going to have a baby." "What now nurse," "no in several month time, we'll speak again,"but what about the birds and the bees." "Doris, I've got some questions to ask, when did you first, do it with your partner," last night she replied, no, before that, when did you first have sex." "Doris thought for a moment, remembering the pillar box, with Johnny, she said, and when was that, oh about eight or ten weeks ago." "Then he is likely to be the father of your child." "I'm confused Doris replied, nurse crackup, took the time to explain in meticulous detail." Shit; I've got to talk to Chrisi," is that your partner," nurse I've got to go." "You need to make another appointment before you go," you don't understand she replied." "I'm in the shit," well in it; you still need to make an appointment, "ok; I'll do that," "now can I go," I suppose so Doris."

Doris hoped that Chrisi was still at the house in Zimmer's room. She was a lazy cow; she thought boarding the tram. God I hope she's there, she kept saying over and over again in her head. She bursts into the room without knocking, took hold of Chrisi by her head shaking her until she woke. "Thank goodness you're still here," "what's up Doris," "get dressed?" "We need to go for a walk right now Chrisi its important." "I am right in the shit, up to my neck, now, please hurry. I'm going out of my bloody mind." "Christi got out of bed as naked as the day she was born. "Doris you've seen me without clothes before." "I know, but what have you done down there," "oh, that nothing, shaved it men like that, turns them on," "bloody hell Chrisi; you look like you have been scalped."

"Now that were are in the park," what's so important, Doris."" "I'm over two months pregnant? Chrisi, what I'm going to do." "Have you done it with Jan yet," "yes last night," "prey and hope he can't figure it out, when the time comes for you to drop your load, tell him your early, premature?" "Hopefully, his math's won't be too good, no big deal." "Chrisi, It's a baby not bomb I'm dropping." "Well excuse me with the expression, pop it out drop it, shit a brick, whatever you want to call it. Chose to have it or get an abortion," "what's an abortion Chrisi?

"With all the men you've had, why're not pregnant, or had one of them abortions." "I take precautions, make sure they don't do it inside me." "Chris, what am I going to do," "did Jan do it inside you? I think so." "Think back to last night, you can do that can't you, yes he did, grunted rolled off, went to sleep, the pig." "Make sure, soon as you can he does it again say nothing Doris," "carry on as normal." "For your sake you have to, in a month tell him you're pregnant?" "Wear loose clothes." "What you brought to the house with Zimmer is all I've got, nothing loose," "a need for some shopping." "I've got no money Chrisi," "don't worry about that, it's your good fortune I have." "I'll treat you in the meantime." I'll draw up some plan of action, leave it to me. Doris took her arm, "thanks, what would I do without you?"

They strolled through the park, catching a bus to the city Centre. Exchanging small talk during the short journey, "markets a good starting place," Chrisi said, "it's where we'll find the bargains and women's larger clothes." "I don't want to look like an old lady." Don't worry they have some trendy loose fitting colourful clothing here, trust me." Doris was amassed, but more about how the time evaporated.

"See you later," "I'd better go home before mam has kittens," "thanks for everything." "Doris go home and put on one of those dresses." "Then make a real fuss of your man, keep him sweet everything will be fine" "I'll see you Saturday, around yours, Zimmer's taking me dancing across the road, Zanzibar time." Doris arrived back home,"bloody room, look at the state of it," she said out loud, placing the clothes on the bed, She turned around, almost jumping out of her skin. For a man who normally made a thumping noise as he moved along the floor boards, could be silent when it suited. He came into the room unnoticed, creeping along the boards towards her, in a deliberate manner. For reasons, Doris didn't understand. "If there's anything you need, anything at all, if your short of money, between me and you only, I can help." Doris felt uneasy with his mood, "I'd like the door fixed please, a bucket, some carbolic soap, a scrubbing brush, some rag, disinfectant or bleach and some wax for the floor." "I'll fix it," "paint if you have any, he stepped back a pace from her, yes, of course." "Between you and me, remember what I said, the paint, I have a man who will paint the room. He'll fix it for you. His name is Yanik." She quickly shut the door as he left the room, Doris felt her heart pounding and that feeling in her stomach,"muttering, I'm in hell. She thought, and this is my punishment."

Maceij returned about half an hour later with everything she had asked for, this time he made that thud along the hall way. "How did you get that leg," "German bullets he replied?" "I have some milk and sugar; I'm making tea in about ten minutes, if you would like some." She wanted to say no, but found herself saying the opposite. "Yes, I'll follow you down" she sat opposite him in the breakfast room. He made small talk, weather, this and that, after the tea, she returned to her room.

For most of the afternoon, she scrubbed cleaned and disinfected the room, and the bathroom, then prepared herself a hot bath, running water. What a luxury, she went to lock the door, another bloody lock that's doesn't work, shit ,she said to herself. The house was as quiet as a church, she had just striped off, stepping into their bath, laying in it, her neck about the water line. She gasped, there he was, Maceij; Doris made no attempt to cover herself or panic; he gazed upon her naked body, taking his time. "This is to scent the water, will help you smell nice." She wanted to scream out, how dare you, but uttered, "thanks" instead. He left pulling the door shut. Her heart was pounding again "Doris get a grip on yourself," she said, things are bad enough. I dare not tell Jan she thought. We would be bloody homeless. She dried off got dressed and decided to confront him. She bursts into the breakfast room he was standing in the kitchen doorway. "Look Maciej," Zimmer, interrupting, "soup, dear it's quite good." Her head spun around, there was Jan at the table, "you were about to tick Maceij off." "Yes, I wanted some fresh air in the room. He promised to come up and open the bloody windows." "Did he," Zimmer said," he properly hasn't come up because he knows that Yanik the useless prick, has painted them shut?" She looked straight at

Maceij, smiling "Zimmer has a low opinion of Yanik. He painted then shut for his information, because they were in need of repair, and he couldn't find a carpenter." Maceij, went to say, but Doris butted in "I know you'll bloody fix it." Doris sat down at the table, the room, erupted into a row, between Zimmer, Maceij and Jan in Slovakian. Jan sat there most of the time just smiling, when the row concluded. Jan said, "soup, my dear, Zimmer not amused. Had said all he had to say, Maceij returning the kitchen, "wish I had never asked," Doris said. "Don't worry, this is quite normal. He takes the money, but puts nothing back into the house." "At some point, point I fear it will come crashing down on our heads, properly when we're asleep." "All the authorities will need to do, place a stone on top here lays a miser and his victims," with that Zimmer left the room. Your soup, "Doris thanks, Maceij."

After dinner, Jan and Doris returned to their room. Jan took a deep breath as he entered, looked around, "different room, we in the wrong room," "no silly, were not, I cleaned it." He placed his hands on his hips "well very good," not questioning anything for a moment, "why no work." "I had to go to the clinic for a routine check." He laid down on the freshly made bed, putting his hands behind his head, "was everything's okay" "yes." Doris removed her under wear, climbed aboard the bed, lying beside him.

She made a distraction from the questioning, by gently kissed him on the lips and took him, pounding him as he had pounded her, he gasped pulling her thrashing hips to his body holding her in that position, when he peaked. Doris collapsed onto his chest exhausted, Chrisi instructions carried out, he gentle placed his hands around her, the pair of them falling asleep. She woke as the sunlight came streaming in through the window, that reminds me she thought curtains, must see my mother. She was still in the same position as he started to wake she wanted to take him again. "No," he said, look at the time breakfast, work," he tossed her to one side like a rag doll and leapt from the bed. Grabbing the towel from the rail on the bedstead, "I wash quickly, then you" kissing her on the forehead, exiting the room. She lay there for a moment, thinking wish I did not have to go to work. I could just lay here, for a moment dosing of into semi conscious-ness, before being suddenly swept to her feet, "look, wash go, now, dress, breakfast," "ok Jan." He smiled, kissing on the forehead, try the lips, pointing to her mouth, "yes, when teeth are clean, kiss there."

Breakfast was the same panic as it was at home, mam would be shouting at her come on girl. She found Maciej was doing no different, perhaps all morning cooks are the same; she thought. The difference was the new surroundings meant that she was arriving ten minutes early each day, on the account of having to catch the tram and then the bus. Doris looked at her money. Most of it was going on getting to work, Doris, Jan and Zimmer's, looked at their finances during that week; with the rent, food and transport, it was going leaving little money over. "I need a better job of work." Jan spoke to Zimmer in Slovakian and then to Zimmer translated to Doris. "Jan has a chance to work in the railway yard. They're taking on engine drivers and stokers, on the account of his build." "He's designed for this job and has a good chance of getting this work." "But he will have to travel where they say, sometimes he may go there one day and come back the next on the long journeys they have two drivers and two stokers." "The stay in a coach drawn behind the train and work shifts on the long-haul line, Scotland and Wales, or the south coast." "The money is good very good I don't mind" Doris said. It might involve the weekends." "It's when the trains are busy," it's up to Jan. "I take the job, if they let me, better life for us," Jan replied. "I have a talk with boss at railway Monday."

At the weekend, Chrisi went dancing with Zimmer. Jan and Doris went to the park for a picnic. On Saturday to watch the cricket and on Sunday, to listen to the band. The days were starting to get cooler. They were already half way into autumn; the sun had lasted. People referring to it as an Indian summer, Doris heard that expression from her mother when she was a child, but never understood what it meant. The nights were drawing in; the room was cosy and had an air of privacy to it. The door had a lock that worked. Her mother made her some curtain. Yanik was due in order to paint the room, and a carpenter was being sorted. So Maceij had stated, Zimmer said at the breakfast table, not to hold too much faith in that, he had heard it before. "Christmas will come first. I think, in England you say, hell will freeze over I believe." Doris enjoyed the banter at the breakfast table; it made the day. The weekend gone so quickly, Monday had soon arrived, back to the grindstone. "You have some funny sayings you English," oh I'm sure you have a few of your own Zimmer, don't you."

Doris kissed Jan on the lips, several times, when they dismounted the tram into town. Wishing him well with the interview, before continuing the rest of the journey with Zimmer to work. The morning sickness had gone. Doris was feeling much like her old self; she was now a fully-fledged member of the gossip circle the gathering of clacking chickens; She preferred to call it, she noticed a new person standing, where she once stood, knowing how that felt, she made a beeline for her." Hi. I'm Doris," "Molly Stringer;" she replied "bugger me. I wish it was a different one." Doris said, trust me that lot are going to have some fun with that name." "If you've come to take the piss, then go back to your little circle of friends." "Molly, I used to stand here, just on the very spot, an outcast, sooner or later either you find a way to put up with them, or stay a loner." "There piss taking bastards given a half the chance, there'll make your life hell." "Fag, I haven't got any," "I'm brasic at the Mo," "I was the one offering," pulling a park drive half way out of the packet, "I'll pay you back no need" Doris said, "bloody murder when you smoke, and you ain't got any." Molly smiled and accepted the offer together with friendship it carried." "You married," "very much so," with that the siren sounded. Bloody sodden thing, they need to bung Ben Grubs arse in that ,to quite it down a notch. Doris laughed aloud, "oh you had dealings already," oh yes" she replied, "nice to meet you Molly" and "you Doris, "thanks, for the fag."

On the way, home, she stopped at the continental shop. It meant getting of the bus and waiting for another; she wanted ideas about, Slovak and polish food. The lady spoke good English. "I want to cook for my husband. He's from Slovakia in the south," Here is a recipe for sauerkraut and sausage soup with dumplings filled with cheese," the shop lady said Doris found the smells delightfully different. The lady gave her a good insight; "I'll come by on Friday. It's when I get paid, I'll buy then" Doris told the shopkeeper.

"So late Jan said," as she walked into their room. "I'm sorry I was at the continental shop and got carried away." "I wanted to get some ideas to cook for you," "good, the job; I have it," "when do you start." "Saturday, come back Monday maybe Tuesday, first stop here, to London, then London to Inverness?" "Then back London, back to here." "When do you go" "this Saturday, "so soon'" better, bigger money. The time passed quickly or seemed to; it was gone to work, eat, go to sleep. She felt like a mouse on a tread mill? Jan kissed her passionately on the lips," see you soon." She wanted to go to the station with him, but rain, arrived it was very heavy at times,"bring back the sunshine." She shouted, waving as he boarded the bus to the city.

There was no one in the house except Maciej. Zimmer was out, calling on Chrisi. She could hear Maceij radio, faintly, and the occasional horse and cart passed by in the Avenue. "Shit I'm bored, she said out loud" I'll have a bath, read the paper and have an early night, or should I do some washing. She just couldn't settle on one thing or another, going for the bath after some deliberation. It was nice to lay in the steam fill bathroom the water up to her neck. Doris had spent a good hour in it, letting a little water out, then topping it up with hot, Maceij, went mad every time she did it, saying it took all the hot water. If there was anyone else wanted a bath, they couldn't. She stood up letting the water out, having pulled the plug. Shit, I've forgotten the towel. "It's on the bloody bed in the room "she muttered to herself. She stood shivering, hoping to be dry enough to bolt down the hall way to the room, right here goes, opening the Doris ran straight into Maceij. She was shell shocked; he had her towel over his arm.

"I went to your room, to see if you wanted some food and wine, I saw your towel on the bed." "I assumed correctly you had forgotten to take it." Doris just stood there, trembling. Maceij unfolded the towel slowly wrapping it around, her body, "you poor thing your cold." "Come the stove is on; it will take I while before it heats the house, the kitchen it's already nice and warm." I didn't light it until late, because it needed a good clean, come and get warm."

Doris still shivering, just followed without any prompting, he wasn't wrong; she thought, joy heat. Doris didn't like the cold at the best of times let alone, being cold and wet. "Sit here on a stool, wait, I'll be back in a minute," Maceij returned with another towel and began to dry her hair, massaging her scalp at the same time, oh that's heavenly. He spoke softly, "the towel you have around you is wet, it needs drying, if you have a bath robe in your room, I will fetch it for you, before you catch a chill." "No, I don't have one of those, never had the need," "if I open the fire door put it on the horse it will dry it quickly." Doris stood up, remove the wet towel, sitting back on the chair naked.

"What, you're shocked Maceij, you have seen my body before," "no he replied, not shocked, surprised." "When I saw you in the bath that day, I thought, you may have said something to Jan, why didn't, you." "I don't know; I'm not uncomfortable with it now either." Maceij turned the towel several times, there its dry and very warm. She stood up, "put it around me then; that's a good boy." "Your teasing me now, it's one thing to see you naked, another to tempt danger," "I'm human, not a machine. The towel was so soothing, but quickly absorbed the heat to her skin, "please Maceij, heat the towel again." Removing it once more, the bulge in his trousers was so obvious he blushed. Noticing she had seen it, once again he turned the towel, feeling it, to see how hot it was. Maceij took the towel form the rail, out stretching his left arm, while staring into the fire, "there" he said, "take it," "no, put around me before it gets cold." Reluctantly, he did as she asked, Doris could see the beads of sweat forming around his temple, "are you hot under the collar." Maceij, he turned looked at her. She took the towel off, patting the towel on his face to mop the sweat. He was bright red. He found himself trembling now, with fear taking a pace backwards. Doris dropped the towel on to the floor. He could do nothing to cover the front embracement in his trousers. She stared down at his trousers, moving forwards a step; he moved back another; he was against the door to the yard, there was nowhere else to go. She stepped forward again." No I can't do this; Jan would kill me." "Do what, you haven't done anything yet," Doris picked the towel from the floor; I am going to get dressed, dinner, wine; I think you said." You're the devil"

"I know Maceij, your properly right, sometimes. I think that, see you in a mo."

Doris was in a daring mood, it excited her. She thought. I wonder how far I dare to go, putting on a loose-fitting flared dress, bought with Chrisi in town, with no bra or underwear, put a pair of slippers on and a cardigan her mother knitted. Not bothering to brush her hair, ran her fingers through giving it a wild provocative look. Maceij was just serving food up as she entered the breakfast room, "are we having wine." Maceij, do you think that a wise move, I don't know. What do you think, stop playing games, please, she smiled riley in response? He placed one glass on the table "are you not having any," "no; I wasn't going to serve you any either." "I didn't want to be accused later of take advantage of you." "Poor the wine Maceij, if I wanted to be taken advantage of, you will be the first to know." Maceij took the bottle to the glass; she noticed his hand shaking; she put hers to his to steady it as he poured, "careful, or you'll over fill it." She took a large gulp into her mouth, then offered the glass up to his lips he responded in kind. Doris took the glass finishing off the rest before refilling her glass. Where are sitting Maceij, "pointing I sit there," "then I shall sit opposite?" The dumplings are good, oh, is that goats cheese, "yes most people don't like it, too rich for them, there's fruit for after, dinner and some chocolate, it's very hard and dark," "I like his voice was trembling, "with coffee or brandy it's quite palatable," "I'll put the radio on, there classical music at this time of the day." She got up and walked around the table sitting on the chair next to him, "it always seems warmer this side and cosy," "that because the heat filters through the air brick from the kitchen, it has its advantages and disadvantage." "The down side the smells from the cooking also filter through" "I don't mind," Maceij changed the angle the chair repositioning himself. "That's better, now I can see you when I speak," Doris got up and did the same.

Maceij broke some chocolate for a thick uneven bar, then poured himself some brandy. "Try the chocolate, Doris took a piece of chocolate and his glass of brandy. "That's quite strong" "only a little." Doris, that's enough, it's not water" "wow" was her response, taking another sip, "my stomachs ablaze, wow that's good stuff," forgetting she had no underwear on she lifted her feet from the floor placing one foot between his knees' on the edge of his chair and the other on the knee of his right good leg, the dress fell all the way down her up bent legs, revealing all, Maceij jaw dropped open, Doris looked down at the fallen dress, making no attempt to cover herself up she looked at his trousers instead and then at his face, his jaw was still open, his face red, the leg that had been between his legs on the edge of the chair, she lifted placing it firmly on the knee his trousers and spread her legs a little wider, Maceij lifted her legs up pushed them to the side, he stood up, without another word, he left the room, she heard the door to his room shut firmly, the house fell silent, sitting there alone all sorts of thoughts drifted through her head, after sitting there for what seemed a lifetime, Doris went to her room, Doris tossed and turned, for a while, the thoughts of her behaviour, skated around her mind, the worry of would he tell Jan.

It was much colder than of late when Doris woke. The windows were running with condensation winters coming, to see clearly she made a circle on one of the pains. It had been raining. The Avenue was awash with leaves dancing along the cobbles, bugger it's cold, slipping the dress on. She had worn, the evening before and cardigan, I need the toilet. She muttered, talking to herself, on her way down the hall way. I wonder if the fire in the kitchen stove is still alight, I'm bloody freezing. Barefoot she went downstairs through the breakfast room into the kitchen. She could see dull embers glowing in the grate behind the glass in the iron door. A tool lay on top of the range. She had seen it used yesterday "I wouldn't pick that up if I was you, it will be hot; you need a glove," Doris almost shed her skin. "You know how to scare people to death Maceij," "you would have burnt your hand, sorry I wouldn't want that." Doris turned to facing him, "come away from the range please; your dress could burn if it touches the iron," he pointed at the stool. "Sit, while I fix the fire," she obliged, "glad you said that my feet were freezing. I should have put my slippers on. In the kitchen, that's good practice, there are splinters of wood on the floor; if you are not wearing any on your feet." Looking down at his feet, she noticed the iron and leather braces, protruding, beneath the long white night shirt. "That's because I'm stupid and was also cold," "do you have to wear the iron all the time," no, only in the day." "Without it, walking is impossible, the pain as well." "I'm sorry for last night, will you tell Jan," "tell him what" she replied, there. It will soon warm up. He walked over to the stood, lifting his night shirt up to his waist, "now we are even, take a good look. I did." "The iron goes always up to your hip," "doesn't it hurt that other legs" "no Maciej replied; my pants have padding, to stop chaffing." "No don't let the shirt down" Doris explored with her right hand "hold the shirt. You could have done anything to me last night. I would have let you," "what about Jan," he's not here and Zimmer, still out with Chrisi, I assume." Maceij scooped Doris from the stool, his giant hands each cradling the cheeks of her bottom. He was about to.

When a voice filled the air, echoing along the front hall way. It was Chrisi, "my bloody sister,"Maceij quickly placed me on the stool, exiting by the back door into the brick yard Doris pulled herself, together, exiting the other door into the breakfast room. "Where's Maceij," Zimmer asked, "I don't know I haven't seen him. I've only just come down was hoping some tea was on the go." "Not that horrible black tea I can't stand that," "Chrisi you get used to it. My feet are cold; I forgot to put my slippers on, I'll be back in a minute." She heard the back door open as she was about to leave the breakfast room. "That explains where Maceij been, getting coal for the range," Zimmer stated, Doris, could feel her cheeks blush with heat, she ran down the hall, taking the steps two at a time, she ran through the door, then shut it and, leapt onto the bed she curled into a ball, her heart was pounding, "that was close," she muttered under her breath, Chrisi entered the room. "You alright Doris, your face is red," I'm fine, are you sure, yes." "Chrisi, did you ever think you were born with the devil in you," "no, not born with it, but it makes life interesting, when you feel that way." "Doris, what are you trying to say, oh, I don't know. It's nothing; I'm missing Jan. That's what it is, you go down." I'm going to the bathroom. "I'll you join shortly," tell Maceij, make my breakfast, don't know about you Chrisi, but I'm starving." Doris joined Chrisi in the breakfast room, yummy sausages, Doris you're converted into a Slovak, how can you eat those spicy fat laden things, first thing in the morning?" "There lovely, there's nothing like a good sausage," giggling aloud. "You should know that Chrisi, who also started laughing aloud, everyone chuckled at the table, apart from Zimmer. "He said you should not mock think of them that have none.", Get off the soap box, they all said at once, he paused for a moment, then burst into laughter, "you know me, too well."

Drudge, Monday was here soon enough. Doris did not like going to work anymore. The journey was tiring. Work was mundane. And the journey home was diabolical, especial for the city to home. This Day was no different from any other apart for the break chats with a new-found friend Molly. It was a boring uneventful time. She was glad to be home. She walked straight into the bedroom striped off her work clothes, throwing them on the bed. She turned there was Jan. Doris hadn't noticed his dirty clothes behind the door. She almost let slip Maceij, thinking he'd walked into the room. Doris flung her arms around, "your putting on weight, too much time at the table." "Quickly taking her hands down, I thought you might have, a kiss or two for me." "Instead, you call me fat, missed you. I love you might have been nice," Jan threw the wet towel he had wrapped around the waist onto a chair, walked over to the piano, picked up the bunch of flowers he had placed there earlier, walk back toward her, then threw them at her. "There, I love you, get on bed I give what you have missed." "Sod you," she put the loose dress on and headed for the door. He grabbed the nape of the dress ripping it from her body, which swung her round. Doris landed hitting her forehead on the top edge of the wooden headboard, the force, cut the skin, dazed and bouncing back of the board, He landed a blow across the side of her face with the flat of his right hand, "party, yes on weekend> dancing in nightclub I see he shouted." Blood was tricking down her face. The left side felt like it was going to explode. "I'm pregnant, having a baby." You are an ignorant bastard," rocking her arms back and body forth on the bed, "Chrisi bought the dress." "That's why I am getting fat." "I'll get fatter by the week." The tears were streaming, the salt from them, stung her cheek' Jan approached the bed.

"Piss off she screamed shouted at the top of her voice don't you dare to touch me." He back handed her across the other cheek, he was about to speak, the banging on the door interrupting him, his hand stopping in mid-air, about to land a further blow. He shouted, in Slovak, "what do you want," a voice answered back in the same language. She knew it was Maceij, "open the door" he said, Jan obliged, then stood in the doorway taking up the whole space, "what's going on" Maciej asked. "None of your business, this is between man and wife," "he bloody hit me Maceij for nothing, for nothing Maceij; she screamed." "He is a bully," "is that so" Maceij replied, squaring up to Jan. Doris stared into the doorway. Jan flexed his biceps; she thought there was going to be a fight, but Maceij backed away. She could hear him going down the stairs. Jan closed the door. "Why you not tell the truth," "because you, shit for brains, you're like my mam, listen only when you want to, assume something else, hit first ask later, you over-sized ape?" Doris grabbed her compact from her bag. The reflection of the mirror couldn't lie her face was swollen. "How do you suppose; I hide this," "sorry he," said she took the wet towel he had discarded on the chair, wiping the blood from her brow the skin was only grazed, but sore to the touch, Happy." Standing up square onto him, "she slapped his face has hard as she could. Doris thought to hit him a second time, but the blow hurt her more than him. "He hadn't flinched "I deserve that, yes" "you bloody did" bursting into tears once more. Jan put his arm around her pulling her to his chest, to console her "I never do this again I swear," kissing her the top of her head.

"I'll get a cloth; with cold water," Jan put the cloth to her cheek, ouch it was tender to the touch."You heavy handed brute, trying to smile" she took the cloth form him; his hand shape was clearly visible on her face. The compact mirror at arm's length, showed the full extent of the impact. Jan had cooled the cloth, slowly it eased the pain, after a few trips to the bathroom. Maceij was shouting " food is ready" "come let's go eat." She looked at him, "are you sure you want them to see this," "it's only Maceij and Zimmer. They know already we had a fight."

When they arrived at the breakfast room Maceij, he was already eating his soup. "Where's Zimmer," "he's at the library, Doris, changing our books. Lucky Chrisi went home or your mother would know about this." Jan looked at her and Maciej shaking his head, "don't you shake your head at me, had my mother known. She would be around here smashing your head in with a copper stick." Jan spoke to Maceij in Slovak, the two exchanging in what appeared to be heated words, Maceij went to the kitchen and brought plates of piping hot food. "What's this," Doris enquired, "chudé hovädzie,lean beef, served with boiled cabbage and dumplings." "It looks delicious," "probably better than it taste's," Doris chuckled; "you're a good cook Maceij, don't you think Jan," he didn't look amused, choosing not to reply, ate his food, without further conversation, perhaps she thought the exchange of words they had, did not please him, the food gone. She took a slice of bread from the basket, mopping her plate clean. "There's no more, if there was, I would give you another plate full," "Maceij, I have eaten enough," she was about to say more, when Jan, abruptly stood up, "bedroom, we go now," hustling Doris into the hall. "Jan you could have at least said good night," they got into bed. He kissed her on the lips rolled over and went to sleep. She thought, while he's in this mood, it's best to say nothing, after a few minutes, went to sleep herself.

Doris no sooner entered the factory it started, "what an earth happened to you." "Ben, so no one else asks the question "I was attacked; nothing was taken; he hit me." Thinking this would quell any further questions. It had the opposite effect, did you get a look at him, have you been to the police, what are they doing, and so it went on, wish I had told them the truth, at break time she chatted with Molly, the only person, to say, "your hubby did that," bastard's men are? They truly are," have a fag Molly,"they say that a lie begets another lie," "what do you mean Doris; you have to cover one thing up with another?" "I still don't understand," never mind, how was your weekend, "much like yours," "except my man tanned by bottom, daren't show your that, hand prints all over it, says its turns him on, that and other things," Doris laughed, "Molly you're a breath of fresh air," as the whistle went, "breath, of what Doris," "nothing Molly, back to the grind stone, hey, girl."

Beat on her feet, it was the end of another day; all Doris wanted was her bed, especially after last night. Jan, on the other hand, had different idea's ideas, on the bed was a new dress. "Get changed, we are going out, across the road to Zanzibar." "Food, drink, dance, home, bed, who knows what, is next," she was too tired to argue. He didn't need to paint a picture, as to the who knows what's next," "How did you guess the size? It fits perfectly." "I Took old one to market," clever boy she thought. Doris; Looked at her face in the compact, most of the bruising, hidden by the makeup foundation, "a little lipstick and I'm ready." Dinner, two glasses of wine; she forced herself to dance. "Jan, I've got to go to work tomorrow." "No work in morning, Zimmer, go to factory, tell you sick." "One more dance, then home," Doris obliged; she lay there in bed, as he pumped away on top, a moment later, the grunt; he rolled off, turned on his side, another minute he was asleep, snoring.

When she woke it was to an empty bed. A red dressing gown, laying where he had laid and a red rose. His work boots, his clothes, were gone, Doris put the dressing gown on. Maceij was having his mug of black tea at the breakfast room table. She went to say good morning, noticing the time on the fire place mantle, "shit ,is that clock right, Maceij" "of course, "bloody hell, I'll get the sack," "sit,'" he shouted as she was about to flee the room. "Zimmer, would have already, visited your place of work, to tell them you are sick, sit to enjoy the day." "Jan, he wanted you to rest. He's gone to work; he will be back in the morning, one day off, and he will work again over the weekend." "To make the money, why, work so hard Maceij," "For a better life, why else," I sometimes wonder, that work, is all there is to life, when do you ever have enough money." Maceij grinned shaking his head, never; you will never have enough because you will always want more." "Welcome to the working part of the human race." "I'm going for a bath no breakfast, no; I am still stuffed from last night's meal, by the time we were served, it was too late to eat, see you later."

Doris loved her bath, wallowing in the water for almost half an hour, dried her self-putting on the new dressing gown. It felt comforting to her skin, laying on the water tank warmed it through. This is a step up in luxury she thought, picking up the wet towel from the floor. She could hear someone coming up the stairs, as she walked down the hall way to her room. "It's you Maceij, in your bath robe, if you're thinking of a bath, sorry I've taken the water again." "Have you, in this house that's a punishing offence, looking down up on him standing on the stairs. "That's bad I just can't help myself, I love my bath, so what are you going to administer, cranking a smile."

He climbed another three steps towards her, "yes you should be punished," looking straight into his eyes, "were the same height now." Maceij reached to the cord securing her robe, pulling it towards him; Doris shrugged her shoulders allowing the garment to drop open exposing her naked body she continued to look into his eyes. Taking his hands placing them on each cheek of her bottom, Maceij scoped her from the floor, she wrapped her arms around his neck and her legs around his waist, kissing him passionately on the lips. He carried into her room, laid on the bed, let his robe letting is fall to the floor, mounted the bed and took her, after Doris lay beside him, they spent any hour or two, talking. Time did not matter, small chat, about little nothings, trees in the park, leaves dancing on the pavement. She had not experienced such passion since Johnny. Doris day dreamed, while Maceij took his bath, after he brought her tea, they kissed and talked some more. I must go and prepare dinner, lay for just a little longer, Doris undid his robe, kissing him from his head down, tasting all she could of his body.

Dinner, Maceij shouted "dinner." Doris joined him at the breakfast table. "Maceij I have no regrets about what we have done, it will stay with us, until the day I die, no one but no one will know."I'm glad you said that Doris," "of course, except for Chrisi, then Zimmer, not forgetting my mother, a few friends." "Doris are you serious," "no; Jan would kill me," "your humour, will be the death of me." "What we have done, must stay with us." "I wanted you the first day I saw you, if you had not been married, I would have tried, to take you away from him." "But you are married and with expected child, his religion, does not allow to divorce or recognize it." "In their eyes marriage is eternal," "I care not Maceij, no regrets I would do it again." "This is a dangerous game we play, caught it would be the chop for both of us." "Enough, I'm hungry Maceij, do we have wine," "of cause we have wine; he replied."

In the early hours of the morning, Jan arrived home, took a bath, got into bed, waking her as he tried to get comfortable, "you alright Doris asked." "Yes need to sleep, I go again tomorrow," "why so soon, because they have someone sick." "I have taken his shift, day-after home out in afternoon, long shift, shift; money why." "You don't have to kill yourself working I know I have to get to work." "Zimmer, he tell factory, you no go back, place in home rest, good for baby." "I like going to work," God she thought I hope he doesn't say ok. I bloody hate work, "No, work, now sleep, Doris, I must, go to sleep." She turned over with a smile on her face that would have shamed a Cheshire cat, a couple of minutes, and he was snoring.

Doris went to breakfast in her robe, thinking what a stupid idea, Jan was leaving he pecked on the cheek, "bye, see you, love you." After she thought, I could have come down naked he wouldn't have noticed. She heard the door close at the end of the hall, got up and checked to make sure. We're alone Maceij; she whispered, yes. The house is empty, have you bathed I have washed, good, turn your chair towards me. Doris took a cushion off the corner chair, got down on her knees, lifted his night shirt all you can eat breakfast, and I'm looking forward to the pudding. The cream is my favourite; we should lock the front door he said, just in case, as a precaution, she lifted her head. That's like bolting the stable door after the horse has left, it's a bit late for that, next time, besides; I'm busy, just be quiet and listen out. Like a hungry cat, she took every drop of cream, licking her lips after, see you later Maceij, off for a bath, he sat there speechless his night shirt around his waist.

Maceij was on his way to the bathroom, just as Doris was on her way back to her room. "After I have had a bath and dressed, I'm going to town," "any special reason; she enquired," "yes to get new locks, to many people have keys." When we're on our own here I want to feel safe in the knowledge that no one is going to walk in on us." Do you want to come? We can do other shopping while were there," "yes I'd love to" Doris answered. She did not need an excuse to shop, even when she had no money, loved to window shop, if money was no object, she would own every clothe shop in the city? "There is no one in tonight, we will have dinner out." "What about Zimmer," "it's his bridge night," "does he stand guard on it or something," "no Maceij laughed, it's a card game, they take it quite seriously," "you must think me daft," "no, different," Maceij, don't fall in love with me, let's enjoy what we have while it lasts, you're too nice a person to die." "I don't recall having any plans set aside for that anyway, get dressed let's go enjoy the day before it's gone."

Maceij would have bought her anything she wanted. Doris turned him down, "saying the offer was nice, but try explaining that to Jan could only raise suspicion," "your right," he agreed. They got home about eight thirty in the evening, laughing and giggling as they opened the front door of the property, at the entrance to the breakfast room Jan stood. "You, he shouted were supposed to be resting; I came back an hour later." "Train was broken route cancelled. House was empty he bellowed out aloud." "Jan it's nothing," "nothing he shouted, another man out with my wife is nothing." "Maceij is not another man, Jan," "your right, he not a man; he yelled," marching up the hall way. She moved quickly, standing in front of Maceij, sensing he was going to hit him, "he was going to town. It was me who asked if I go, she said no, I insisted." it's not his fault she screamed, is, it right yes. She answered. "Not you," Yes Maceij bellowed back I saw no harm, so I said ok." Next time, you go town with me, no other man, I only." Doris forced on the water works, Jan ignored it brushing past, her."I go get ready for tomorrow, for work, no play, your room now." Maceij, spoke Jan in English, then switched to Slovak, the tone and aggression, enough for Doris to know, the jealous persuasive nature and vile temper Jan had as she climbed the stairs, Doris thought it would continue when he came into the room. However, he was as nice as pie, she couldn't get her head around the swing in temperament, cold, hot, cold, hot and a mixture of all of it; he was unpredictable, as how far he might go. Maceij right; This dangerous game to play.

She woke as she had the day before, alone, the bed and the room empty. Something in her gut told her to get dressed, have breakfast. Maceij was having his black tea as Doris entered the room, Doris was about to speak, when he put his finger to his lips and his eyes towards the kitchen door." Good morning Maceij," do you want some tea, please but not that stewed black muck though," she sat at the table opposite him and had barely sat down when Jan walked in, "your dressed, why" he said, for work of course I still have a job, therefore, a duty to go, I can't just leave and say nothing." 'Why, they would sack you." "No "think why, what do you, owe them, you no work; you stay in house I work." Raising the tempo of his voice, said, "When baby comes you have a job, look after baby, Jan, this is not a prison, I'm not a prisoner, no you're my wife, when I come home, then we go out, when I work, you stay in the house."" "I have a family, a mother and father. I would like to go and see them." "Then we go when I come home, together, they are now, my family, as well." Doris burst into tears, running out of the breakfast room and up the stairs to her bedroom. A minute later, he came into the room, slamming the door behind him, "in my country, a woman, does as she is told." "You're not in your bloody country. You're in Britain." She cowered on the bed drawing her arms up to her head, as he raised his to strike her, stopping an inch or two from her face. "Go on" she said, "be a real man and hit a woman who can't hit back." "I will go and see my mam and dad, when I chose to go, not because you say, let my father hear what sort of a man you are." "Jan backed off from the bed, shaking his finger at her, "am I so bad he asked," "yes Doris replied this is not love," this is being a bully; you understand a bully. "No." "Why does that not surprise me, when you make someone, do what you want by force, against their will," I don't understand?

Doris opened the door and shouted done the stairs, "Maceij, please come here," there was no response. "Maceij you coward come now" she shouted again, "I am coming," she dragged him by his shirt into the room, "explain to my husband; she shouted, what bully means in Slovak." "Doris please; this is not my place," tell him she yelled," after Maceij had spoken. Jan put his face to is hands, as in shame, shaking his head from side to side, "now I know" he said, "I have much to learn," she pushed Maceij out the door.

"You can go," shutting the door firmly behind him, "yesterday your jealousy, today, well that's today, what of tomorrow." Jan looked up, "sorry,." What did you stay behind from work, just for that, no? I don't go until later five, this evening." If you want to go, see your mother, father, go, tell them, my fault, as if I need, then can see, look at my face. Doris stopped short, of slapping his face again, remembering how much it hurt her hand and thinking to herself. She had the upper hand, leave it at that. "We need Maceij," taking his hands in hers." "To plug this gap, between us, a bridge Jan, "yes,'" I need Maceij to explain so you can understand, "yes you're right." "All this new, you my first woman, only woman," His eyes had watered over, sorry, when I don't understand, I will ask first, come let's go eat some food."

They returned to the breakfast room. Jan spoke for several minutes to Maceij. "I have told Maceij I to look after you when I work and talk here together when I home." "I will learn, how to be good British man." Maceij looked across the breakfast table nervously at Doris, fidgeting with his hands, not sure whether to speak or be quiet. Now and again, he looked if he wanted to say something, then continued to fidget some more "you ok Maceij." Doris enquired, "yes this is a big responsibility." Jan has placed on me." Jan butted in speaking in Slovakian" I'm to go with you, when you go out, Jan has asked, this big thing of me, for his peace of mind; when he's at work," "Jan said I trust Maceij." Doris, however, had the feeling he did not.

Over the next one and a half months Doris and Maceij, behaviour was strictly landlord and tenant. Jan went to and throw, home to job; to home, everything had settled down to a rhythm. Doris went to her mother's house. Maciej sat and had tea, remaining silent, only speaking when required. Weekend's she went to the park. Maceij accompanied her anywhere she wanted to go. Doris did not trust Jan one bit. She had Maceij stay two pace's behind, just in case he was having them watched, she had become paranoid. If they kissed it was upstairs between the bathroom and the stairs, never in front of any window, the front, back door locked, chain on, entry door bolted. Maceij told Jan there were people in the area stealing from sheds and out building. They were after work after tools, in recent times next door had the shed riffled. Jan swallowed the story whole, having spoken to them just after it happened. They were both careful to the extreme. It proved to be a wise move. She found a bill, tucked into the lining of his work coat, a bill she was not supposed to find, from a private investigator. Doris was looking for dirty gloves and handkerchiefs. She knew he stuffed in his pockets. Doris put everything back as found, when he returned from the bathroom, she asked him, "Jan have you got any gloves, shirts, handkerchiefs, for the wash."

Doris put everything back as found, when he returned from the bathroom, she asked him. "Jan have you got any gloves, shirts, handkerchiefs. For the wash, she watched as he took everything out of the pockets of the jacket and trousers being careful not to remove the bill, from a private investigator. When he went to work again, she told Maceij in their usual place, the hall to the bathroom, whispering the conversations, it was clear, Jan was capable of, anything, they decided that, would limit their encounters, to five minutes, even then they were both nervous and unsettled. "This is ridiculous Maceij. He can't see through walls can he, if we make no sounds, how would he know, as long as we do it up stairs on the hall way to the bathroom?" "Make sure the house is empty and secure, there's no way he could know, of course unless we tell him Maceij." "Are you likely to do that I certainly am not? I can't go on the way things are. He's an animal." "Whatever you teach him, is a waste of time. He'll do it his way." "He jumps on me, a minute later, rolls off goes to sleep and snores; even that parts not regular or loving." "I need what we have," "Maceij agreed a plan of action was needed. The hallway in that part of the house was dimly lit and had not a window, but the floor is hard. We need something we can't put down and take up quickly, placing it out of sight."

Over the next week, Maceij constructed a false ceiling in the airing cupboard above the hot-water tank. The ceiling went up at least two and a half feet, Jan or anyone, would never have any cause to look. Maceij finished it in a Colour as it was, then dirtied it to give it an aged look. In case he had Yanik the painter, to paint the box room to disguise the smell of paint of his project. He had him, paint the hall away and stair well, including the hot-water tank cupboard door. It's brilliant work. He showed Doris she thought it had always been like that. In the following week, Maceij went to town. Buying a light-weight quilt, when folded length ways in three it was a half-decent mattress, it fitted into the false ceiling with ease and was quick to put away. He got Doris to go through some dummy runs soon "Maceij. She whispered you have gone to a great deal of trouble and expense." "There will be a time when we can't make love, not because I wouldn't want to, because it might harm the baby it would also become uncomfortable for me." "My mam, told me to tell Jan, that, men don't understand women, they just want their way."

They went for their usual work in the park. Doris knew Jan was likely to be home at some point that day what happened next totally shocked her and Maceij. A table and two chairs appeared in her room; Jan was not in her room, Doris,went downstairs, thinking Maceij was responsible. On reaching the bottom of the stairs, she could hear a heated conversation going on between Maceij and Jan. "What's up. Doris asked, walking into the breakfast room, Jan abruptly, answered that, from today you eat up stairs in the room. "Why, I like eating here," Jan swiftly, walked towards her, pushing her back into the hall shutting the door in her face. The heated argument continued, a few minutes later.

The breakfast door opened, with such force it repelled back and shut again in her face. It opened a second time, Jan holding it open with his left hand. She could partially, see Maceij, wiping blood from his nose.

"What an earth is going, she demanded with some authority; he grabbed Doris by her hair."What's going on, you and him kissing in the park," he slammed her head at the hall way wall, you don't lie to me pulling her head back "your mad. She shouted I've done no such thing, that ridiculous I swear," "you swear he shouted in her ear." Maceij came towards the door, to aid her. Jan momentarily let her go to challenge Maceij, another heated exchange of words in Slovak, between them was in place, Jan threw Maceij onto the breakfast table; he landed with a thud. "Stop it, she screamed, stop it; he's done nothing," in the background the front door knocker was being banged heavily. Police, a voice shouted, open the door; a voice shouted, repeating the words Doris ran towards the door to open it. "No, Jan said, walking down the hall towards her, upstairs now." Open the door, this is the police, pointing at Doris. Jan used his finger and pointed indicating, to go up the stairs; he also showed her his left hand, his fist clenched. Doris stepped onto the stairs just out of his sight; he continued to the door opening it. Doris peaked around the corner of the stairs. She could make out the uniform, Zimmer the coward had come out of his room, his being at the front of the house close to the front door, looking as if he had just woken up, but the noise had been enough to wake the dead, later he said he stayed in his room, because he did not want to get involved. Zimmer joined Jan at the front door, then

Maceij also did, whatever was said. It had smoothed things over, the policeman leaving.

Doris quickly scooted upstairs as the front door closed. She sat there on the bed staring at the table and two chairs, five minutes later Jan stormed in, "you do not talk to him." Maceij stood at the doorway to their room "you eat there." She wondered if Maceij had spilled the beans, she could see him shaking his head behind Jan. "You're doing it again Jan, bully boy, see this bruise, there a police station at the bottom of the road." "I'll be going there to show them this, pointing to her head, so, what. This is an assault Jan." "No" he said Zimmer saw you fall, hit head on the wall. I think Maceij, and you have, argument. I hit him; we shake hands, after he makes no complaint." She slumped back on the bed. "What sort of men are you?" She blurted out, "he hits you Maceij, for nothing, hits me for nothing and gets Zimmer to lie for him." "You stand by him; all three of them looked at her. Maceij and Zimmer left, Jan, said sorry, putting his hand on her, "don't you bloody touch me, don't you dare." She left the room and went to the bathroom, returning she got straight into bed, not another word was spoken. In the early hours of the morning, unable to sleep, her forehead painful to the touch. How she thought did he suspect anything. We were so careful, as for Maceij; it was clear he had been attacked by Jan, as for Zimmer, why did he side with Jan, with no hesitation, were we not careful, enough? It did not matter? Doris decided to leave him, I'm going back to mam and dads, if I stay here, the chances are I won't live to see this baby born. She swung her legs out to the side of her bed, standing for a mere second the room spun; it's the last thing she remembered.

When Doris regain consciousness, a Doctor was standing over her, ouch, it's only a flannel, you, tripped and fell hitting your head, it's properly a little concussion, keep the cold flannels coming, it will ease the swelling, Zim, its Zimmer, are you her husband. "No, he's just coming, but his English is not so good. I will explain it to him, I'm his friend, well Zimmer." "I need to examine my patient, to see if, there no other problems, a little privacy," "it's no problem. She won't mind, maybe not," "but I will both of you out the room please." Doris went to get up, "no, my dear; you must stay there for the next couple of days or so, or chances are, you may faint," "but what if I need the toilet" "I'll ask, see if they have a chamber pot." "Stay there don't move I need to check you over."

The doctor left, returning a moment later, "the best they can muster is a washing up bowl." "It is not ideal, but it will have to do." I need to check you over, to make sure the baby is ok." "Everything seems to be fine. I'll get the district midwife to check you over again, tomorrow, have you had your pre natal at the infirmary clinic," "Pre what Doris replied, pre natal," "you must have that done as soon as possible; I'll bring them back in now," "Zimmer can explain it to her husband," "no." "I want my mother. Shush, just rest my dear, I'm sure your mother will be along soon," the doctor explained the situation to Jan and Zimmer and left.

Jan sat on the side of the bed. He placed a fresh cold flannel on her head. Doris flinched, the thought of him hitting with a shovel from the shed, was printed on her mind. "Don't you touch me, you bastard," "I would have the devil himself touch me rather than you." "I'm sorry, what I did, I can't it take it back, no. She screamed out you can't." "Whoever told you, I kissed Maceij, is a liar" "I know," Jan said. "Someone told me, he said that you kissed, they were mistaken. The picture looked like you and Maceij; however, they were someone else." "Bastard she screamed. You had us followed and photographed. You are sick with a bastard." I'm jealous, ok. I love you; I can, not think of you with someone else." I am sorry they are no longer going to do that, I am not allowing it again."

"You hit me Jan, then Maceij, bullied Zimmer, or maybe he's the one that followed us," "no." "He has favour for me, to repay; he has paid that debt now, who are you Jan." "Who are you," a bad man, who loves you too much." "It's a funny way of showing it and what confession did you beat out of Maceij." He said nothing, my action was enough. I put fear into him to keep him quiet," "Jan it will be, hard for you to forgive me," "I pray you will; I'm sorry."

Two or three day's passed by, Doris lost track of time. Jan had waited on her hand and foot and when he went to work Maceij took over. Was he doing this out of loyalty or because of fear, she thought, many things passed through here mind, as she lay there? Only getting up to relieve herself in the bowl, she needed her bath and use of a proper toilet, groggy, she maneuverer herself along the walls of the hallway to the bathroom, glad when she reached it. She wanted to get in the bath, knowing she would she would need help. She shouted out, "help please," a moment later Maciej appeared. "I want a bath please," "Jan is down stairs I will get him," "no, don't want his help," "Doris you must, I told him nothing he whispered," "do as I ask please, she muttered quietly," I will speak again it's safe," Maceij went downstairs, downstairs. It forever before Jan appeared, "what took you so long, getting a new camera person no doubt," "I will never do this thing again," "you will never hit me again, remember, that short short-lived promise you made." "a mistake, everyone can make a mistake," "yes, your right" "Jan; your mistakes, however, likely to be fatal."

He helped her from the bath, dried her and then sat her at the table. "Dinner is coming" "I'm I still banned from the breakfast room." "no; he replied I want to put everything back, if I had been magic" "I would do that."Tears flowed freely down his cheeks. If it's one part of Doris that was forgiving, it was seeing a grown man cry it had not happened many times. She remembered her father crying when granddad died, he told her, then when a man does that it is from his heart, It was a pleasant change to be waited on. I could get use to this. She thought, men waiting on me, like I'm was royalty, as Maceij walked in, "another tea my mam." She was about to say something but Jan was behind him, shit, she said, in her head, that would have put the cat among the pigeons. "We have to go to the infirmary tomorrow," Jan said, "I have to go to work; Maceij will have to take you." "He will say he is me, pretend he knows little English." "I hope that will work. I cannot, stay, or I may lose job." "My job she said smiling, my job," "yes" he replied.

Doris hadn't realized how close to home the infirmary was. "What's that big castle looking building across the road Maceij." "It's the prison; many bad men are in there, killers, murders, "they are the same thing" Maceij; my English is corrected. I was trying to get into the acting, for the hospital sorry." Maceij didn't have to do any acting, the nurse, asked is this your husband, "yes," sit there pointing to a row of chairs, ten minutes later she was back. "That it," "no Maceij that was for blood and other things, I have got to wait to see the genealogist, or something like that," Maceij looked at a sign on the wall with an arrow pointing down the hall, !I think it's a gynaecologists,"is that what it is I wonder what he does," "I have no idea Maceij said," half the bloody morning, will be wasted," as she said that the nurse called her, "sit there, Maceij and act dumb, for you men, that shouldn't be a problem." Doris was back ten minutes later, "what happened he asked, don't ask, you don't want to know. "I hope I don't have to come here again."

"No public kissing remember, Maceij," "why not, don't you want another beating." They both burst out laughing walking along the pavement back to the bus stop. It was as if there was not a care in the world, until Maceij, noticed one of Zimmer's friends on the opposite side of the road. "Doris, don't look, there is what I think is one of Zimmer's friends walking at the same pace as us over the road." "keep on walking as if it's nothing, on the bus they sat down stairs facing to the back, Maceij wanted to see if he got on. He did, leaving it to the last possible moment. He upstairs, when they got off, Maceij looked through the privet hedge behind the wall of the front yard, indeed the man had got off the bus and walked pass the house. He could hear his steps continue along and then stop.

Maceij said nothing to Doris and didn't look back either, when they entered the house. He put his finger to his mouth, indicating for her to say quite, "sit on the stairs" he whispered. Maceij went to his room returning with a key. He carefully and quietly opened the door to Zimmer's room. Aware that the bay window faced onto the front yard, Zimmer should be at work he thought as he opened the door, what if he's not gone went through his mind. He took his chance the room was empty, on the side cabinet a reel to reel tape was slowly turning, passing through part of the machine onto the opposing real; a large microphone on a stand was pointed towards the ceiling in the direction of the stairwell, and wires going out through the air vent. He quietly shut the door again looking it, he tip toed back to the stairs where Doris was still sitting. His finger over his lips, whispered, "follow me," they went into the breakfast room.

In a loud voice, Maceij said, "tea, it's nearly ready," he beckoned her to follow him into the kitchen shutting the door behind him."It's Zimmer," "was he in his room," "no, he whispered he's at work." "He's the one spying on us? He has a machine in his room, for catching sound. I saw one in town once in a music shop, they had some sort of exhibition." "It was when I went to enquire about getting the piano fixed in your room, it didn't get fixed, the man who came said it would cost more than it was worth, it plays, but it's out of tune and some of the keys don't work. "what, she blurted out," "hot'" he replied "I'll bring some more milk," putting his hand over her mouth. She couldn't believe her ears.

Maceij thought long and hard as they drank their tea, in total silence, in his head, I've got it. He put the radio on, then beckoned Doris back to the kitchen, whispering in her ear, "tomorrow when he has gone to work I will turn the electricity off and have a good close look at this machine, perhaps we will have a better understanding of it." "I will take notes, in the meantime stay in your room, except for food at dinner." The next day, when Zimmer went to work. Maceij switched the electric off at the fuse board. in Zimmer's room, he was being very careful not to disturb anything and not to make a sound. The machine was not moving, out of the front was a lead, it went to a box on the floor. The microphone was in the same place as was the day before, its lead went into the box, there were two others, where did they go. he wondered? Maceij didn't want to disturb too much in case Zimmer noticed, one lead went out through the air vent in the wall, the front yard side. He went outside; the wire came out of the vent. It was quite thin it ran up the back of the drain and under the stone sill of the bay to an air vent leading into her room, the bastard he muttered, Maceij didn't want to poke around out the front, in case he was being watched.

He went back to Zimmer's room, checking out were the other cable went. It went under the rug behind the book case, through a small hole in the wall, into the entry, that ran from the back yard to the front of the house. Maceij went and checked it out, in the entry the cable was tacked onto the lime mortar,and almost the same colour, unless you were looking for it, it would go unnoticed. It turned the corner along the yard into the air brick into the breakfast room. Maceij went back indoors to his room got a torch, got on his hands and knees removed the tape and paper that was put over the vent to stop draughts in the winter. There inside the vent was a microphone, small in size, the bastard he thought again. He replaced the paper and retaped the paper over the vent. "Doris follow me; he went up to her room' put a finger to his mouth, for her to keep quiet he did not know if it still worked with the power off for certain. He peered out from behind the blinds. He could see no one in the street.

Maceij got down on his hands and knees to the vent near the bay. It had been papered over with wall paper, It had partly peeled away. It was enough to see the head of the microphone, the bastard,he crawled back staying clear of the window's once outside her door, signalled to her to join him, quietly they made their way down the hall. He has microphone's in the vents, your bedroom and the breakfast room, the bastard she whispered, exactly what I said to myself, who the bloody hell is Zimmer and Jan, did the work for the Germans in the war, Maceij shrugged his shoulders, who knows, what we are going to do, I don't know, yet, he said, I had better close his room and put the power back on, if he asks we had a power cut, you say I don't know, what a power cut, just act dumb, who said I have to act; Maceij smiled, back to your room, stay there till dinner.

Maceij heard Zimmer come in, gave his usual call up the stairs to Doris. Dinner, she was sitting at the table, when Zimmer came in, Maceij was in the kitchen, "did we have a power cut today, what's a power cut" Doris asked, "never mind." He asked Maceij the same question, "oh, that might explain why the light went off in my room." "I was going to look for a new bulb, while you had your dinner, but I'll check my room, a minute later he came back, "good the bulb; it is working fine."

"How's Chrisi Zimmer," "how the hell should I know, how the slut is," "what did you say." "Doris you heard me just fine," leaving the table abruptly, "what's a slut? She asked, as he went to the door, "it's what you both are, ask Chrisi I'm sure she will elaborate." Doris thought It's Saturday tomorrow; I'll go and see mam and the following morning, in the kitchen. "She whispered her intentions to Maceij." I'll come with you as far as the town," "no; she said, I'll go by myself, as not to raise any suspicion." "However, why are you going to town," "to check out how one of these tape machines work, make sure you're not followed? We don't want Zimmer getting wind of what we know, she agreed; they went their separate ways.

When she got on the bus, she remembered the man from the other day he got on, going upstairs as he did before, he got off the bus behind her. Doris could see his reflection in the shop window. He followed her to the tram got on that and got off again when she did, she had used her compact to touch her lips up, so she could see him, he walked about ten yards behind her, his shoes giving a distinctive sound on the pavement; he followed her all the way to her mothers.

Christine was in her bedroom. Mother was busy cooking she went up and saw her first. "Hi Chrisi, Doris what bring you over, she spoke quietly. "What's with you and Zimmer," "entirely my fault, went with a regular down at the chip shop, got an infection?" "When Zimmer told me he was peeing razor blades." "I knew what it was goner head or something like that." "I went down the infirmary, got an injection, before I could tell him, he had already been to his doctors, they told him, what it was and how he properly got it, and as I was the only one he'd been with; he dumped me." He called you a slut Chrisi, what's one of them," A woman like me, who goes with too many men? He had me followed. He found out, pity; I liked him?" "Chrisi he said I was one as well. I don't go with lots of other men." "Doris he's mad at the world, besides that, there's something not quite right, about him, couldn't put my finger on it." Doris thought I had better not tell her about me and Maciej, in case this house as a bloody microphone shoved into it. "I came over to see how you all were, Jan's at work; you've got a good one there Doris, bugger, if only she knew, went through her mind. Doris had a cuppa with her mother, then set of back home. She had only just gone around the corner, to the tram stop, there it was, that distinctive shoe sound a few yards behind her. She got off the tram and onto the bus, once again the man going upstairs, getting off the shoes were there as well.

She went straight in and upstairs, Jan was home, asleep on the bed. She didn't wake him, looking at the time it was almost dinner. Doris went down to the breakfast room, all though it was early, she fancied a cup of tea.

Zimmer was sitting with his head in a newspaper. Maceij asked how she was "I'm fine, could I have a cup of tea if it's not too much trouble," "it's no trouble," "been to see Chrisi,' Zimmer asked 'I had." "I suppose she told you, that your no longer together," "yes, shame," "she said nothing, what were you expecting her to tell me." "The why" "as far as I know, it is you that broke it up. That's it, if you go and see her, you'll properly both make up, lover's tiff." "I expect. It can be fixed, all you need to do is talk to one another. They're simple," "you, think; that's it." "Well, if there's more and you want to tell me I'm a good listener," Doris knew she had the up hand, Zimmer would hardy want to tell her he was pissing razor blades. She thought. I hoped it hurts good,"thanks Maceij, can I have a little more." She was just about to say milk when Jan walked in, "hi I didn't wake you thought I would let you enjoy the sleep as you work so hard." He kissed Doris on the cheek, "been out, yes I went over to see, mam, dad and Chrisi; they send their love." While you were there, spoke to them about, anything else," "what is there to tell," "what happens between man and wife, is not my parent's business or my sister's, for that matter, although she told me, Zimmer and her had broken up, I told him to go and talk to her and fix it, just like me, and you sit down?" And talk.

It was clear not what a bewildered Zimmer expected, probably Jan hadn't either. I've got the pair of you now; I can play your game. Doris smile at Zimmer, "don't know about you, but I'd famished." "What having you been doing other than visiting" Jan asked. "I sat in our room lot, thinking. I should get some wool and knit, clothes' for the baby. That's what my mams doing, that was the other reason, for visiting." "I knew she had spare knitting needles, as I didn't have any money, apart from bus and tram fare, I knew she would lend me some." "She gave me some wool, pink for a girl and blue if it's a boy," Doris portrayed the look of an excited mother. It was a front, to side step them. She knew it was working. She just had to be careful not to overdo it; Jan rocked is head from side to side, as if he had a stiff neck, "you have done well. I make sure you have money for wool and baby's things. We need a pram she said excitingly," "it will have to go in Zimmer's room; he'll have to move upstairs. You won't mind will you Zimmer; you would be closer to us. The room opposite ours is empty, well I believe it is."

Maceij, said, "it's a mess in there. It would need decorating" Zimmer almost choked on his food, "no, he said, his mouth still full, I like it just where I am," even Jan laughed. He thought it was funny, "Doris; he will not move from there. You will have to use explosives." "We will get a pram, in good time will clean the shed to make space," "we can't put the pram in the shed; it will go rusty; my dad did that to my mams pram, that went that way." "We will fix something, maybe Zimmer and the pram can stay in the room," Jan; Maceij and Doris laughed, the only person who didn't think it funny was Zimmer; "I'm going to retire for the night" swiftly leaving the room.

After a cup of tea and a chit chat with Maceij. Jan went up to bed, what a different atmosphere. They laid on the bed together, talking new words to improve his

English. She was going to ask when he was going to work again, but thought, that might prompt him into asking why, would I need to know. She didn't because perhaps he might think I'm up to no good. During the late morning, Jan took her into town, they window shopped for a pram, had coffee. Walked around the market, bought a little fruit, it was a joy. They held hands walking along through the cobbled streets. Doris started to feel it on her legs, as soon, as she told him, he became the concerned father, sit down rest for a while, it was another side of Jan, a nice side, but she knew underneath. He could quickly become another person. Unrecognizable, from the present Jan, when they got back, Zimmer wanted him, go to the room he said. I'll be there; in a moment, she did as he asked went to the room got down on her hands and knees, put her ear to the floor, she could faintly hear them talking; it was in Slovak. She got back up and lay on the bed, no doubt he was reporting to Jan, ten minutes later Jan came up. He was still in the same good frame of mind, at least Zimmer hadn't drummed up any lies. He lay down beside her while she looked at the brochure the pram salesman had given her, he put his arms around her, need a sleep, too many window shops, a moment later; he was snoring.

Before they went down to breakfast, Jan told Doris he was going away that afternoon. "Work well, be safe she said, kissing him good-bye that afternoon, she shut the front door and went through to the breakfast room. "Hi Maceij, I need a cup of tea," "you sit down at the table I'll make it, while you drink your tea. I'm going to try my new radio, my old one; the volume was no good, in the kitchen. I couldn't hear it." She watched with interest Maceij put it right next to the air vent, when he switched on it didn't sound that loud but certainly louder than the old radio, but not loud enough that it would disturb anyone else in the house. Maceij pointed to the kitchen. He gently pulled the door to, not closing it altogether. "The noise is loud enough to screw his tape machine up. The machine will record the sounds from all the microphone; the loudest recording will over shadow the rest; this is what I have been led to believe, you need to get a radio in your room, put it next to the air vent. He might as well throw the machine in the dustbin." She smiled, "you clever boy," go back to the table, say that's got a nice sound to it, I'm going to my room see you at dinner." "Then go to your room, carry on till we have this fully taken care of this problem."

Doris done as, he said, stayed in her room. Knitted, so there was something to show, did everything, so that Zimmer, would not be able to tell Jan anything. When Jan returned home, she was the perfect wife. "Jan can I have a radio; like Maceij, she asked, when I'm up here it would be nice to listen to the music." Maceij switches his off, from here I can hardly hear it anyway, can't see why not, how much does one cost," Jan asked? "I don't know perhaps you can ask Zimmer or, Maceij, how much they are," Maceij just bought a new one, Jan went down stairs, five minutes later. He had Maceij old radio." There is a plug near the bed," Jan can we make the lead longer, so it will sit on the floor near the table." "I have to go to work, but I will be back tomorrow see if Maceij can do it for you." "We can go to town if it's nice," "yes I'd like that," The next morning, when

Doris went down to the breakfast room, Maceij knew what time to expect her; it would be at eight, then twenty minutes earlier and the ten minutes later, giving no pattern or routine. He would have the radio on from seven thirty each day. They planned this in detail. The next morning she went down as planned, into the kitchen for any private conversation. "Maceij, Jan said, you can put a longer lead on your old radio, so that I can put it on the floor near the table," bloody good idea he said. They then went to the breakfast table, with pre planned chit chat, weather, politics, events, a variety of conversations. Maceij went to town that day bought an extension cord when I was in town, go connect it up you know what to do with my old radio, it's not very loud, but with mine on and yours, it will blow Zimmer's mind."

"Now all we have to do is make sure they go out, but do not come back in unexpected. I'm working on that as well." When Jan went away on the next two and half-day trip, Maceij told Doris of his plan of action. "Here is a pair of field glasses, they're good quality. Maceij showed her how to operate them, Doris learnt quickly. "I have put a mirror in the bushes just across the road, when you look through the field glasses into the mirror you can see from one angle along the road this side if you look to the other mirror, you can see from the other angle, when I placed the mirrors. Stand behind the curtain anyone looking can't see you." "The Zanzibar won't know, and neither will anyone else. They would need to be looking for them; they may need a little adjustment." You look. They might be ok. They're working already she said, there the man, a few gates down from us. When the radio was on in her room, they would mouth a conversation, just like when she worked, she taught Maceij the basics, he had a few improvisations of his own, hand language, between the two, they worked very well, their love encounters were back on track.

She heard Jan and Zimmer frequently talk in his room. What Maceij and Doris couldn't work it out. Why did the guy, outside, turn up day after day, what was he hoping to achieve, they weren't going out? When they did they went separately and why did he only follow Doris. It was a mystery that was soon to solve itself, at five in the morning that Thursday; Doris was suddenly woken by was sounded like an explosion down stairs. It was the police. They were knocking so hard, she thought they were going to break the front door.

She was ahead of Maceij in letting them in, there were policemen all over the house, going through everything. Maceij, Zimmer and Jan in handcuffs, in the breakfast room, they sat Doris on a chair away from them. A plain clothed policeman shouted down the hall way, "we haven't found anything, ask them where it is." They started with Zimmer "where have you hidden it," he kept saying, "I don't know what you're talking about." They weren't listening. They kept on and on at all three, then me, I told them the same. "I don't know what you're looking for, so how can I tell you where it's hidden." They took, Zimmer to his room and questioned him for appeared to be forever, then Maceij and Jan to his and our room. Then Jan, Zimmer, Maceij was brought back to the breakfast room. They question me, in front of them, we know this. The plain clothed policeman said; we had you followed,"so where did you stash it." The guy who had followed me around identified me to the man. He appeared to be in charge. They went over and over the same thing, three hours later they accepted that we knew nothing, but they still wouldn't tell us anything about or what it was they were looking for.

"Zimmer, you have an interesting hobby, recording music, played in other parts of the house, or are you just a pervert, who gets his kicks that way." We are dismantling the microphones and taking your equipment to the station." I'm sure they would like to know," we, sat there in the Breakfast room, looking dumb founded. I could see the smirk on Maceij face; it was two in the afternoon, when a policeman ran down the hallway. "We've found it governor two doors down." The plain clothed man said, "ok un-cuff them," Maceij, first, then Jan, but keep that Zimmer cuffed. "I want some explanations from him about his equipment, make sure we have all the tapes." Zimmer "they might need you to explain it, later." Maciej tea everyone, the policeman said, "no thanks the men are leaving." I was referring to them" I wasn't asking you.

"Maceij, one more thing, Zimmer's door, to his room you have to leave it, for now." "There's tape across the frame, once we have finished questioning him, we may require to search his room again." "You mean he was spying on us," Doris said, "yes mam," replied the plain clothed man. She was finding it hard not to smile, worst still burst to into laughter. "We're sending some people over to check for evidence, that might take some time," "what about Zimmer, "he's under arrest." "He may or may not be charged, if he is charged, he will appear in court tomorrow, or the next day, then he may or may not be bailed." "What's bail,'" Doris asked "let out mam, until he has to appear in court again, also you can't cut any wires" "wouldn't even know where to look for them." Maceij said."We'll show you when we have finished our enquiries." "It's never dull in this house is it, let's have that tea," Maceij said.

Zimmer, wasn't released until, the following day. Maceij was shown where the cables ran and the microphones, he put on the most amazing face of, being totally shocked. Doris smiled, sitting in the breakfast room, watching the day unfold. It was restful she thought. Jan was enjoying a hearty early lunch before work. The mirrors hadn't been discovered, Zimmer's antics at an end and the man following her, turned out to be a policeman. "Peace bliss-ful peace," "what" Jan said, "nice lunch," "yes, food is good, very good," he ate like a man who hadn't had food for a week going for seconds and would have had thirds had it been available.

"Hello Zimmer," "hello Doris look," before he could utter another word, "piss off Zimmer," "I have no room to piss off to." "Should have thought of that you pervert, where you trying to hear me and Jan doing it." She caught Jan shake his head to Zimmer out the corner of her eye. He knew what Zimmer had done, but she went on with the pretence, got you again she thought to herself, "get a few grunts to turn you on." "Doris leave it;" Jan butted in, Doris being Doris put the last word in, Zimmer. I will never trust you again, you are a bastard." "Doris leave it." Jan repeated, Maceij joined in where Doris left off, you all this time, I thought you were my friend." "I should throw you out," you can't do that, I have ten percent of this house." A very small part, the authorities may allow me under the circumstances to buy you out," "you don't have the money." Maceij knew he was right, but bluffed, the bank said they would lend me the money, if I could get one more lodger." "I asked some time ago, but I said no, Zimmer is my friend, that has been undone, you traitor." Zimmer was placed on the back foot. He wanted to call his bluff, look; he went, in a sheepish tone. "We can work this out start again," "why should I Maceij said, "because I have no one else, I'm sorry" putting his head in his hands. "I'll think about it turning away from Zimmer. Doris caught his smile as he went into the kitchen, he's got you Zimmer, just where he wants you and so have I she thought.

That afternoon, Jan went to work. The police took more tapes and equipment from Zimmer's room giving it back to him, when they left, a case was made against him. He was cautioned in front of Maceij, but it was up to the police and Maceij, if he was to be prosecuted, Maceij wanting to keep the upper hand, told Zimmer, he would think about that.

It was Sunday. Maceij and Doris decided at breakfast. We would go to the park and listen to the band. There was no fear on this day; listen to the band play sitting together, Maceij said, "we must continue to adopt the plan we set in place; we still don't know, what Jan or Zimmer may do next." "I don't trust them, as for

Zimmer. I have bluffed him; he may as yet see through that, without his money and the fact; he owns a small part of the property; it would all be over." "I don't like it, but I have to tolerate him, make the peace." Be careful Doris, slowly, make the peace." "That way we will win him over, she agreed, "now let's enjoy the day, while we can."

Peace and quiet in the house were short lived. Monday afternoon when Jan returned. It was with the raw of a motor bike in the front yard. Zimmer doing a rapid exit from his room, the noise vibration must have shaken his room to the core. "What's that he blurted out exiting the front door. "A motorbike idiot," Jan said. "You can't leave that there," "why not," " Maceij joined in, nice bike, Zimmer repeated again he can't leave it there, why not Maceij said, Doris was on her way down the stairs, "wow, what a machine, what's it called," called Jan, looking at her bemused, "called,'" "it has to have a name," "Triumph, name on the side,"" pointing to the word. "It's blue; we will call it blue boy," Jan laughed, "not our boy I hope. You don't call him that," you're sure it is going to be a him," "of course." "How are you going to keep the seat clean wearing your work gear." "I have a plastic cover over seat, "this is not for work." "For us to go on holiday Doris," "can we go out now, no I will wash and change. We go," Zimmer, chirped in, "when the baby arrives, you will need a luggage rack to strap him on." "I will also need rope to drag you by your neck Zimmer," "good call Jan," Doris chuckled, as did Maceij. "I will have side car, when baby comes," "where's that going to go, under your window Zimmer." "What," Jan was joking, "I had side car in army,would have to take privet and wall out." Tea Maceij laughing his head off. Jan took Doris out into the country side away from the city. They stopped at a village pub, had a drink and returned home, "if I don't remember to say I had a good time, later; I did, thank you."

At the breakfast table, Zimmer was still harping on about the noise and fumes from the bike. How, if he left his window open, the gas might kill him. Maceij was quick as a flash, "you never open the window, that's why your room smells of snacks you have and the booze you share with no one; not even at Christmas or other occasions." It's because you are a cheap person, Zimmer, just for Zimmer." "This is not true; you presume; I do this secret drinking, behind them door. I ration my drink to make it last." "I haven't got money to just throw away, Maceij, "no I have noticed that, when we have gone to town together on rare occasions, stopped and took a coffee, your wallet, is sown to your trousers; that's because it is sown to the lining," Jan laughed so much, he needed a toilet, laughing loudly. "Maceij knows you to well," "rubbish; you've been out with me Jan was I tight with my money. "Yes, you were, one round in three, look this is all I have in my wallet excuse." Maceij said, "the rest is probably hidden in your room, so well I bet the police couldn't even find it." Jan could be heard laughing from the outside toilet; Zimmer vacated the breakfast room; Maceij laughed, "that's the first time Jan. I've seen him lost for something to say."

"Doris, still laughing its Easter bank holiday, next weekend," If you feel you can manage it. We can take the bike to the coast, stay in a bed and breakfast, "what she screamed with excitement." The sea side, the beach, sand and sea I've dreamed about it, but I've never been," you still don't show too much, along as you're not un-combatable we can take a break or two along the way." "Don't go to fast Jan, that will scare me, I have to see the midwife on Wednesday, if she thinks it's alright." Then we will go, yes; Jan smiled, "yes we will go," "where though." Hunstanton, "is it far, not two far, I looked on a map. He spread his thumb and index finger apart, "it's about that far," she ran over to him, leaping into his lap. He caught Doris, threw her up into the air catching her, then plonked her on his lap. She could feel his him through her bottom, "come on she said let's go to bed," they made love. It wasn't the usual press up's, grunt and roll off; this had passion and felt intense.

Wednesday, she told the midwife her intentions. Doris "she said, you hide the baby well, it to do with your height. It's due in eight weeks' time may be less I can say you shouldn't, there's no reason to, but at the same time, it's not wise either," "so what are you saying." it's up to you." "That's all I can say; I'm not the Doctor; I know what he might say." "When the baby comes, I won't be able to go, why not there the train, buses. It's a different thrill not a motor bike; I can't explain it "Doris said. "I know I was young once, enjoy yourself, bring me back a stick of rock."

Wonder, she thought, if I can have a dip in the sea, well feet at least, she couldn't stop thinking about going. She also thought about what the midwife said it could bring the baby on early, premature she called it, could be just the answer to my dilemma. I won't tell Jan, then if it happens great, he will think it one of those things. Men are stupid according to Chrisi, shouldn't be a problem; she dismissed it from her mind. "What did they say at the clinic Maceij asked? It was ok to go." Doris, "what did they really say?" "Go enjoy myself, the house is empty. We could; she put her finger on his lips; we could not; I've got to start being a wife to the husband he's becoming." "I agree, I told you it could be a dangerous game. It almost was, go be a wife" she cuddled Maceij, "thanks, if it goes pear shape, you'll always be my friend."

"I've got you a present, it a size larger than you might need. The sleeves will be too long, bottoms should be alright and the waist line is adjustable."They're sheep skin lined. It can be still chilly at this time of the year on a motorbike in the raw wind; you need to keep warm "waller" Pulling a package form under the breakfast table, leathers, "oh my god Maceij. I never thought how I was going to keep warm, shit, why didn't I marry you?" Because I'm too ugly, your mother can perhaps can do something with the jacket sleeves," I'm going up stairs to try it on, the trousers fitted well, Maceij was right about the sleeves, they are four inches too long, mams sewing machine wouldn't cope with something this thick, she thought what about work, they have an industrial sewing machine in the finishing shop, I'll go there tomorrow. She went down to the breakfast room to show, Maceij, the trousers fit, but the sleeves are too long as you said. Maceij. "I'll take a ride over there tomorrow," it looks like I bought well" "however, you will need these gloves and boots to go with the leather's machine. "I sneaked into your room and got the size, hope you don't mind, "I don't, why don't you come up and help me take them off." " Doris you are a bad girl, "I still have the radio; next to the vent," "I don't trust that bastard Zimmer, "I have the same opinion" "come on Maceij, one more time, hey, Maceij." He couldn't resist, after, Doris washed, got changed and dressed. "Tea my mam" "if you please, dinner and certainly, maybe a little wine," "why not," "we have Zimmer to put up with," no it's, bridge night; he never misses that, he goes there straight from work; I use to think he was paying for a woman once a week." He dragged me along once, that was enough; they take it so seriously."

They spent the evening, in each other's company enjoying the chit chat, a final tea before turning in for the night. On her way past Maceij room,"wait she said, I've never been in your room," oh you don't want to do that it's a junk store, let's see." She pushed him against his door forcing it to open. The single bed was length ways in front of the door. Doris pushed him back till he sat on it, kicking the door closed, with her right foot, she put her hands on his chest, as he fell . The noise of the front door closing shut, echoed in the long hallway. Maceij leapt from the bed, "shushed her" with his finger. He exited his room rapidly having pushed Doris to one side. It was Zimmer, "I thought you were at the bridge,"" "I was, but one of the bridge partners felt ill, there was nobody to take his place, so it was the end of play, got most of the evening playing." "There's a bit of a draft coming down this hall, Maceij wonder where that is coming from its quite a draught, weight it's almost stopped," felt like it was coming from your room." Maceij was standing in front of his door, but had the sense to realize Doris had climbed out of the bedroom through the sash window, "yes of course. I remembered opened my window earlier; I was cleaning inside the sash; I have forgotten to close it." "I'll do it in a minute. It's only slightly cracked open; it will wait; I'm having tea first, you," "yes why not it freezing outside it will warm us up," "you sit I'll make it Maceij said. Doris quietly opened the toilet door, fortunately he always kept the key hanging on a nail.

He hoped that Doris wouldn't open the door, shouting through, "sugar Zimmer," why ask, you know I always have sugar," "age'" he said, "when anyone flushed the toilet, it made a right racket, especially at night. It's why there were night bottle's and chamber pots made. It could be cold enough sometimes to freeze a brass monkey, Its freezing out there Zimmer remarked, who's that stupid to be out there, of course Jan, then Doris walked in try her hardest not to shiver. "Gents don't go out there for a minute, if you know what I mean," "are you mad," Zimmer enquired; "it's that or stink the house out. Zimmer," "tea Maceij asked," "hot please; the toilet is not my favorite place, when it's really cold, in particular, particular, if you're having a job to go," "oh for god's sake Doris, Zimmer yelled; we don't need the details."

The next morning at breakfast, "Doris, that was quick thinking on your part." "What if the window didn't open; it was Jan instead of Zimmer," "well it did, so no problem." "Doris I told you that it could be a dangerous game, were playing it, no more," "oh go on, she teased him, once more," "no Doris, I don't like life on the edge of a razor," "go on you want to," Doris, no, now I know you mean it." You can whatever you like when you're mad at me," your teasing me aren't you," "yeah, I guess, I' am, thanks for the leathers." With that she went to her room. Knowing Jan would be home tomorrow afternoon or early evening.

The next day straight, after breakfast. Doris took the bus to town and then a tram to the factory. It reminded her how uncomfortable the wooden seats were. She couldn't believe the warm welcome she got, instead of someone they use to gossip over. It was like they had lost a long-lost friend. Megan, was the first to shed a tear or two, despite his snarling manor so was Ben. "Bloody hell girl won't be long you'll be a mum" It's going to be a girl. Ben soon as, she is older enough, she is coming here to work, Bloody Nora, with that" He was legged it out of the canteen. "Megan, now I have seen the girls and their back at work I came to ask a favour." "Doris don't ask I can't knit, "no, can you alter this leather jacket, just the sleeves," "no problem, have your tea and take it down the finishing room." "They have an industrial sewing machine; they'll have that done in a jiffy, fifteen minutes later she was back, their job done brought the ruminants; "in case you ever had to patch it," "you're a gem." Doris bring that baby to see us all when it's born and the weathers nice; where are you going now?" "To see my mother, good girl, do I owe anything for this, "yeah forty quids," "what."Joking Doris you owe us nothing. This place owes you plenty's yeah."

"Doris had nice memories to take with her of the factory. She was glad she had come, the compound across the road where it all started, new buildings were going up, the sign of changing times. It was the nicest walk from the factory to her mother's. She could ever remember. "Hi mam,make us a cuppa," "make your bloody own; I am still not your skivvy," "love you to mam," "oh come here you big dope, dads at work; How's that strapping son in law," "he's at work?" "He'll be home later today, so I can't stay too long I don't want to get caught in the cold, oh that frost was an odd one." "Forecast tonight is mild, warm and sunny at the weekend, make a bloody change it neatly always rains." "What with the heavy bag", "it's a jacket." "I won't get it out it's a nightmare to put back, that wasn't her real reason," "had she told her, there would have been forty questions, why do you want to do something that daft, thank God, she didn't insist?

They got off together; Jan took her big bag; it was only a short walk from the bus stop, to home. "What's in the bag, wait and see, it's a surprise. She opened in their room and put it on, the sleeves. They're perfect now, "where did you get the money for that." "I didn't; Maceij bought this, trousers, boots and gloves. I nicked one of mams woolly hats she doesn't know yet." "I went to the factory where I use to work and got the sleeves altered, they were too long. They did for free." "Maceij said it would be cold on a bike; I never thought about that he did, maybe he's been on one." He's right Jan said, I didn't think about that either." He opened the door and shouted down the stairs in Slovakian moment later Maceij arrived. She thought oh shit there's going to be trouble. Jan spoke some words, hugged him like a long-lost brother, kissing one cheek then the other, "it's good Doris that someone had the sense to think, how much do I owe?" I don't know. We will talk about" that, Maceij straight away in English, and I could only assume he repeated in Slovak. He didn't want any money "it was a gift, to you both more for Doris, the gift, but for you, for peace of mind on the journey?" Apart from Zimmer's face, it was a pleasant, evening around the breakfast table. Jan had walked down to the off licence and got a bottle of polish brandy, he and Maceij shared; it's probably why Zimmer had such a long face. They were only doing what he would do, bring a bottle and drink it himself, Maceij prepared something special, in the kitchen don't know what I'm going to do if I have to cook, Doris said, it's been so long I've forgotten how to cook, Jan. You can't cook, Zimmer's only words of the evening, trust me, Maceij and I have tried his food, it's terrible, if you want to kill yourself and that baby, then by all means eat it, Jan, took a glass from the centre of the table, filled it pushed over to Zimmer, he's right, he deserves a drink for that, he just save your life, it was the first timed Zimmer had laughed for a while, then they all joined in and laughed, the meal was to die for, polish hunters stew, Maceij explain to Doris, it is the national dish of Poland, hearty long simmered meat and sauer-kraut, it goes back before my grandfather was a boy, you normally have it at the beginning of the hunting season, the recipe, today you could ,properly find down the continental shop, then it was made, using the family recipe of barrel cured sauerkraut, with any game vegetables and other meat you could find, my mother use to make it and I paid attention, it was delicious

Maceij, very, very good Zimmer and Jan said, She drink gone Zimmer left the table, returning with a bottle of aged brandy from his room, Maceij grabbed his chest with his right hand, pretending to have a heart attack, not convinced with the acting, do it again Doris said, on that I'll get the afters," Doris said, cheese biscuits, coffee, "all fine with that, and some playing cards."

Sea, sunny skies, sandy beaches we are here, worming the way through the traffic into Hunstanton. Jan spotted a fish and chip shop. "Doris, fish and chip," Jan said, "please I'm starving." "There will be a wait look at the line. It's not raining, and we have somewhere to stay, don't we." "No, but we can sleep in the park or tent," "do we have anything like that," "yes, small tent, and two sleeping bags, in leather panniers." "Plenty of of pubs and inns we find somewhere and food is everywhere." "How romantic," "you sit on the bench," "and I will get fish and chip," "vinegar and a little salt on mine Jan."

After they had eaten, they walked down a side street. Luck was on their side a small bed and breakfast had a room free, a cancellation only a minute or two ago. They took it straight away, just as well, others soon came knocking, the owner, put up the vacancy sign in the window, but still they knocked. "We rest, an hour, then we go can explore" "this is exiting, my first visit to the seaside." Other guests, hearing her, said you would think it's the moon she is visiting. It's only the sea side, one elderly man said, Doris said, "when you haven't seen it before she replied, it's as good as heaven," "yes your right, the old man said. "I bet I'll be visiting that before you do."

There was one thing and one thing only on her mind the next morning, it wasn't breakfast, or exploring the wonders of Hunstanton, putting her feet in the sea. "Jan that's what I wanted to do the minute we got here and walk on the sand, the feet didn't stay in the water for too long. Doris couldn't believe how cold it was "Shit, Jan it's freezing." Bare foot on the beach didn't fare much better either, "Doris it's still early in the year it's not summer; It will be cool;" "I've put mine in now you. I'm not moving until you do," in one swoop. He whisked her off her feet, carrying her back onto the parade walk, and "I'll get you an ice cream. That will balance the temperature," "funny, hah hah," there was a gentle breeze blowing along the promenade chilling the air, the walk was pleasant. Thanks to the leather jacket that Maceij kindly supplied. "What's that over there, look Jan, it's a walk way out to sea, men fishing on it." Doris asked one of the men, fishing, if he had caught anything, but couldn't understand a word he was saying. She once heard a girl at the factory, she was from Birmingham. Doris couldn't understand her either. She shrugged her shoulders and walked on, some of the attractions were not open a lady said, they were being renovated, ready for the summer season, there were beach huts painted being painted, their owners painting them a different colour from the next, which made them stand out, "time to go" Jan said, it all ended too soon, there was a tear in her eye as they headed back for home, "we will come again, Doris. This is the first journey of many journeys for us." Doris thought, how sweet, that's the first time he has used, the us word, On the way back they stopped at sandringham, a guest in the bed and breakfast place, told the it was the Queen's summer house. They stopped outside the main gates and in the village for a while before continuing, stopping once more in Uppingham, for some light refreshments.

Maceij came storming out to greet them, recognizing the sound. "Tell all" he shouted over the noise of the bike, Zimmer to was pleased to see them and the bike. "Jan turn that bloody row off, Jan revved it up some more just to any him." "Maceij, it was wonderful, have you seen the sea," "yes he replied, when I came here as a refugee, on a fishing boat. I was sick with every inch of the way, very nice. "Well I enjoyed it she said, but the sea was cold, bloody cold," yes I remember that Zimmer said, it was winter when I can, also on a fishing boat, I too, was very sick." "When we arrived I had a bad cold on the lungs, they said some had died from it." "That was unfortunate Zimmer," "Doris your all heart." "In the transit camp, we were in tents, that didn't help either, there was only one doctor, for so many of us, us; children perished. The weather was harsh, old people as well, it seemed only yesterday." "I can still hear them in my head," all of us sat in silence, as Zimmer told his harrowing story. There were tears in all our eyes, for all the victims of war. "Maceij, said war is a terrible, thing it took away the full use of my leg. I was lucky to keep it" where many had lost theirs. "It's because I pleaded at the time I was fortunate," your all brave having fought, for our peace." I'm going bed; it's been a very long, day and you my love, have work tomorrow; Jan got up," "she is right, work tomorrow."

At breakfast, Doris told Maceij, in full detail, about her journey to Hunstanton and the one back. She told him they had stopped at the Queens summer house. I have a book about Sandringham. After breakfast, she spent the day in her room reading it reading it, falling asleep in the chair, she was woken, suddenly. Maceij was shaking her "wake up Doris," half asleep still, she blurted out "is the house on fire," "no he said in a solemn voice, there has been a terrible accident, Jan, she screamed." "No, Chrisi is downstairs. She has come to see you," "what is it Maceij," "it's your father; It's not good news." "Where's Chrisi, in the breakfast room," "Doris, pulled herself together," "Chrisi, what's happened to dad, is he hurt," "more than that he's dead, bursting into floods of tears," Doris following suit." "Tea Maceij said, tea with sugar," "how, did it happen, at work something to do with the machine he is working near; he was killed instantly where is stood." "A man from the factory, came to the door." "where is dad now I don't know; mam is at the mortuary, waiting for dad." A car took her there, once the police have finished at the factory, investigating what took place." He will be released to the mortuary, mam. She will have to identify the body. It is the normal practice, they told mam, I've come, because they were worried, the shock, and the baby, it's not good for you. Mam is coming here, with Uncle Ken, Denis" "I'll get more cups Maceij said and some biscuits and handkerchiefs."

Doris smiled at him, crying profusely," he's a really good man Chrisi," they sat there consoling each other, for what seemed hours. The light was fading, when her mother arrived with Uncle Ken and Denis. "What happened mam, they say your dad was walking by this machine when a belt broke, and struck him on the head. The guard had been removed earlier in the day, to get the machine ready." Dennis said in an angry manner, "they bloody knew the belt needed to be changed, but they wouldn't stop the machine." Because they would lose production, ken sat next to her, putting his arm around her shoulder." Zimmer came in at that point, saw everyone was crying and walked through to the kitchen, Maceij, was making tea, told him what had happened. "Where's Jan," Chrisi asked, "at work on the railway. He won't be home until the day after tomorrow." "What does he doing on the railway," "he Stokes the fire on the steam trains, he hopes to be promoted to an engine driver, it was better pay; than the demolition site, it's made a big difference." "He bought a motor bike. We went to the seaside on it," "in your condition, are you mad, her mother blurted out. That's typical of you my girl." "Mam this is not a day to pick I fight, and this is my home; this is where I live, what I do, right or wrong are my choices."

It was the first time, there was closure with Vi, "your right, sorry Doris." "Tea is served," Maceij, placing filled cups with saucers in front of everyone; her mother wasn't quiet for long. "what's this? Where is the teapot and cosy." This is not how you make tea my boy, do you have a tea pot?" "No" Maceij replied, "well I've got a spare one, next time I come here I will expect you to learn how to make tea properly." "I'll get Chrisi to bring the pot over, so you can practice." Maceij was speechless; "cat got your tongue boy," "no mam." Maceij quickly retreated to the kitchen, in order to avoid any further dishing's of tongue pie.

"If I wasn't so thirsty, I wouldn't have drunk this excuse for tea," "mam you'll hurt Maceio's feelings." "This is polish tea," "rubbish Doris. Tea is tea, the taste, is a question of how you make it. I should know the British empire was built on tea," sorry no it was not Zimmer, jumping into the conversation, see Doris, a man who is not afraid to disagree with me. You have tea because you stole it, not you personally, that's why it's a British thing, tea." "Zimmer are you polish, "no he responded," "are you from the Czech republic, "did we ever own that place; Ken shrugged his shoulders. I don't know Denis," Zimmer interrupted him, before he could say anymore. You don't own anything. Your marched up the beach, stuck a flag in the ground, then called it British. You stuck your nose in everywhere, including Germany and Poland, starting, in effect, the second world war, no need to be so hostile about," Maceij said. "Don't worry Maceij, Vi replied I'll get Frank to sort him out." Realizing what she had said, started the water works off, the others added to the tear flow, your intolerable at times, Zimmer, "sorry Chrisi, sorry Violet I did not mean to upset, you, I get a bit carried away with politics." "That's fine, I know you didn't son, it's alright, really," Zimmer got up, to leave the room, you don't have to go on account of me, "its ok Vi I have some books to read."

Chrisi followed him out of the door, shutting it behind her, Zimmer," I'm sorry I don't intend to make a spectacle of you," "he said I should have been more sensitive. I'm sorry for you and me." "I don't do that anymore, men, for money," "your mother ever knew you did that." "No she, would be upset," "that would be a very mild way of putting it," "Zimmer, I miss you. She said, really miss you, not as much as I do, he said." "I regret, it every day. He took her hand and kissed it. She took his head planting a full kiss on his lips." "Chrisi remember what's going on in the other room, I know I'm bad, but at the moment, I'm more interested in what's going on in this one." They almost tore the clothes off one another, so frantic was the engagement; they had forgotten to shut the door." Back in the breakfast room, "Maceij, why has Chrisi gone after Zimmer," "to console him, I would think Vi, he, is, very sensitive?" He's properly upset with himself over the political outburst. I'll go and see." Maceij walked down the long hall wall to Zimmer's room; he could hear the puffing, panting and squeals half-way down. He could have shouted and danced his way down. The pair were totally oblivious, going at it like a pair, of dogs." Maceij shut Zimmer's door and went back to the breakfast room, yes he said, with authority, she is consoling him." "Vi said, poor man," "yes indeed," Maceij replied, "more tea."Not so bloody likely," VI said, as soon as she's finished, with Zimmer, we'll make a beeline for home." "if the spare room was usable, it is badly in need of decorating I would have offered it to you." "Not on your nellie, Maceij, if tea is anything to go by, God knows what breakfast, would consist off, it boggles the mind to think, what my poor daughter is eating." "Doris stood up, mam. The food served here would put first class restaurants to shame. I think you have over stepped the mark mam, once again the tears flowed, sorry mam."

"Maceij she's right, were all on the edge today, Vi said, "I'm hurting the nice people, you all here. Doris is clearly doing alright on what you feed her, as long as she's happy that's the main thing." At that point, Chrisi walked back into the breakfast room. "What an earth having you been doing girl ,your hairs all over the place." She quickly responded; Zimmer's glasses fell behind them," the "what girl," "mam, the, furniture; his hands were too big." "So I got on my hands and knees squeezing, myself between that and his bed. "Did you get them, VI asked, oh yes," "Maceij, interrupted, "he's always losing his glasses, somewhere?" "Right, well she looks like she's been in a wrestling match, not been wrestling with Zimmer have you." "Maceij had put his hand over his mouth, mouth. He disappeared into the kitchen." "Well, let's be off, I this Zimmer is ok now, Chrisi, mam; I think so." "Can I stay with Doris for a while, it's getting late and dark, well if Doris doesn't mind I could sleep here, in her bed?" "Jan's not going to be home. I don't mind mam it would be company for me, is that ok with you Maceij," "no problem, Vi." "Let's be off then, Ken and Denis hadn't said a word virtually, apart from hello and good bye, as Vi left. Zimmer was coming out of his room, "glad Chrisi was able to help you find your glasses, hope to see you another time, Zimmer," You look like you've been in a wrestling match as well., bye, bye."

"You pair of animals, "I came down and shut your door, what if her mother had instead." Your mother Chrisi and Zimmer's, face had no show of shame, almost as, we wouldn't have cared, on all days as well, Maceij went on saying." "She has lost her husband, you a father, where's the respect?" "I'm waiting by breath." "My mother would have said that, Chrisi replied I made a mistake letting this man go, because I was stupid." "Today I was making amends for that," "try talking to each other next time? It's exhausting."

"Its past time, dinner will be late tonight," Maceij went to his kitchen. "I don't have any clean spare nighties was going to the laundry tomorrow won't need any, me and Zimmer." "We sleep in the raw, too much detail." Doris shouted, "what's for dinner Maceij," quick English dish today, Cumberland pie." I was going to make something else, but I would have needed much more time. Apple strudel and custard to follow, no wonder Doris you look so well, if he feeds you stuff like that, told mam, he's a bloody good cook?" Chrisi shouted "am I getting fed, Maceij said of course Chrisi, you're a guest." "I'll feed you later; Zimmer chirped in." "I think you two need to get a room at the Zanzibar."

The house wasn't quiet tonight, after dinner Chrisi and Zimmer had gone to his room. "That reminds me; I must get him to replace his bed with a quieter one. The springs on that thing are positively Victorian, if one off them broke, straight in the backside." She knew what he was doing, trying to lift her spirits, Maceij good at that she thought, however, her thoughts were with her father, sitting there; her love for her sister was diminishing. "Maceij how could she do that, knowing our father is laying on a cold slab" "ever thought. It's maybe her way of dealing with life." "She is high spirited; it will hit her all of a sudden. She will need your shoulder. I've seen it to many times; loss is heart wrenching, if not today, tomorrow or the next day or

the day after, different people, grieve in different ways."
"Maceij you should have been one of them philo
sofiters, if you know what I mean." Smiling he got up
kissed on the forehead "I'm going to bed, me to, night
Maceij," "good night Doris."

Doris as always was down for her breakfast before
it had even finished cooking. "Maceij, what magic is
going on in the kitchen, bacon, eggs, fried tomatoes,
mushrooms and toast and for a change fresh coffee."
"Sit it will be ready in about ten minutes," coffee immediately, there's someone at the door. I'll get it, as she
opened it, her mother stood there, before she could
say a word. Chrisi was coming out of Zimmer's room in
his dressing gown, be back in a mo. Hun, just need a
pee and some of that coffee. I can smell." What she was
looking for this time, his false teeth, cause he's going to
need some," Chrisi turned in shock, the dressing gown
falling open revealing her naked body. Zimmer stuck
his head out of the bedroom door, "shit," the door shut
quickly the key could be heard turning in the lock.
Chrisi bolted up stairs straight to the bathroom, locking
herself in. Vi stormed past Doris into the breakfast
room. "You Maceij, what sort of a whore house are you
running. One with decent coffee, this morning, care for
a cup, look, before you speak, these are lodgers; they
rent a room, with breakfast and evening meal, who they
bring, what they bring, is not my business, as long as
they pay, and they don't burn the house down." "Breakfast, you look like you could use some." It was the
second time in two days. She had the wind taken out of
her sail, "a bit of that toast and some coffee wouldn't go
amiss; I didn't sleep a wink."

Maceij, listened as Vi poured her heart out. "I miss my Frank; Maceij pulling a clean handkerchief from his pocket, "here. I knew, somehow it would come in useful today." "Sit I'll get you a cup of tea; a dressed Zimmer crept into the room, Vi she butted in, "you're going to tell me, it's not what it looks like. Well, I know exactly what it is, and it's clear she is older enough to know what it is." "Were you about to tell me something different," "no, I suppose not." Then get my daughter dressed please. We have to go down to the mortuary in two hours' time. I'm not doing that alone, think you can see to that Zimmer," "straight away," "Maceij; it's a changing world, "yes Vi it is."

Doris, starving as always, "these days, I'm waiting for this man to feed me." It's coming, Maceij said. "Coffee Vi, I hope is to your liking," yes very good. I'm a tea girl, but I believe; this wakes you up or keeps you awake, so I've heard," "when all have eaten and the bathroom is free. I will shave, put a suit on and accompany you, if that ok, Vi, for support, for respect." "I'd like that Maceij. I'm going to need a strong-arm today." "I would have asked Jan had he been here," "so I thank you for your offer and I graciously, except," "it will be my pleasure."

Suited up, Maceij, looked like he was straight out of a gangster movie, hat and all, just the carbine was missing. Chrisi was down and dressed, but reluctant to see her mother, sitting in the breakfast room enjoying a second cup of coffee. You'll have to go in. I know Zimmer; she knows about us now. "Nice to see with some clothes on, Chrisi, I've told lover boy," "I don't want to hear it, not today." "You've made your bed; he had better taken care of you now." "I hope you're up to that Zimmer, and I don't have to come here with a borrowed shot gun," "No, Vi you won't need to do that, but I also can't promise what will happen in our future, it's a two-way street. We both must want this relationship. It must not be built on just lust." "You're clearly not a stupid man, Zimmer. I'll accept that, because it was carefully thought out."

Ken, Denis and Matida were waiting outside the mortuary, "where did you get Capone, Vi." He's Maceij? You will address him as such; he's a nice man offering me a strong arm, which is surely needed." "He is also Doris and Jan's landlord." "Chrisi is with her man, Zimmer." "She's a bit young to settle isn't she, Maceij said, they've done it together. I'd say that makes her older enough." Zimmer didn't quite know where to put his face. "Were not here for the cat gossip, where here to see to my Frank." Maceij, was the quick draw on hankies, beating Denis hands down; it looked as they had come well prepared for the expected. The skill of the mortician was evident; you would never have known he had part of his head torn away. In the accident, a director's representative was also present. He spoke to Vi, before she went in, he had stated that, he was there to ensure the costs were met, and that she had a free hand, within reason, for the arrangements. Doris had left Jan a note in their room on the table should he come home early, the question when he was coming was soon answered. The note of the bike engine she would have known anywhere it was so distinctive. He had also taken time to make himself presentable, Vi burst into tears the minute he walked in; "you were Frank's favorite; he had liked you like as a son."

"Hi Doris, I can't believe it." "Doris tearfully, hung on to Jan's arm for all its worth, they've made him look so nice." They all walk through together and then individually. Maceij, was well prepared with a stock of hankies, after they all sat through in reception, while the directors' representative and Vi dealt with coffins and stones. "Everyone we are going back to mine, for tea, Maceij has agreed to help me." There are others, to deal with Doris from your dads works, I'm going to need some help with that." I can do this Jan, said," "I don't know what's going to happen with the allotment," "I will come over, until you can find someone," Jan you have work to attend to and Doris. Maceij stepped in, "Vi; I have nothing but time and I like to cook, in fact; I live to cook, an allotment, can provide a lot of food, if that's ok with you, I can come over in the day-after breakfast and maybe at the weekend on the bus. Doris can come with me, if it's alright with Jan, she can keep you company while I see to the ground," "fine with me, Maceij, thanks Jan," what about you, Vi you're not young." Maceij, I know. It will be something I want to do, "Maceij I accept your offer." "After tea and cakes at Vi's everyone went their separate ways, Doris, Maceij, Chrisi after she, got some clothing and Zimmer, went back on the tram, Jan stayed a while longer to make sure Vi was ok, "I will arrange for the time off, at work, with my boss, will you be alright." "I'll be fine Jan, there's no need for you to take time off, except for the funeral," "go home and see to my daughter," Jan left on his motor mike.

"Was my mother alright Jan," "she seemed fine Doris are you ok," "for now, its next Thursday? That's when I'll need you," "I know, I'll be there." "Maceij going over to see mam and sort the allotment and the garden." "You don't think it will be too much for him, he not a spring chicken," "what is spring chicken," "Jan it's someone young, with lots of energy, oh you mean like Chrisi? She will keep Zimmer young I think, but not a spring chicken, when she has finished, he will be no good, for nothing."

"The noise below, it reminds me I need some oil, to lubricate the bike and Zimmer's bed." Doris laughed " not funny Doris, how are we supposed to sleep through that," "cotton wool Jan, put it your ears," "no more worries, for you perhaps," "if we can put up with the Zanzibar on a Friday and Saturday, Zimmer's bed is a piece of cake?"

Miserable weather, and sobbing miserable people, it's what's most associate with funerals, that was the case on this day. The heavens opened up during the early hours. It didn't look like stopping for a second. It's the sky, when you look at your window, you just know it's a day when you want to stay in bed but can't.

"The flowers Jan, they have got to down at Emerson's for the funeral parlour." "Maceij and Zimmer want to go with you; they have a reef to get from a different flower shop, there only a couple of streets apart." "I'll telephone his factory Forman, to remind him where to take the flowers and the girls want to send some from my old works" "Doris stop panicking." "They already know" "I know; everybody knows." The tear works, were in full swing today, "sorry; I'll make sure ok."

"Did you ask Maceij for an umbrella, yes? He has bought six of them; I have no idea, and how he knew we would need them in the first place." "Chrisi and Zimmer they're at it again. Jan someone needs to throw a bucket of cold water over them two." "I'll go knock the door, there is no time for this today." "I am going for breakfast, what about you," "no; I couldn't manage it. My stomach is in knots. I'll be down, it a minute." "I'll just put my face on," "war paint," "no Jan, makeup, war paint."

"Nice suit Jan." "I'm cooking breakfast of the cuff this morning. I don't think everyone may want it, Jam." Yes, porridge please, and coffee, black. The rain looks like it's in for the day, good call by you." "I had this premonition, no, not really. It was a fifty, fifty call; I would either be right or wrong." "Jan, did you knock Zimmer's door, twice. They were at it last night and now this morning." He'll be very lucky if he can stand up," "on the contrary, Zimmer said bursting through into breakfast room, looking full of the joys of spring." "What a wonderful, day," "how do you, figure that out," its pissing down with rain, Doris said, and we are burying my father." "See you have your sister's tongue for vulgar expression," "I assume you want breakfast, toast, sausages, eggs, the works you'll need to go do more press up's, not a bad idea Doris." "Do we have time," "Zimmer you are the pits?" "Tea please Maceij," please take notice the teapot, with the cosy I'll just get it from the kitchen. The tea is brewed to perfection, as instructed and taught to me by your mother." "I have laboured to succeed, Waller, for you, one fine China mug, Vi did say cup and saucer." "I, thought that was a step too far, besides you drink more than you can put in a cup, I thought of a chamber pot. I thought that a step to much as well." "Maceij, don't ever change when I'm down, you know just how to pick me up," "talking of picking up, flowers. We know Zimmer everyone said at once," "oh."

"Chrisi, come on, it's time to get on the move," Zimmer shouted down the hall, "or we'll miss the bus," "just a mo. I'm doing my face." Doris was like a cat on heat. She couldn't stand; she couldn't sit. "For God's sake Chris come on," "keep your hat on, ready, heaven's sake Chrisi you look like you're going to a dance." "You need black or dark clothes, "why; dad can't see them, what difference does it make." Doris slapped her face; Chrisi replied in kind; they both burst into tears and then hugged each other. "I haven't got any dark clothes; except this mac, Zimmer bought me." "Let's hope the sun doesn't come out, hey," we have to repaint our faces. Jan calls it, war paint, if we looked in the mirror, we would look like them Indian squaws in the movies." They both started crying again as they ran for the bus, just making it. "It's becoming hard to run, when I do I want a pee." "Doris, I think that's more info than the folks on the bus wanted to hear," she whispered look at my face, Chrisi." "The mascara has run; I look like something out of a horror film." "No, Doris, you looked that way before the make up."

"Bugger the trams not running, Doris." "They've roads shut, someone just said, a tree came down," "Chrisi. I can't walk all that way, don't worry; I'm thinking, wait. I'll ask; Someone's bound to know a way around it, that man over there." "He's talking to them others waiting; I'll go ask him." "No problem Doris, but we have got to get on two buses, the first to risborough crescent, up on the Brandon estate, and then we can catch a bus to your old works and walk from there." "Great Chris sounds like a plan, where do we catch the bus,"? "That's the downside, it's a ten-minute walk to the bus station, starting from there," "these high heels are killing me now." "I'll never make it, shit, bloody shit, got it, got any money on you," "about three bobs. I've got about four, take out the bus fare money." "Bingo, that's that's about what it'll cost, for a pair of flat shoes, there a shoe shop over there, come on let's go." "Please Mrs. I'm pleading on your generosity, look you can see my sister pregnant, the roads blocked. The tram is broken; we need to catch a bus; she can't walk to the bus station." "For pity sake, look at the shoes she is wearing, it's it too far she needs the cheapest pair of bloody flat shoes you've got." "My dear, they won't last five minutes in this weather, weather. The and navy store is fifty yards down the road, first left, left. They look very, elegant, but they will do the job," "spit it out Chrisi said, wellingtons." "Perfect, new fashion your setting, a few minutes later, "I look ridiculous," "but your feet will stay dry, think about that hey." "No they won't, the rain is running off my coat into them," "never mind. It's what we can afford, thank the Lord, for wellingtons."

They made it just in time. "Where have you two been," "mam, it's a long story, see her feet. That's the story, Wellies." "Chrisi, Doris will tell you later, Doris sat on a chair, turned her wellies upside down, about half a pint of water emptied onto the floor." "Oh shit" she said out loud, don't do it in here. I'll make the place smell, smart arse said. "The Hurst and limo's will be in a minute," "what is Maceij doing, mam, in your kitchen? A miracle." "I was in a right state, when the boys got here," he doesn't look bad in that pinney." "He's doing sandwiches and whatever; for everyone coming back here, after we." Vi couldn't hold her tears back. Jan grabbed her arm; Zimmer got the other one; she fainted. "Sit her in the chair, near the fire," Maceij said. "I'll make some tea. Plenty of sugar and a little polish brandy, one of you men, there is some brandy around here, it will steady the nerves." "Don't worry Chrisi said,"Maceij already has it covered." "Vi doesn't drink, it not for just for her; it's for me. I feel a bloody wreck." "Maceij, you need to get ready, to go the limo's here. "I'm not going Doris," "I need to finish here, there are cakes in the oven and tarts to go in after," "Chrisi won't fit in there." "I heard that Doris, that was under the ribs," "Chrisi, but true, "yeah your properly right," "not really you're a diamond, glad you were there, with me in town." "I would have sat on a bench stayed there for the day and howled," "like you doing now you mean." "I can't help it," "come on no one can today, but try, think of the stress, that poor baby's getting."

"See you in an hour or two, Maceij," "no problem," waving as the Hurst set off slowly down the Avenue in the pelting rain. The two limo's pulled up outside saint john's church the walk to the church doors were amassed with reefs and flowers. Despite the weather under the parade of brollies, people Vi, had never met from Franks work had turned up, by the score. Jan took her arm, under the canopy of the umbrella as she mingled. "All these people Jan, I, never knew there would be so many, it's a send-off he would have been proud of." "He always said, Jan, just throw me on the compost heap, down the bottom of the allotment, that was Frank." "He was liked everywhere. By everybody, I was the only one who made his life a misery." Zimmer, he handed a handkerchief to go with the rest." "No, I have seen you with my own eye's, Doris is always correcting me, how he looked at you. he loves you, anyone could see that, come let's go." The church was packed out, just the front rows made up by family, the rest people from his work, the union and factory bosses and from where Doris use to work. After the short service, they followed the precession to the grave yard. The heavens opened again as the coffin descended out of sight into the grounds. The vicar said the final words of comfort, then the handful of soil thrown into the pit, one by one. Starting with Vi, brought it to an end, as they parted from the graveside, Doris looked back from the church, only Jan and her mother, were standing there, the last to depart.

It was amazing how many people, turned up. "I'm dumb founded," Vi, said, when she got home, Maceij had put on a spread fit for a king, "wow." "I didn't have stuff, certainly not to do all this." "I brought one or two things with me, and an arrangement with your local cake shop helped." "He opened up his shop and helped brings some things here." "This must have cost a packet, let me know, and I'll pay you back," "let's call it rent; for the allotment," "I would be happy with that Vi," "Frank favorite place your know," "sorry;

I didn't mean to upset you. I wasn't thinking; I just like gardening, and I don't have one, so that was a bit presumptuous of me." "Not at all, Frank, he would have been proud to have you as a friend, I know he would." "I have much to do; your guests are arriving."

Vi invited close friends, family and neighbours. It was still raining the house was packed to the rafters. People were in the scullery, kitchen, stairs, lounge, everywhere except the bedrooms, with the exception of Chrisi and Zimmer, Vi went up to see who was up there. She did not go into the bedroom instead came back down and spoke to Jan. "That boy want's to learn to keep his pants on, there a place and a time." "Jan you straighten him and my daughter out," no problem." Jan went to the kitchen, Vi followed him in, "Jan there in the bedroom" "I know," "I'll sort the washing up later. It's not for that," Jan ran the cold water, filling the bowl, "I'll be just a minute." She was somewhat bemused, when he took the bowl upstairs, "Arhhh, are you bloody mad," rang out. People chatting stopped for a brief second, "now get dressed and clean the mess up." "Jan the bowls empty," "yes Vi, "when two dogs are stuck together, cold water will quickly separate them." Chrisi appeared at the top of the stairs "I need a towel mam, that bloody brute has socked us in freezing cold water." "That's a pity. They're all in the wash I needed cheering up Jan."

"What's with you and Maceij," "right now, that was the tonic I need, your mother needed, bloody serve them right, hah?" As people were starting to leave, the sun came out. Maceij had sense to borrow plates from the neighbours. He had put little stickers with sellotape on the back, as not to get them mixed up, the down side for the owners of them, they had to take them home dirty. No one complained about that. Zimmer and Chrisi, Maceij ordered them about like a military general. Right assemble those still here its clean up duties, "who made your boss, I did." "Now get on with it," he set uncle and aunts and the one or two neighbours, on cleaning up duties sending Vi to her bedroom for a needed snooze. When she returned the place was spotless, Maceij was sitting on a dinning chair he had taken from the lounge a sandwich in one hand and a glass of wine in the other. The strength of the sun was warningly pleasant," I don't drink Maceij, except a sip on the rare occasion, could you fix me one of them." "Sure, with the sandwich, it makes the package sit," "no you were sitting there." "I'll get another, then we can sit and drown our sorrows," "I've got plenty of them at the moment."

"Where is everyone." "oh, I sent them to the pub." "They were getting on my nerves I think they may have also, got fed up, with me, bossing them; I was glad to see them go." They didn't put up any resistance," "this is pleasant," "yes Vi summer is not a million miles away." "I think there's some things that need planting; the ground needs turning over." "I have a tool in my mind for that, it's called a rotivator it has an engine, to make work quick." "I was speaking to the man three doors down. His allotment is next to yours," "I think you can call that yours Maceij, the garden even too much for me." "I may need your help with that, sorry you were about to say." "He's is giving his up, I said

I would take it over," "bloody Nora, how are you going to manage both," it won't be a problem?" "You'll see, but that is more than we can eat, I know that as well, I have an arrangement with the local veg shop and the café." "This year won't be a bumper crop, but come next year, you and me, will make some money." "I have other idea's also, but they can wait." "Can I have another glass of that wine, what's it called," "merlot, its soft and fruity, pleasant to drink, it's supposed to be good for you, but don't take my word for that?" back," mam, it's that wine your you're" "don't sound surprised, Chrisi, us old folk can drink as well as you youngster's."

"I don't have to ask you Zimmer if your leading my daughter astray." "Or are you going to tell me it's the other way around." "I properly think it is, it was Chrisi on top this morning," Vi laughed out aloud. "I and merlot, might become good friends, really mam, Doris, the day been a bad day and a good day, if it wasn't for Maceij, and you Jan. I couldn't have coped, so cheers, and leave the bloody wine bottle. I might let Maceij have some," "no, I have to go cook dinner," not today Maceij, Jan's getting an Indian take out; it's something new." Zimmer knows about it; they're going to get in a while, mam before you speak, it already ordered, apparently you can, warm in the oven." "can't say I've ever heard of that, the chip shop Chrisi use to work in would have been nearer." "Not unless you want to join dad," Chrisi blurted out, then realizing what she said, broke down and sobbed. "Chrisi, I'll be with your dad sooner enough. He's there waiting for me, when it my turn, well, until then we all have to carry on the pain will lessen." "It will never go away. How it?" Chrisi ran out to the room and up to what use to be her bedroom, Zimmer, went to go after her, when Vi called out, leave her to cry it out, besides." "I've already seen some of your consoling ideas. So just sit son, she'll be down when ready."

"If you don't mind, mam, I'm going to make me and Jan a brew." "Doris you know where everything is, why don't you Jan stay the night." "We can't mam; Jan had to shift is work around to get yesterday and today off?" "He's got to go to work tomorrow." "Well, you know you would have been welcome." "Chrisi and I could stay if you like. "No Zimmer, not you two, no, you go back to your home." "My Frank would turn in his grave, if I let you, do that carry on, under this roof, not that I don't like you son, because I do, it just wouldn't be right."

"Ok, food is severed," "Zimmer; you can smell it all over the house." "That's the spices, of the east, some are hot and others mild." "It's serves with yellow rice or white rice, quite frankly. I know the difference." Zimmer stated, that's because your Colour blind," "try some Doris, bloody hell Jan, give me some water, quick, that's burnt my mouth and throat. "What's that called," "v ido,vinno,vindaloo." "That's where it should be down the loo."

"Bugger that was hot; I've drunk a pint of water, and it's still rattling around my mouth." "You try it Jan," "being that hot I thought it would shut you up." Zimmer, next time see if they have something hotter." Doris thumped him in the arm, "don't know why

I thumped you." "I knew that would hurt my hand more than you" "this stuff's quite nice Doris, this tastes of coconuts." "How the hell would you know what a coconut would taste like." "Chrisi I didn't think the served that down the chip shop." "Mam, at the fair I tasted some there; they were giving samples out." "This bread is nice that came with it Doris." "It's Nan bread Vi" Zimmer said, "Nans bread, did someone's Nan bake it." "No its was they call it, there lots of different flavours and types, their best severed hot."

After dinner, Maceij, said his good-bye's to Vi "have to get their breakfast for them, then housework, then I can go see a man about a rotivator, for tomorrow, that will be enough." Remember, last bus is in fifty minutes. Jan, make sure you drag them two with you." "Vi, see you tomorrow sometime" "you have time for a cuppa before you go. The next morning Breakfast was severed. Jan already had gone to work, "Doris. What are you doing," "oh, I've got an appointment at the clinic?" "Right I have prepared dinner. I'm off to see a man about a rotivator," "yes I know Doris said see you later," "give my love to my mother."

This is a big adventure Maciej thought, setting off to buy his machine, after spending an hour at the guy's machine shop in Shaftesbury way. He set of with it as long the pavement, it was a good two mile walk, the machine, had gears, and it could go faster, however, Maceij was apprehensive. A steady pace is all that's needed he said to himself. It was all going well until a policeman stopped him. "Hello, hello, what do we have here then," "a giant rabbit," Maceij replied, "sounds like a joke. It's not it's a machine for turning the ground over; I can't stop it because, I might not be able to start it again." "You're a comedian then," "I wish; the pay would be better," I stopped you for two reasons, one you're on the pavement, two you're going up a one way street can't allow you to continue, so you'll have to turn around." "But that Mr. policeman, will put over half a mile on the journey," "that's bad luck," "there's only a hundred yards to go, then I would be on the road." "Sorry the laws the law, if you continue, I would have to give you the ticket." The worry, I, have, is, Maceij thought, will the fuel last. "I'll take the ticket and argue later, if I don't, this will run out of fuel and be stuck in the road," "it would seem. I'm left with a dilemma then, make you turn around or let you continue, the road up ahead narrows and its busy, these things not coming back." "No" Maceij replied it's going to an allotment. It won't be leaving again," "right I'll walk in front, once you past this one way road, on the road, not the pavement and get out of my sight," "no problem." Half way through the afternoon, worn out he arrived at the allotment. By the time he had drank his cuppa, it was time to go home and do dinner.

"Boy did I sleep last night, as soon as my head hit the pillow." "How was my mother, in good spirits made a cuppa, then I had to leave?" Maceij told her how the day had unfolded. "I needed cheering up; she laughed her socks off. You got there, eventually." Doris, I was, as you put it, knackered." "When are you going next?" "I wasn't going to go until the day-after tomorrow, because of yesterday, I need to clean the shed out. Then get some fuel, get generally sorted." Then I want to get back there and plan out planting for late in the summer food and flowers." "Plan next spring's planting." "You're taking this quite serious," "yes I suppose I am." "Jan and I are going-away bank holiday weekend in three weeks," "oh where you're going." "York, in a bed and breakfast, on the bike Maceij," do you think that wise, it's probably not, but I'm going anyway." Well, peas, beans some lettuce, wall flowers, if I get a move on these can get planted. "Busy week for me. I wanted to go see your mother today." "I was going to go tomorrow; I'll leave a note for Jan" "he can come over on the bike" "I will make dinner at your mothers." "I know Chrisi is out at some do with Zimmer," "perfect. I'll put it in the note, what are you going to cook, Maceij, because I can't to save my life, wait and see?"

"The doors unlocked but where's mother, mam" Doris shouted there was no reply, "Maceij," Doris screamed; mam's gassed herself." There was a hose attached to a gas outlet meant for an extra burner, Vi had it in her right hand. "I'll go to call an ambulance," "no, Maceij said, wait, she is breathing, besides. The gas is not turned on at the tap and the tap on the end of the hose is also turned off." "There's an empty wine bottle next to the range, she's drunk, Doris, get a blanket. She has laid here a good while, Vi is very cold to the touch." "Is she going to die Maceij, I can't lose my mam as well," "get the blanket. I'll put her on the couch?" "Maceij, she is diabetic; that's why she doesn't, drink." "I've seen this before, the cold has properly helped," "make some hot tea, get a water bottle." "I assume she takes that without sugar," "as far as I know" Doris replied" let the tea cool, get me some Luke warm water." Maceij taped her face, with the palm of his hand, "wait Maceij. She has a washing sort of a bag with a syringe in it I think, she injects." "Get it let me see, Maceij took off his, tie, ready to use it as a tourniquet. Vi started to stir, Vi, slapping her face at little harder, "Frank, is that you, Frank," "give me the water. Doris, her mouth will be dry," Vi took a little, "she's drunk; that's the problem." "The empty bottle is dry red wine; she just needs to lay there and warm up, feed her a little water Doris, when she stirs keep the mouth lubricated." "I'm bloody cold, has the fire gone, out," "mam ,Maceij, is sorting that out, you've been laying, goodness knows how long on the kitchen floor." "Doris get her to drink the warm water as much as she can, there another empty bottle on the table." "She has hit it, heavy," "Mam. What was you thinking of, you never, drink; I just wanted to be with my Frank." "What where you doing with the gas hose" "I found it in the shed, I was going to use it, you're lucky you didn't blow the house up?" "You'll see dad soon enough. He wouldn't want you to do this, tell he Maceij," Doris, is right, a bit of a mad idea." "How was the wine, making my head thump," "good,'" "I was sick in the toilet, don't go in it's a mess, I'll clean it?"

"Maceij please just leave it." "Have some tea, if you can remember how to make it." "Tea it will help trust me," "insulin Vi, do you need it," never mind that, I need the toilet, Vi went to get up, bloody hell my legs won't work," "I'll take you." "Maceij you can't do that," "Doris, I had to look after my grandmother, she was in a chair; it's not something I haven't done before, it's not a problem." "I'll get her there, then you can sort her out, when she is ready to come back to the chair." "Then, give me a shout, in the meantime I'll prepare dinner, by the way," "I forgot to say Vi, I'm need to use your kitchen."

Maceij made his first job, discarding the hose, when he took the hose off, he laughed. It wouldn't have worked anyway the tap was soldered at the nozzle, good job. "Mam did you need to use that injection thing," "surprisingly not, considering the wine I drank." "Bugger me, one thing I could do without is the bloody thumping head; it has given me." "Promise you won't do that again," " your heads in a state, who knows what you might do Doris." "If you're thinking, of doing that again, I'll get Zimmer and Chrisi to move in," no god forbid, I'm cured." "What's Maceij doing in my kitchen, whatever it is it will taste great?" mans a genius with food," Maceij, Vi shouted, "what are you cooking." "If the snares have done their job, then it will be rabbit stew." "I've prepared vegetables, for whatever, give me ten minutes. I'll know, just got to go down, then end of the allotment, there're some new potatoes, ready. I'll be getting a few of them, see you shortly?"

Ten minutes later, Maceij was back with three rabbits and a bag of new potatoes. "Doris you scrub the potatoes," "I assume you have a nail brush," "mam, where's the nail brush," "in the shed with the carbolic soap," "you see to that Doris? "I will skin them, the skins I'll dry. They make good lining for slippers." "I brought some pepper corns, bay leaf, spices, garlic, bay leaves, olive oil and some cider vinegar, oh, and some butter," Maceij having prepared the food. Now some tea, English style, then I have work to do" "I must go to the garage, get some petrol and get the rotivator on the go."

"I'm going to walk down the allotment, Doris, you coming." "I'm intrigued to see what Maceij is doing." Vi couldn't believe how quickly the allotment next door had been incorporated in hers. The fence had gone, not that it amounted to much, there he was going into the corner, Maceij was three quarters done. "Machinery, Doris, that's the future," "that would have taken Frank weeks" Vi said. Maceij stopped and walked over, "if this is planned properly next year we will see it turn a profit," I'm going to the livestock market next week and get some chicken's and a hen or two depending on cost." "There enough material around here. that's been left, to build runs." "I notice the next allotment as well looks a mess, as though it is not in use." "That's Winnie's. She lost her husband just days before the end of the war, like the rest of us, she's old, it's just become too much." It's a bit ambitious so soon Maceij said, There is good solid shed, I could use, if I don't strike now someone else will." "Be careful Maceij, you don't want the council to get wind of what you're doing." "Don't worry VI, where the fence has come out, I'm re-establishing that with gooseberry bushes, black current and black berry, if I can get that allotment I will leave the fence." "As it open I'll go see her now, a supply of veg from time to time will be my negotiating tool," "seems he's got it all figured out Doris."

"The smell, it's to die for." "I must have fallen asleep," how did you get on with Winnie The allotment is now mine?" "I have much to do, but it will be worth it, never mind that," "Jan's here." "I was about to say, when will it be ready to eat," "in about two hours time can't wait that long." "You're, kidding," "Vi, too soon it won't be right." Give us a kiss big boy, not you Maceij? Jan, I've washed and changed, before I came," "I didn't hear the bike." "I switched it off in the road, and pushed it into the front garden, where's Doris." "Upstairs making the beds up, go up Jan, treat the place as your own." Vi wished she hadn't said that, Doris was bound to tell him. He was down, almost as quick as he had gone up. "Is this right Maceij? If what happened today is correct, Doris has told you, then the answer is yes," "we will stay here, for a while." "I should have thought it was too soon to leave you alone." "Jan I'm fine Vi insisted." "He was having none of it, "well if you're going to stay, I'll sleep in Chrisi old room you, have mine." "I should have done that yesterday" "I probably would, still sat down here drank and pickled my brain." Zimmer will be here soon, " he has some money for me, from my last job of work," "good Maceij said, if you're staying, I'm going out to sort the shed I had started doing that earlier." "I will have a word with Zimmer. He can look after the house and he own food and Chrisi for the next three days." "I can sleep in the shed; it's warm enough and has electric. The dinner in the meantime will look after itself, rabbit stew." "Jan, can you go back to the house, get my sleeping bags, I, have one in a camping bag in the corner of my room, take out the sleeping bag and the army, bed; it assembles to make a canvas bed, you'll know what it is when you see it and a blanket, oh and my washing bag, can you get that on the bike. "Yes,

I have panniers, "good that's settled," "you could have slept in Doris's room," "no. I prefer outside thanks Vi," "I can get ahead in the allotments and go to garden centre, for my plants and seeds.

"Wow, Maceij, where did you learn to cook like this?" "That's the best rabbit stew I have ever tasted." "Vi, moggies taste's just as good." "Maceij only joking, Doris, my grandmother was a wonderful cook and in the army, I had to make meals out of nothing." "I enjoyed it, until the Germans shot my leg up, for fun, they had been drinking." "It was me or whoever, whatever, would be in their sights. I was in the wrong place at the wrong time." "They captured my unit. We were target practice, that was until their commander realised I was the cook." "Their's was dead, the substitute's cooking was terrible, so bad leg or not. I got the job, there were no poisons." "Unfortunately I had to feed them and what was left of the unit, until, they were sent to the concentration camps." "The Germans kept me. I pleaded for them to save my leg, there be doctor fixed it, or I would have lost it." "so, I, cooked for them, after the war when they were captured, their commanding officer told them I was a polish prisoner, a cook, he told them how good I was."

"I ended up being a British cook; the army wanted to keep me as a cook, after the war, for a while." "I stayed on because I needed a home, I had three diamonds; my mother gave me. They were hidden, don't please ask where," "When the time was right I sold them, bought a house with Zimmer, and put some away for a rainy day, like now and my new garden business," "If it is successful, I will buy more land and grow more.

People will always need food." "You could set up a cafe Maceij," "no Doris, there is no future in that, too much hard work; for the reward, supply and demand, that's the market," "have you got any relatives Maceij," "no? They are all gone," "what about you Jan," "Vi I have two brothers I don't know if they are alive or dead, we all joined up for the war, but we all ended up in different places." "I hope they are alive, and I will see them again one day, "that's sad," "war is sad Doris."

Maceij was up at the crack of dawn. He had done two hours outside and got breakfast as well. "The man is a machine, to look at him. You wouldn't think he had the stamina." Breakfast is served, Vi; I know your diabetic; I have done some egg on toast and beans." "For your full breakfast for Jan, fresh English tea, marmalade and coffee for me." "The price of that, is more than gold dust, but I like coffee and tea, flowers on the table." "I can't remember the last time; there were flowers in this house. "Vi, I got them when I was at the garden centre" "I can see why the army wanted to keep you." "You're a credit to anyone" "thanks Vi," "tea please" returned to the allotment, having prepared vegetables for dinner. He hadn't out there for more twenty minutes, there's always something, "what's wrong Maceij?"

"There is a bomb in the allotment, I know the procedure. I'll phone the police; they will phone the army." "I will get nothing done today, Doris you take your mother, tell the neighbours. I'll call the cavalry." The army bomb disposal team where there within the hour. They evacuated all the occupants of local houses to the church. The bomb was soon identified as a dud, previously made safe but not removed. The officer had the Avenue cleared, as a precaution surprisingly they were very quick. While we sat in the church singing songs for a couple of hours. We could go about our business once; it was confirmed that it was already defused, wish they were all like that. The office confirmed the lads will be here for a while, while they get the casing out, we will keep this one for training. Maceij asked, "can I go back to my allotment, don't see why not."

"A bloody dud, Vi, anyway I'm glad they're taking the case away, one thing lest for me to worry about." Maceij cracked on it was time to do dinner, "Vi was feeling a lot more like herself," "what are cooking to day Maceij," "stuffed sheep's heart, not everyone likes them. The can be chewy, but if they're not cooked right there tasty and cheap?"

In the three days, he was there Maceij, had sorted all three allotments and got his chicken and hen coup built. As they were the last three houses at the end of the Avenue, with allotments, they were not going to bother anyone. At the weekend, he sorted out Zimmer and Chrisi, who were quite happy to have the house to themselves. Maceij returned to Vi's, The shed was his second home, "what are you building now Maceij," it's a cheap cold frame, Vi the glass is from the local glazier?" "it's called horticultural glass. It's cheap, but you have to be careful if it breaks you can cut yourself." "I need this to bring plants on early, and another for growing tomatoes." They want sun, but not too much, so I'll paint some of the glass, to defuse the sun, like this one I did earlier." "It will be a small farm, maybe in a year or two. If I could get my hands on those two fields, "I would get a tractor. I'm getting a bit ahead of myself," "Vi. I have to go home." "I'll have a cup of tea, with you," then I'd better go check. Zimmer and Christi see they haven't burnt the house down."

The house was intact as he got off the bus, it had a crowd outside, that concerned him. It sounded like a murder in progress as he got closer to the door, "excuse me please I live here." Maceij opened the door and was met by a plate just missing his head, "Zimmer, stop throwing things." "It's not me; it's Chrisi" "it's Maceij." He shouted, "stop throwing my plates," "then tell that bastard to stay out there and stop beating me and let me go." "That's because you're a whore," "stop it both of you, now, in the breakfast Zimmer," "I don't want to go in there the whore," "Zimmer a few days ago we had to throw cold water on you two, what's changed?"

Maceij sat down in the breakfast room; Chrisi ran upstairs. "Charging a friend, for sex, that's what's changed." "Surely your mistaken," "go ask her," "Chrisi," he shouted up the stairs. I'm coming up no missiles. It's Maceij," Zimmer started to follow him down the hallway, "Zimmer stay your end in the breakfast room please," "no," "Zimmer do it or I will hit you," I have a good name in the place I want to keep it," "I don't want a policeman at the door or the house destroyed, now stay your end, or go to the hospital your choice," "Chrisi come down, good grief," she slowly walked down the stairs, her nose running with blood, torn clothes and a series of scratches and bruises. "What an earth have you two been doing to each other and have you no respect for my things." "Sorry Maciej," he just started hitting me the minute

I walked in." Maceij asked, "is it true what he's saying, "yes,'" "what, are serious," "I was broke, have you done this before, yes, lots of time and I'll probably do it again." "Does he know that, no, not all of it, but I expect he will now," what did you think, he would say." "I know, what he'd say, let's have a good time, then when it's, no longer good, that's it. He made that clear; I was a bed partner, not a long term proposition." "He never intends to commit. He likes his money, his time on his own, when its suits, his things, there's no sharing with Zimmer." "I can't survive that way, so it's over, he' got his money worth before he throws me onto the street." "I've been keeping him, not the other way around. His wallet is sown to his pocket and do I love him, yes. That's why I'm broke." "My god, does your mother know, no clue" "and she won't, Maceij stated."

"Zimmer please come here," "not, with her in there," "you'll come in here, if I have to drag you by your hair." "Let's make that clear and you know I will, sit down," "slut," Zimmer said. "Enough, you clearly don't want her is that correct," "I don't want a whore." Zimmer shut it; she loves you God knows why, because you're an ass hole." "In this world, you think it's you and no one else matters." "You use people, to get what or where you want to go, when it suits you dump them." "You're going to let her get her things; for the next three or four days, she will have my room." "You, will not touch her; that's time enough hopefully, to let nature cover the mess you have made of her." "After that, wounds healed or covered with makeup, she will go home to her mother." "You will never speak ill of her again, to anyone, because if you do, I will make you

sorry you ever drew breath, is that clear." "You have
had your fun, and she has had hers, unless you have
anything to add, Zimmer, "no," "Chrisi, "no," "good,
that's settled then, tea." "One thing Maceij, where are
you going to sleep," "not with you so don't, worry, in
the rat hole of a spare room when I'm here?"

"Remember I have an allotment to run." "Zimmer
I want your word on this;" "you have it." "You madam
do not antagonize him, stay in my room, out of sight."
"If Jan comes home unexpected, I don't want a confron-
tation taking place this applies to you as well Zimmer."
"Should anyone ask, Chrisi is out," "you'll be at work
in the daytime?" "It's only at night, for the next four
days I'll make sure I'm back here on second thoughts."
"I'll fix it with your mother. I will tell part of the truth,
that you had a row and have parted, a lovers tiff,"
"Chrisi no more of what you do, find a nice man,"
"I thought I had," "there are others Chrisi," "it's hard
for you to understand perhaps Maceij," "he might be
a rat," "but he's the rat that gives me that, something
you can't explain, that has taken me long enough to
find it and just as quick to lose it," "do you understand
Maceij," "does Zimmer," "she's right, I am a rat,
I haven't the same feeling's, a boy with a toy I brake it,
then throw it away and look for another toy, I won't
hurt her anymore and I can't love her either, what we
had was lust, her love was going down a one way street,
I'm sorry," "Zimmer, for what it's worth, thanks for
that bit of honesty," "thanks Chrisi," "you kids, I'll go
make the tea, someone clear my broken crockery up."
"We'll both do it, ok, alright with you Chrisi, fine, just
fine Maceij."

"There's a little problem I need to talk to you about Vi."
"It's Chrisi" "she not hurt is she, "No.'" "Only in the
heart, a lovers row, they are in separate rooms." "It will
lead to more arguments, and I cannot be in two places
at once." "Maceij. What do you expect I should do,"
"allow her back home?" "I know exactly what Chrisi
is, do you think in a small community like this; people
don't talk." "You don't want to hear, about the name
your daughter has been branded with." "When it's
more than one time, you know it has the ring of truth
behind it that's like a knife to the heart." "I should say,
no, if Frank was here I would, if she comes home, it will
have to be on my terms." The minute, she treats this
like a hotel again; she's out, Maceij you need to make
that clear." Doris had been listening; she knew what
her sister was, experiencing it first hand, it's how she,
got into the predicament. With a cloud over her head,
constant fear, If should Jan discovers the truth. God, we
will cross the bridge when it has to be faced, with the
unknown consequences it may entail, she didn't want to
think about it, until the moment, it did not didn't exist,
for now.

Chickens I have some, but how to get them here, easier
said than done, Maceij thought. "I have to see a man
about a horse and cart," "how many chicken have you
bought." "Fifteen. It should give us about sixty eggs a
week, in the meantime I have some planting to do, then
I will go home and short Christine out." "I have a job
for her, that will keep her busy for a couple of days." "I
have a new lodger, come house keeper to interview.
I have to fill the house to make it pay." "See you have
made the shed like a small home," "Vi. I want to spend

more time here and less elsewhere." Jan and Doris, will soon go back to their room, Chrisi will be company for you and a worker for me." "I have to make a lot of things work I can't burn up my savings for ever."

"Tomorrow, Maceij, I have to go to the city, the solicitor acting for the factory." "They want to see me, will you come; I have no idea, what to do," "have you a lawyer, no." Let's see what they say, then, after you may or not need a lawyer, they have admitted that the fault of the accident, the guard to the machinery, was missing." "The walk way, was not shut off," "unless they make a generous offer, don't except anything without advice." "Maceij, went home after the customary, cup of tea, Zimmer was at work." "Chrisi, I have spoken to your mother; you can go home under her conditions." "Chrisi, she knows; she has for a while, continuous gossip, like any story, a ring of truth about it." "What I can't understand is the insatiable appetite for sex, it not just with Zimmer, please explain it, because you said that you would do it again, last time we spoke." "Chrisi this time you can't, screw this up, that's why you're going to take a job in the allotment." "This job I'm going to pay you for, please don't get excited about that, I'm balancing a lot of things in the air." "I have a new person coming to see me on Friday, if she takes the job of lodger and cook." The must is; I fill my rooms to make it pay, live and stay in the shed at your mothers. I have to make the allotment pay as well, a crop of flowers and whatever else I can sell; this year will help."

"I have to do this for your sake, because if you break the line once your mother, will throw you out." "So an answer to my question, if you please." "Maceij you're a good man; with a good heart, I can see that with how; you have picked my mother up and Doris; everybody likes you." "I have a disease Maceij it's called nymphomania; I can't help myself; it's not all the time." However, there a need for sexual relief," "I don't have any disease down there. It's in the head and there's no cure." The relief is a man, so I thought, why not take money, it's the oldest business in the world." "Maceij butted in but can lead to venereal disease and death, no money is worth that." "It paid well, Chrisi said, Maceij, I know your trying to help me, but it's the way God made me." "Do you enjoy it," "sometimes. Zimmer was special. He forgave me once, but he's an unforgiving person a second time around?" "You can't blame him, Chrisi, I can't tie you to the bed," "Maceij, kinky, if you were younger," "age is nothing Chrisi. All the parts still work." However, I'm older enough, to have been your father," "more kinky thoughts," "Chrisi, stop it." "Maceij, I can't help myself, if you were all that was available then, I would do my best to take you, not because your young, old or attractive, got money or none." "I just have to," "how often does this, urge to take place," "it's unpredictable. Chrisi moved closer to him, laid her head on his chest. She cried softly, do you think I like being like this." I don't know how, but we need to find a solution, for the sake of a roof over your head." Promise me you will stay here and not go man hunting, not for now." "There's only one solution Maceij, but I promise. I won't go man hunting; it's that time of the month." "I don't get the urge then; it's a few days after that and just about any other day." "In the morning, I have to go to your fathers place of work, with your mother to see their solicitors I think they want the matter dealt with quickly." "I have a job for you. It's not nice, for a change. I need your help to clean out the spare room and the house in general." "I'll get the painter in next Monday hopefully, Mira Hurdish, will take that room and do the cooking, then if I can persuade her, will you, help me please." "Maceij, it's the least I can do," "Zimmer's in, good. I need to prepare food for you and him, breakfast." "He will sort himself; you will also have to help yourself, any rubbish from upstairs, put in the back yard; I'll deal with it, tomorrow afternoon."

"Thanks' Maceij for coming this is the solicitors, let's go see what they have to say." "Mrs. Buntie, you know we are and all who knew your husband truly sorry." "A terrible loss of a well-liked man." "I speak for the board. We will continue to pay, his wages, for the rest of your life; we will set that up, so the money goes directly into your bank." "He has a pension, that will be paid in addition and a lump sum cash payment now." "It's more than generous; you shouldn't want for the rest of your days, if this went to court, it would drag everyone through the mud." "We, as I'm sure you want this matter at an end, "Will Mrs.Buntie get that in writing, please, in a language that the common man can understand." "The documents, it's already done," "Maceij it appears to be a generous settlement, it won't bring my husband back," "it will not Vi; the money seems fair, but it's your call." "I hope steps. Gentlemen have been taken to ensure another person's husband is not subjected to the same pain." "I accept the offer; I'm too upset and tied to fight," "I understand Mrs., Buntie;

Frank was a good personal friend to Harry's Smith, a director of the board. He was grief stricken, at the lost." It was he, who insisted that this settlement be a fair and just settlement, without prejudice." "Please thank him for me, they will be no need. He is waiting outside in person, Mrs. Buntie."

"Harry's Smith I presume. Frank often spoke of you." "I didn't know you were close friends," "on union nights. He was my drinking partner only man I could have a conversation with." "He would, just listen; he was my sanity," "was it a union meeting," "Mrs. Buntie. It was not, "Vi please." "I would spill. Whatever was ailing me, and he would, give his answer, if any end, it was always a straight answer, never around the bush." "He was very good man thanks Harry, Vi; he tipped his hat, and they all left." "Home, cup of tea, Maceij, I think I may invest a little in an allotment and Maceij, shut up." "Before you say a word, I'll speak to you later about this in private, after a quick chat with Doris." Jan was at work, after Vi had spoken they had decided to stay a few more days and Vi was glad of their company, Maceij headed home, "I'll see you tomorrow."

Maceij arrived home to, the classical sound of a radio playing up stairs. He could see light was spilling onto the landing from the spare room. There was Chrisi in a skimpy pair of knickers and bra, cleaning the window. She had emptied the room of its junk, washed it down, the bare sprung single bed the only item remaining. "It's a good job that window backs onto a solid brick wall, or goodness knows what people would think, of the view." Maceij knew what he thought of the view, if the ache in his pants was a guide. She had noticed as well, "now Chrisi you have that look, stop it," the wrong time remember," "that was yesterday, Maceij," "Zimmer might come in or Jan," "Zimmer at bridge and Jan is not home until the day-after tomorrow." "You said we had to find a solution, by the view I have; I've found one." Maceij tried to back out of the room, but he was pinned against the frame of the door. Chrisi un buttoned his trousers "wow this leg hasn't been shot at; your temperature seems to be rising Maceij." "Chrisi no," your two tall to kiss, without bending down," Maceij found himself speechless and frozen to the spot; the easiest thing would be to just push her out the way. Instead, he lifted her from the floor. Her legs wrapped around him in a vice grip her hand slipped down, directing, as he lowered her. "Yes, Maceij, yes she muttered softly," they made love where he stood, after they took a bath together, she bathed him, a luxury he had never experienced. "There's not a lot of room for two, and if we fill the bath anymore Chris, it will be over the floor." Maceij you will have to be my solution, Maceij; I can't have a home; I've got no one else that would take me." "No one except my mother or you, if you're going to let your room, well, where I am I to go." "That's why I'm living in the shed, I can't say that I didn't enjoy what has happened here, I'm human, your mother has my trust, it also a friendship, I have come e to cherish, discretion will have to be absolute." When that urge you have comes, it must not be so obvious, and take place out of sight," "deal Maceij." "God I solve one thing, get out of one fire and climb straight back into another." "Time to get dried," "can you manage it on a nice bed, or are you passed your best."

"You little devil, I'm in my prime, my bedroom now, oh and bring your clothes."

Maceij had missed the warmth of flesh on flesh and the passion that went with it. Chrisi knew how to take a man to the ceiling and back. Zimmer he thought was a fool, had he treated her better she would still be in his bed and would not have wandered, he a bloody idiot. He looked at her perfect body, not a blemish anywhere, model material, lucky me. The thought also was a curse, if her mother ever got to know or anyone else, that would be a disaster, at all cost. I can't let that happen. I must get dressed and sought some dinner; he thought. "I trust for the time being your appetite is dampened, for now I have to give it to you Maceij, credit where due, that was as good as I have had," "sod dinner, for a minute." "Maybe I'm catching this disease you have, nincophanier, something or other." "Now I really must get dressed," "Maceij,'" "shut it Chrisi, after dinner, Chrisi, be good." "Do you have any paint in the shed, yes, lots of it?" "Maceij, didn't think to ask why, see you tomorrow, leave Zimmer alone," "don't worry, he is no longer an endangered species she whispered. Zimmer, knocking his door on the way out, "see you tomorrow, ok."

Maceij had a good day; at the allotment, his chickens had arrived, and he managed to plant out the allotment next door. The third of his allotment; he had cultivated, but money, was tighter. There were other things, more pressing. "What are your plans for this allotment," he hadn't notice Vi with a pair of wellies on, standing behind him." What's needed is half of the fruit trees,

plums and apples, in the middle and to the side, to
provide shade, then rest strawberries, grass? I agreed a
small lawn at the front. For her to sit on during the
summer; it will make it easy to maintain. Flowers down
the two borders and to the rear will provide Colour and
seed, well the trees. "When will you plant them, ideally,
weather permitting September October, no later," "I
will pay for them, no argument Maciej, and find out
about that bloody field hey partner?"

When Maceij got back on the tram, he was over-
whelmed with joy, it was further boosted, by the smell
of fresh paint. There she was in her knickers again; all
the wood work was bright and fresh. He was shocked
didn't expect this, "just finished she said, walking over
and close to him." I want you to bathe me, also I want
my reward now, after a further session in the bedroom,
it was a mad rush for dinner." "Help Chrisi with the
serving," they were done just as Zimmer walked in
the door. "what are you doing tomorrow, the walls
then it will be done I've found some paper for that,"
"do you know how." "I do, who do think did the
papering at my mother's, definitely not my dad,"
"do a good job, because that will help me." "I can
cancel the decorator" is he nice, is he young," she whispered in his ear,"Chrisi behave." "Remember you can't
do this tomorrow night. You're at your mothers," "then
I want my reward before I do the work." "look this
lady, for the lodging and cooking is also coming tomorrow, and Jan will be home, be careful; he whispered
back, see you tomorrow." Zimmer said, knocking the
door on the way out, "see you tomorrow, good night
Maceij" he was off to bridge.

There was always work to do, on land, chicken's the eggs needed to be collected. Maceij had made a rack up near the gate in the front garden, with an price and a price, per six. Today he was clearing and burning, rubbish from around the perimeter and attended to a compost heap; he knew its importance. He encouraged the neighbours to put their green's waste and potatoes peelings onto it, a benefit that would pay back later. Half way through the morning he took a break, walking down to the farm, to have an uninvited chat with the owner of the two fields he had in mind to purchase. With Vi's help, the week was full of surprises. He couldn't believe is luck; the farm was up for sale. A couple from London wanted to by the house and the fields that lay that side of the road. However, they were trying to negotiate into not buying the four fields on Macie's side of the road. Good fortune for him, he and the farmer struck a fair price, Maceij said he would be back within the hour; he just needed to speak to his partner. It was an opportunity to good to miss; Maciej had a clever vision. One day not too far in the future, the land at the road side, would or might be needed for houses. That would turn a good profit, interim sales in terms of crops, would help to generate income. If Vi agreed to this, proper papers of sale and ownership would have to be drawn up, he would have to be honest about, his future thoughts. It would be a time to visit his bank, the cost of a tractor, was something he would need to explore, a plough and cultivator, was a must to handle the task. They would have twenty two acres, to handle, that needed planning. He saw the farmer had a Ford major. He hadn't asked, but perhaps he would sell that and its attachments.

He couldn't contain his excitement. "Vi, you know the fields."

"Well, we can buy four fields instead of two," over the usual cup of tea, he told her of his plan's cost and a possible buy out of the farm implements. They spoke of drawing up documents, because they would need to and his intended visit to the bank, she put her hand on his. "Maceij, the money, from Franks settlement is more than I could have dreamed." "There was also a letter today about, a cash pay-out from the pension fund, its small potatoes, compared to the money that farmer wants." "If you say that it would be a good future investment, then I want you to have it and the machinery you need. I'm an old woman." "I'm not in need of riches, but I am in need of the father figure you have become and friend to me, if only she knew he thought, to say no to this generous offer, but it was a dream, as long as he could remember, to farm land of his own, so he accepted, "I'll go tell the man I have to ask, when and how shall we pay." "Through your solicitors, I'll come with you, cash it will be Maceij, go tell the man." Maceij had never walked so quickly to convey news. He was able to strike a deal for what he needed. The farmer gave him a full inventory together with the details for his solicitor, Maceij, assured the man, giving his solicitor's detail's, that on their handshakes, they would conclude the deal quickly.

He left before time that day to his solicitor's office in the city. Having phoned his secretary for a prompt appointment he arranged while he was there, an appointment for a weeks' time, when having spoken briefly on the phone with the farmer's solicitor, who had already conveyed his intention. "Mr. Berderick, looks as if we can conclude this business swiftly, when can you deposit the money with us," "tomorrow?" "You will need to bring your partner." "will by then have a full break own of legal costs regarding our fees and transfer of ownership of land and machinery."

From the city, he went home. Chrisi had finished decorating. He couldn't believe the quality of her work. I'll get her to do the rest of the house in time. He thought walking down stairs to find here. She was on his bed, laying there naked. "We can't today Chrisi," "yes we can," but be quick though; I have dinner to prepare," "already done and the decorating," "oh boy, can you cook," "cook no just prepared it, buys a little time for my reward." He didn't argue and put in a supper fast performance, "wow, that was full of aggression, more of that please." "No, you bad girl not now, get dressed." "I'm going for a bath, Maciej," "pack your bags, be ready to go after dinner." "I'll fill you in on the bus, really, with all the passengers be watching," "Chrisi, your intolerable at times come on get a move on." "Ok, keep your hair on." He explained about their land sale, but not about the money or who was paying, Vi had made that clear, Chrisi asked what have you planned, "in honesty at the moment, I don't, know." "but I will be working on what will return the best profit, for the least to do; sugar beet perhaps is one consideration, some livestock, not sure is the answer." Maceij told Vi what he had told Chrisi, was what they had agreed. The next morning, Vi and Maceij went to the solicitors. Another surprise was in store. Vi said "I don't want my name or signature or any involved part in the transaction, apart from the bill. I will be paying all receipts and ownership to Maceij he conducting this matter, with my blessing." "Neither do I want a return in the future of any kind." "My arrangement with, Maciej, that he, takes care of my family, should anything happen to me."

Vi was adamant, despite leaving the office for a five-minute break. The business was concluded and a fast transaction assured, in the afternoon Maceij went back home, concluded his business with Mira Hurdish. She had accepted the position as agreed and would be moving in on Monday, all he had to do on Monday evening, tell Zimmer, what a day as he headed to Vi's, having fed Zimmer.

Out of respect in the morning, Maceij took a walk down to farmer Haroston, out of courtesy, to tell him that the money and contract had been signed. Chrisi went with him. He already knew, "I will get the equipment out and moved, where are you going to keep it?" "I saw there was an old barn at the head of field two, if that is serviceable, I'll keep the machinery there." "I saw it was part of the sale, yes very much so, he said it's been there since eighteen thirty, there's a few dates and names carved into the oak. It's your fields now, oh, there's also an old, concrete century box from the war." "I'll take a walk around there."

If only walls could talk, when they got to the pillar box. "Maceij, its urge time, there's no one around," before he could say boo. She was in there, knickers off, Maceij took one look and obliged. "They got reacquainted with their clothing, "Chrisi, don't you think the barn would have been a better place," oh there as well," "we haven't set off from here as yet," the walk will build your energy up." When they got back, Chrisi went up to her room, Doris was sitting on the edge of the bed waiting for Jan. "Doris guess where I've been surveying with Maceij" the land, there a pillar box in a field three and a barn in field two," "Chrisi, she beckoned her over whispering in her ear, that's where me and Johnny did it, that's where I got pregnant." "Shit, Doris, Chrisi thought had she known; she wouldn't have done it there, on the other hand; I'm a liar, so I would have done it there. Bloody hell, If only Doris thought, you knew, what I had been doing and with people. If thoughts could be transmitted, it would read, Chrisi, if only you knew what I had done with Maceij."

At dinner, the topic wasn't landed. It was York, that was Jan's, dinner conversation on where to go next weekend and where to stay. Vi went mad when she heard. Doris was going on the bike, "mam. I'll be fine. I went to Hunstanton; I was alright." That might be so. However, Doris you have grown a bit since. After ten minutes, she gave up realizing it was falling on deaf ears. They had a book about, bed and breakfast, and a map of the area.

They decided on a one of three near the river off bridge road, this time. Jan was making sure there was a place for the bike, and the room was safe. "I've telephoned them, the rooms sorted, next weekend we're off." Doris made a list. From the York book, "Doris, we're going for a bank holiday weekend, not a month, stick to the city." "All these Jan are in the city, "oh, well we will see what we can." "Who cooking dinner Maceij," "Vi is, ok, "I have an early start tomorrow, Jan's" first time he will get to drive an engine in the shunting yard?" "To me, it's a toy as Chrisi put it, the one that all boys want to drive toy." The rest of the week the air was full of York's conversation, they were going to go here and there and everywhere. Anyone would think they were going on a world trip."

On the Friday morning after breakfast, the set off, stopping for fuel and rest, it was a little more uncomfortable this time than it was when they went to Hunstanton. However, the pain was offset by the spectacular scenery, "Doris, Jan this is breath taking." It had been a long trip, when they got to the bed and breakfast, the pair conked out on their bed, the weekend like all weekends when you're enjoying yourself passed quickly, Doris had been struck in ore at York Minster. She had never seen something as magnificent. They left it the last minute before saying their good bye's and departing, promising to return again, there was so much more of York, they would have liked to see."Doris We will have to go a little quicker going back." "I have to go to work tomorrow know Jan, if we have to stop I will, just shout," "ok Jan." They stopped for fuel and a rest outside Worksop, before continuing, there was more traffic than normal, Doris had commented, that's probably because it's a holiday weekend, "think your right Doris." You are alright," "Jan fine."

They had just gone over a bridge on the Kegworth road towards Loughborough. When a black car pulled off its near side verge into the path of a cream looking car. Causing it to swerve into Jan's path, to avoid it, he had no option but steer the bike to the curb of the road in the process. His right leg hit the cars wing and bumper the bike hit the curb, and was launched, through the bushes towards the trees; it happened so fast the bike went away from him. Jan narrowly missed a tree; his immediate thought was not the pain or the thorn hedge row he was implanted in, it was Doris. He couldn't turn around to see her; he called out her name several times but there was no answer. She had landed on the soft verge, landing heavy on left hip. The impact had winded her; she could hear Jan, but could reply. She felt wet, the thought on her mind as she lay there was if she was bleeding and for her baby, someone placed a blanket over her. She could hear the bell of the ambulance ring, getting closer with every second; she tried to move the pain was intense around her hip.

Doris screamed out; it was the first sound she had made since the impact. Doris, are you alright, I don't know, what about you, my leg is broken, and I can't move, at that point. What looked like a nurse started to exam her, "can you hear me, tell me where it hurts, "my hip she" replied. "I'm wet am I bleeding," "No. You're lying in water, "my baby," I'm listening for a heartbeat, don't worry; we are going to get you to the hospital."" We are, going to lift you in a while onto a stretcher, Once a doctor arrives on the scene, examines you and administer something for the pain; he's on his way." My husband, he's fine a medic is attending to him, try to lay still; the Doctor has arrived, after checking here over, he gave her an injection in the hip for the pain. "Does it hurt anywhere else," "side of my head a bit, "that's a bump you took when you hit the ground," we are going to put a support around your neck as a precaution."

Doris could see police men around her and in the road, she caught a glimpse of Jan and firemen, before being loaded into the first ambulance. "How's my wife, Jan kept asking, Don't worry she's being attended; you don't mind if I call you Jan, I heard your wife call you that." "that's fine. He could feel a man working around his leg, how bad is it, don't worry. It looks worse than it is, there is going to be some discomfort, the angle looks badly swollen and is trapped in this v shaped bit of the tree." The doc is going to give you something for the pain, when that kicks in, the fire boys will cut the tree, don't fight anything, just try to relax." "Is there any other pain" "only the thorns from the bush," "they're going to clear them in minute, once they get a board on your back; the was excruciating" as they started to cut the tree, it was over quickly," "Well done Jan; you don't mind if I call you, while were getting you ready, to transport you to the hospital." "The doctor will check you over to see that you are stable."

"Before we set off a policeman here wants to ask, what do you remember Jan." "what happened" "yes," the driver of a black car, pulled off the grass into the path of the cream car. He swerved and to avoid him; I had nowhere to go, head-on into him or the verge." Jan was told later, the driver of the cream car, which turned out to be a zephyr, stopped immediately, assisting, with the traffic. the black car was never seen or traced, but an anonymous call was made from a phone box not more than a minute away, people later describing a black car, but was not sure of its occupants or what vehicle it was. They were both take to Leicester general hospital. On arrival. Doris could hear lots of hospital stall talking around her, "were going to lift on one, two three. She let out a scream,"Doris good girl, were going to take a look." "Your pelvis might be broken, don't worry. We will check on baby, but we want to look at the hip first."

"It will be a bit uncomfortable going to put a drip in. The nurse is going to cut the clothing away on this side." "try to and stay still, the hip is bruised and the thigh. The Doctor is going to send you to get an x-ray, doctor." "It won't hurt your baby, so we are doing it now." It seemed a wait forever for the results. Doris was stuck in the one position, if she tried to move a fraction, the pain was awful. "The hip is not broken Doris, but it is compacted." "We are going to administer some pain relief and transfer you to a ward." A consultant will come and see you later, to check you over and the baby." "Never mind that, now I know I'm fine, what about my husband." Relax Doris, he's here in the hospital; his leg is badly broken; he's in theatre at the moment." "He's not going to lose his leg is he," Doris started to fret; I can't tell you anymore than I have I know you're anxious, but try to stay calm and relax; we need you to do that for your baby's sake."

It was no fun laying there, trying to relax, that was impossible. Her thoughts were racing all over the place, what are we for God's sake? What will we do for money was one that plagued her mind, will the baby be normal, did it suffer brain damage, how will I cope with a one-legged man and a child? God I was stupid getting on that bike my mother was right; I'll get my ear bent forever, the pain, that played on her. The breaking point was reached. The tears flowed, "I want my mum" a nurse quickly attended to her, "shush now." "Do you want us to inform your family. Doris thought about that for a moment, "no, not just now." I wanted to know how my husband is first, "could you do that, find out, "yes the nurse replied."

Later, that evening the news his wife was alright. Delivered by the surgeon who had treated, Jan. "Can I call you" Doris, yes, I prefer Doris Doctor," your husband is in a men's ward, he is fine, his leg is set, in a brace and plaster, recovery will take a while, and he will regain full use of his leg." However, he will need to where a truss, "what's that," "it's to support the hernia; your husband developed during the accident, once he is fully recovered; he will be able to discard apparatus?" "The consultant with me, is here to talk about you," call her Doris thank you doctor any particular reason. Head of the chart, yes I see, Doris, let's discuss you, firstly, the obvious, your very lucky, these accidents."

"Where motor cycles are involved, the consequences are far worse." Lucky I say because I have been informed you land on soft wet, very wet grass, that's what saved you, had you landed on solid ground. The pelvic region would have suffered catastrophic damage." "That aside, you have suffered some compression and heavy bruising, the good news your baby is fine." "The bad news is I cannot allow a natural birth at this stage your pregnancy. Therefore, I conclude C section surgery the only safe option." "What a C section Doctor," a caesarean section is where we make an incision, removing the baby through your stomach, because you cannot pass it naturally, as your baby was due next week. I propose Thursday, we take you to theatre, now next of kin would you like us to inform them, "one question first Doctor is the operation safe," "yes Doris it is," "can my husband be present, no it a surgical procedure, requiring a sterile environment." Besides he won't be out of bed that quickly, but I will inform him, not about the baby though please, religious you see." "I'm not allowed to discuss anything without your permission." "Thanks, tell him I'm fine." "Jan may I call you that, you may still feel a little groggy from the anaesthetic." I have just seen your wife. She is fine, what about the baby Doctor," That's fine also, nothing for you to worry about, relax, you're both in good hands."

"Vi they should have been back. Jan has to be at work this afternoon." "They're cutting it fine," at that moment, there was a knock at the front door." Maceij answered the door. It was the telegram service, "do you want me to wait for a reply sir, one moment please." "Vi it's a telegram for you." "This doesn't sound good she said," it wasn't, "Maceij Jan and Doris are in the hospital?" "Where, Leicester General, now don't worry, let me tell the, telegram man he can go." "I'll give him some change; we go, It's probably she is in labour," "of course Maceij, your properly right I hate telegrams is reminds me of the war; they never brought good news," "your cheerful Vi," "when they got to the hospital it was clear. The news was a motor cycle accident, as much as Doris, tried to say it wasn't Jan's fault. She She was talking not listening, he was being blamed; it took her strength to raise her voice loud enough. "Mother get out, go," out now she screamed, "you don't listen to anyone but yourself, go. I don't want you here." A nurse was quickly in attendance, to settle Doris back down, escorting her tearful mother from the ward. Maceij came across from the men's ward having heard the commotion from there, to comfort Vi first he explained what happened; pointing out Clearly Jan wasn't in any way to blame, he told her had he not taken the action he had, the accident would have been, much more serious, maybe even fatal. She listened to Maceij, but had not her daughter, if she felt bad after, Doris had shouted at her. She felt worse now. Vi pleaded with the nurse to let her back in she would not, saying it was too stressful for Doris, but she would convey her message later.

"Vi, you wait here for a minute while I go speak on the telephone to Jan's work, tell them what has happened." "He thinks he can go to work in two or three days, he an optimist I have to say." Maceij returned ten minutes later, Vi had fallen asleep, "come, there is nothing we can do let's go home. We can come back tomorrow." Chrisi was becoming a real gem. She watched Maceij prepare food and assisted at times. Dinner was cooked and ready to be served. Maceij had no worries for Zimmer. He was getting on very well with Mira, "so young lady. "What have you created, cottage pie and vegetables, with gravy?" "It looks good to me. Vi are you ready" "I don't, fancy food at the moment Maceij." Try to eat a little, Vi trust me? She will be fine tomorrow." "It's been a stressful day, the accident, the worry, being pulled around. A good night's sleep all round."

"I'm going look at the field up near the barn," "can I come Chrisi asked, yes I could show you how the tractor works," "according to this note, tractor and implements. They were put in the barn today together with the implements and other things you may find useful, thanks for the quick sale." "This package came for you while you were out," Maceij, had a truly joyful smile on his face, it was the deeds to his land. "Now we have a real start," he said out loud, "we have enough loose timber in the barn that can be put to good use I'll have a look, when we walk over their Chrisi." "Will you be alright Vi?" "I'll be fine," "I'll have some tea and sit here with the moggies." I know why you agreed to come Chrisi, to the barn you want feeding, damn right I do," "what's with the timber? You'll see."

"The barn, has a door, with a block for a lifting hoist." "So, Chrisi, it means it has or had a floor, look that Hessian cloth; that hangs from the top beams, there's a ladder Maceij on the wall, behind the tractor." "let's get it out and up against that lower beam, so I can take a look, sure enough there was the floor."" "Maceij tested it out; it was sound, come up Chrisi, there a spy hole you can see down the fields towards home." "We can clean out this old hay, get a matter, then you can get a comfortable service." "Maceij she replied I don't care where I get a service as long as you keep giving me one." "Maceij, what's with the wood, to create pens for horses, we could have a horse riding school, use the head of the land it would give the horses good exercise, and income, to get a crop of some type going next year, and a job for you'd enjoy that Chrisi." The number three field I hope we can sell that for building development, not now but later, with that money I would then negotiate for the seven fields that wrap around to that old factory Doris use to work at, keep this close, its secret." "However, why Maceij do you want to do all this," "to make enough money Chrisi, so you and I don't have to work ever again." The canaries near Spain, constant sunshine, all year around perfect for me and you." "Why have you included me," "I can't go on doing, what we're doing and not make a decent woman of you?" "I went to your mother, my age, your age, what do you think her reaction would be." I don't want to take a guess Maceij," but if you don't like that idea of some wealthy guy, I'll rephrase that, some elderly wealthy guy on your arm, just say." "I want to rip your clothes off Maceij," "of course, one thing." "I must warn young lady no lies with each other, no messing around with other men; I would properly kill you." "Have you messed with other women" Maceij replied, "I'm no Saint; "as your local vicar would put it a sinner, anyone I have known, anyone you have known?" That's the past, new slate, from today, and by the way, I love you. "You do, wow, pinkies," "What," "Maceij we get our pinkies our little fingers like this around each other's and swear it." "Then Chrisi I swear it," after making love in the barn, Chrisi had a new spring in her step. She put her hand in Maceij's, "Chrisi we have to carry on like nothing is different" "I know," no one can see us walk along here." "I wanted us to walk just for a moment as lovers," "by the way, I don't see you as an old man, in his fifties." "I see you as the man who fills my heart, it's what I needed?" "It will be hard work at first this farm to be, but it will be worth it, in many ways It will satisfy me because it's what I always wanted, stability," "together we will create that for each other." "By the way Maceij, I love you."

The next morning when they when to the hospital, Maceij said, "let me in first to see Doris, trust me on this, ok Maceij," "I trust you on many things," "will she see you, Doris will think I put you up to this," "it will be fine." "Doris," "Maceij," if you don't talk to your mother, she will be heart broken, if you saw the state of her last night, if it was your daughter, you would do what's best; you wouldn't be any different." "Be truthful this is me your talking to, Doris." "You can have many lovers in your life, many men you could call dad, but only ever will you have one mother." "Did she put you up to this Maceij," "I put myself up to this," "Hell send her in." "See Chrisi you can make your peace with anyone." "Grandmother to be and daughter together let's go see Jan." Tomorrow, 'I'm going over to your old room to sort that out, for decorating so you can get someone in there." "Then what about the attic, the dormers need renewing before anyone can go up there." "Maceij, if we can keep the beds that will save a little money. when the allotments pay this year and the horses, we will have the money, Chrisi to finish the house and have it full with lodgers."with the rest of the summer the rest, I hope, make the money back, there is someone interested in renting a small corner of field four to put the grand-daughter's pony." Every penny we can get this year will help to make next year better.

"I've worked out the tally for this year." "What's needed to produce hay?" "We will need that Maceij for horse feed," "and it's about the best; we can achieve Chrisi," "Unless I can put it out for grazing of sheep with farmer Jackson, in Holliston, he asked me the other day when he was in the Baker's shop." "It's the bakers granddaughters pony." "Jan how are you,"

PETER ABBASOVA

"fine Chrisi, Maceij," "how's Doris, she fine." "Vi is in
there with her, mending fences." "Jan; they had a falling
out; it's all straightened out now, a few tears here and
there." "What's with the leg," they wanted to keep me
here for a week? I will go mad." "They are bringing
the bike back to yours Maceij; the insurance has sorted
it out."I hope to be at work at the weekend." "You
can't stand and work with that," "its fine." "They are
letting me work in the shunting yard, if I'm up to it,"
I will be sitting mostly I can handle that, it's only the
lower leg broken Maceij not my head.

"Glad to see you're in good spirits." Maceij spoke in
Slovak, to Jan brining up to speed with the allotments
and the land, but not giving him the how did he do it
and where did the money come." "Vi go and see Jan,
have a chat with him try to make him see sense." Chrisi
and I will quickly, see Doris then we'll get ourselves
home." "Doris, everything sorted with you and your
mam, yes, Maceij,"it wasn't exactly true, she was telling
no one about the baby and the operation. least of all
her mother. "See you the day after tomorrow, Doris."
Vi and Chrisi sat together on the rear bench seats,
Maceij, sat opposite them, "Jan is mad going back to
work so soon, yes I told him, but Maceij he wasn't
listening. He was in a world of his own, thinking what a
lucky bugger I am to have someone so beautiful as
Doris wanting him, will it last, who knows Maceij."
"Sorry Vi, I was miles away, were here, home." Chrisi
had been ironically thinking the same, at the dinner
table when Vi spoke, "Chrisi, have you two got the
same illness today." "Sorry mam, it's been a long day,"
"we have a longer one tomorrow. I'm decorating Maceij
room at the other house."

"Maceij coming over tomorrow to sort out what he wants to get rid of or take out of the room." "The next day I will be going over, Maceij will come over in the afternoon and help me finish off." "Then what are you going to do with the room Maceij, rent it mam," "The extra I get from there the more I can put in here. You're both determined to make this enterprise work." "I can see that," "Maceij, yes Vi," come here. I'm an old woman, but not a stupid woman." "I see the way you look at her, see the way see looks at you; she's in love and so are you, when she speaks of work Chrisi uses the both; we will not Maceij or I." "Maceij don't say a word please, there's no need, it's what she needs, if I were younger, it's what I would want, a strong man to lead and protect me, a man that will always be there." "I believe you to be such a man, what I'm saying, I approve," you do Vi, you're the most astute woman I have ever known." "Fifteen eggs today Maceij, rushing into the lounge, "Chrisi, yes mam," go take his hand with my blessing, "you told her Maceij," "no I did not." "I think they call it women's intuition; they should bottle it. I would make a fortune." "I'm right Chrisi, "yes; I love him mam," "does Maceij love Chrisi" "he does, Vi" you lucky girl.

Jan was determined to go back to work. He had already enquired about self-discharge and was persuaded to at least see the consultant. Congratulations, "Doctor for what; your wife delivered you a son last right, now if you're still thinking of discharging yourself, I have the forms." "I could get a wheelchair organised and have a nurse take you up to the maternity ward, your choice." "wheelchair." Jan replied, "how soon," "Jan, ever heard the saying patience is a virtue," "no," "never mind then," "nurse," "yes doctor," "can you get a chair and take this man up to room three, maternity ward." "He is in a hurry nurse, to see his son." Doris was half asleep and in a lot of discomfort, despite that she put a smile on her face when Jan was wheeled in. "Baby, where's the baby," never mind the wife," "nurse can you find out where he is, of course," "thank you nurse," a moment later he was wheeled in? The tears flowed down Jan's face, "our son, What name; we give him;" "I thought John, after his father," "my name but as said in English good name, John," Doris, "and Frank, his middle name after my father," "that's also a good name." Two days later, Jan went back to work, "Doris I need money now for our son," "that's a reason to risk, damaging that leg," you worry too much," I'll be fine, Jan find out when I can go home, I've asked the doctor said when you can stand, a few days more, a few days more was three weeks, the doctor said in view of where they lived, on a upper floor, although Maceij had offered his room, Doris knew it was much smaller than theirs, everything had settled, normal life was being resumed, Doris and young John where at home, his wooden was next a window, Chrisi and Maceij, had a room together at Vi's, two horses had started their dream and the potential sale of the one field for house development was in negotiation, the other fields Maceij wished to purchase where in full swing, Zimmer had a new love, in Mira, Vi was visiting her grandson, every other day, the summer almost over, Maceij was planning a new year, Chrisi was talking of marriage, Vi was talking to Maceij, about the ground floor room, at his house, so she could be closer to her grand son and daughter,

Jan smothered his wife and son with love at every opportunity, his leg was on the mend, a promotion was promised him, a main line route, as an engine driver, it was utopia all round.

Doris, I have an appointment to see the consultant, something to do; with the truss, I may not need it any longer. He wants to check it, ok honey, see you in an hour or two or three, maybe more, go on, with you, gives a kiss, come back safe. Jan was sitting on the rows of seats, waiting as so many do, Jan, hello doctor, how's that son of yours, I was your wife's surgeon? I saw you briefly when, you visited your wife in maternity, oh yes, Jan replied. The truth was. He couldn't remember him, must be three months now. It is doctor. He has grown well and strong, for a baby born so early. Jan no, he wasn't early; he was full term, no Doctor you are mistaken two months early. No Jan he wasn't premature, if he had been, we would have thought twice about the delivery, well he's healthy; Jan, the Doctor replied that's the main thing, yes of course, Jan the nurse is calling you in for your appointment, Jan, good luck, thanks doctor.

"Jan you don't need this truss any longer." "I'm happy that the hernia has settled down, but take it home." "keep it on hand. If you feel the need to wear it again, make an appointment." Doctor, Jan asked." The full term for pregnancy is, nine months, "yes" "I have a question, to ask." If I'm able to answer, I will." "If a pregnancy was over the time or early, how well could you tell, the time either way, having examined the person." "Oh within a week or two, you couldn't be wrong." "Jan why do you ask, is there a problem," no, just wanted to know, for a friend." "Well you can tell him Jan, with a degree of certainty, max two weeks either way, premature, that's before time not a concern." "Late after two weeks, a concern, but still nothing to unduly worry about," "what about two months late." "Jan your starting to concern me now, if your friend has no doctor, get her to see one now." "Straight away, no Doctor, she goes to the clinic. It's just me." "I just wanted to know, out of, interest." "That's fine, no other questions no Doctor." Jan smiled, "absolutely none."

Jan hid the rage within him well, as he was boarding the bus for home to spine Avenue. His head was pounding with questions, that had no answers he wanted to hear. As he walked into their room, Doris was sitting at the table by the window. John was asleep in his cot in his blue romper suit. Jan walked straight up to her, "I am going to ask you just one time, who does that baby belong to and don't lie. It was not early, the doctor told me it was on time, a second doctor, not knowing the conversation of the first doctor confirmed that also. This baby if it was mine should have been born at the end of June. Not the end of July It's not my baby. Who's is it, the questioning had been calm until that moment?

Doris was about to stand up and tell him the truth, but in her heart. She knew; the family dream was about to be shattered. "He screamed at her, tell me." No chance was given for her to speak, his patience gone a back hand sent her crashing to the floor. She tried to clamber from the floor using the chair as her aid, another blow struck her on the side of her head sent her to the floor, laying there, trying to compose herself.

She could see Jan walk to the cot; he looked down on John; grabbed him by his clothing, picking him up he then, threw him one handed across the room in the direction of the door. Doris used the table and chair, to get back on her feet, there was no time to think. She took the long tined fork from the table. "No! She screamed out, before plunging the fork into Jan's neck, a stream blood spat out onto the window, he staggered back, clasping his hand to the wound, falling to his knees.

Now What.

Lightning Source UK Ltd.
Milton Keynes UK
UKOW03f1527070514

231270UK00001B/5/P